P9-DDS-706

Entangled

Other Five Star Titles
by Tracie Peterson

Controlling Interests

Entangled

Tracie Peterson

Five Star
Unity, Maine

Five Star Christian Fiction.
Published in conjunction with Bethany House Publishers.

Cover courtesy Bethany House Publishers.

c.\

January 2000

Standard Print Hardcover Edition.

Five Star Standard Print Christian Fiction Series.

The text of this edition is unabridged.

Set in 11 pt. Plantin by Warren S. Doersam.

Printed in the United States on permanent paper.

Library of Congress Cataloging-in-Publication Data

Peterson, Tracie.
 Entangled / Tracie Peterson.
  p. cm.
 ISBN 0-7862-2228-X (hc : alk. paper)
  1. Political candidates — Kansas — Fiction.
 2. Widows — Fiction. I. Title.
PS3566.E7717 E5 2000
 813´.54—dc21

99-046905

To Judith Pella

For your friendship, your teaching, and for just being a lot of fun to be around. Here's to many years of writing together!

One

Cara Kessler slowly came awake to the gentle sounds of classical music. Refusing to open her eyes, she reached across her side of the bed, touched the empty pillow beside her, and sighed. It was a ritual that had haunted Cara for over five years. *Jack isn't here. Jack will never be here again.*

She opened her eyes and sighed a second time.

Five years of widowhood had yet to foster familiarity, and in moments like these, Cara wondered if she would ever again know what it felt like to be whole.

She shut off the radio alarm, then rolled over to press her face against Jack's long-deserted pillow. After multiple washings from tears and launderings, it no longer smelled like him. But somehow it didn't matter. It was still Jack's pillow and it was still Jack's bed and she was still Jack's widow.

In the early mornings she tried to remember every detail of his face, but as the years wore on it became increasingly hard. She'd listen for a memory of his voice, but that too had faded into silence. The only good thing was that the harsh stabbing pain had faded as well. In its place was a numbing lonely resolve Cara could never quite figure out how to handle.

Sometimes she wanted to hate him for leaving her alone. Yet deep inside she knew she could never hate Jack, just as she knew she was never really alone. There was always God . . . and Brianna.

"God will be with you even after I'm gone," Jack had whis-

pered in a dying voice. *"I'm not really dead, remember that, Cara. Remember it for Brianna's sake. Remember it for your sake. Find someone to love you and Bri. One day, we'll be caught up together."* And then he had closed his eyes and slipped away. Away from her loving touch. Away from the five-year-old daughter who needed him. Away from their youth ministry work. Away for good.

Some days were harder than others, even though Cara had tried to face each one in a positive manner. Today promised to be one of those hard days.

"Mama!" Brianna's voice squealed as she dove onto the bed.

Taking Cara by surprise, the lively ten-year-old had no way of realizing she had rescued her mother from certain despair. "Brianna, my little ray of sunshine," Cara said, mussing the already disheveled brown hair. "Come cuddle with me." She threw back the comforter to admit Brianna. Pulling her daughter close, she sighed for the third time that day. This sigh, however, was one of contentment.

"So what's our plan for this particular Saturday, Mistress Brianna?" she asked her daughter conspiratorially.

"You promised we'd go to the zoo—to see where they put Daddy's brick, remember?"

Cara nodded, remembering the zoo's fund raiser. A brick bearing the name "Jack Kessler" was now a permanent fixture of the new children's section at the world-famous Topeka Zoo.

"I remember. So we go to the zoo and then—" Cara's voice was interrupted by the ringing of the telephone.

"Oh, great," Brianna moaned.

"Hello?" she answered, noting her daughter's frown. No doubt Brianna worried that the caller would take Cara away for the day.

"Cara? It's Melissa Jordon. Used to be Melissa Cabot back in Hays."

The voice was strangely familiar. In the silence, a memory and an image came to mind. "Missy?"

"Melissa, these days. My grandmother named her rat terrier Missy, and that put an end to my nickname."

Cara laughed. "I haven't talked to you in years. I can't even remember the last time." But then she did remember. It was at Jack's funeral.

Melissa seemed to sense the meaning of Cara's sudden silence. "How's Brianna?"

"She's great. Ten years old and a star fourth grader. Plays the piano like Mozart himself."

"I'd like to hear that. It doesn't seem possible for so much time to have slipped by. Wasn't it only yesterday you and I were in school together? I guess a lot of water has gone under and over the bridge since then."

Pause.

"So . . . you're married?" Cara asked, desperate to fill the awkward silences creeping into their conversation.

"Yes, I married a wonderful man named Peter Jordon. We met while I was doing graduate work in New York. We married right after I received my masters in journalism. It's been three years now."

"I'm so glad for you. Are you living in Topeka?"

"No, we live in Lawrence. It's halfway between my job here and Peter's need for the international airport in Kansas City."

Brianna wriggled out of the covers and took off for her room, obviously no longer threatened by the telephone call. "I'm going to get ready!" she called out.

"Was that Brianna?" Melissa questioned.

"Yes, we're going to the zoo today. Jack's name is on one

of the new memorial bricks and I promised Bri we'd go see it." As hard as she'd tried to avoid the subject of Jack, Cara was amazed at how easily he slipped into their conversation.

"Cara, I . . . I hope you won't think me out of line, but I want to tell you that I felt really bad when Jack died. I felt even worse that I didn't try to get together with you. . . ." Melissa's voice faltered, but after a moment she resumed the conversation, fully composed. "The car accident was such a shock. Jack was alive one day and gone the next. I just didn't know how to deal with it."

"That makes two of us," Cara said softly, but then she added, "Without God I'd have never made it."

"Your faith must have been pretty strong. I've kept track of what you've done with the youth ministry. It's because of HEARTBEAT and your work with the kids that I'm calling today."

"Really? Why?"

"I work for *The Capital-Journal*," Melissa answered, referencing the local newspaper. "I mainly report on the governor's office and the political scene around the state, but I've been given the go-ahead to approach you about a story."

"What kind of story?" Cara was immediately wary. She'd been interviewed on more than one occasion and had experienced some troubling results.

"Actually, that would depend on you. You see, we're featuring a special multipage insert on Kansas youth. I talked to the editor about how your work has inspired young people all across the state. I told him we couldn't possibly do the project without including your various ministries at HEARTBEAT and he agreed."

"I see." Cara felt less than enthusiastic.

"You would have final approval over the article and I'd fight anyone who changed a single dot. I want the piece to promote what you do, Cara." After a breath of hesitation, Melissa continued, "I mean, I feel like I owe it to you . . . to Jack."

"Why do you owe us anything?" Cara sat up in the bed and tucked a stray strand of brown hair behind her ear.

"I guess I feel like a deserter," Melissa admitted. "We all used to be so close in school. I thought we would always be friends, and, you know, live forever. . . ."

Cara smiled in bittersweet memory. "Yes, I know exactly what you mean." They were Hays' original "brat pack"—or so they thought. Jack, Cara, Melissa, and half a dozen others pledged to be lifelong best friends and nothing would ever tear them apart. At least that was the plan.

"Anyway, since I couldn't find the courage to spend time with you after Jack's death, I wanted to somehow make it up by doing a great story on the ministry you both loved so much."

"It's not necessary, you know. This call is more than enough." Cara felt a tender tug for the woman who'd once been her closest friend. "Melissa, I appreciate your honesty more than you'll ever know. When Jack died, a part of me went with him and I wouldn't have responded well to you back then."

As if to clear the air between them, Cara changed the subject. "Do you and Peter have any children?"

Melissa seemed taken off guard. "Ah . . . well . . . no. I can't have children. I had some physical problems and it resulted in a hysterectomy."

"I'm sorry," Cara said, and she truly meant it. Brianna was a critical part of her life, and she couldn't imagine having to endure the days without her "sunshine."

"Me too. But maybe one day we'll adopt. Right now I travel quite a bit with Peter. He works with a New York publishing house that sends him to all corners of the earth. We've had a lot of fun we might not have otherwise had with a family." Her words sounded convincing, but not her voice.

Brianna appeared in the doorway, dancing around with a package of donuts. "I'm gonna have this for breakfast," she chanted.

Cara rolled her eyes and shook her head, but Brianna didn't appear to notice. "Look, Melissa, I'm going to have to cut this short, otherwise Brianna's going to have a bowl of sugar for breakfast. But, tomorrow at five, the local television station is running a short special on HEARTBEAT. Why don't you watch it, and if you still want to do the interview, come down to my office on Monday."

"That'll be great! What time?"

"Say around ten. That way I'll have time to explain things to Joe Milkhen. He's my partner at HEARTBEAT."

"Ten sounds good. Thanks, Cara. This really means a lot to me."

"I think I understand. I'll see you Monday." Cara hung up the phone and threw back her covers. It had been years since she'd thought about Melissa and the fun times they had shared. Cara smiled. Sometimes memories weren't so bad.

Two

Heavy blue smoke hung over the conference room like a vaporous noose. Seven pairs of eyes were riveted on the seemingly stoic expression of the eighth man. But Robert J. Kerns was far from stoic. He was fully capable of feeling, and delivering, both pleasure and pain.

Here in the conference room of Kerns and Dubray, Attorneys at Law, Kerns intimately knew each of the men before him. He had structured them, molded them, created them. They were his men, both willingly and unwillingly. Some had come to him as desperate men in deep trouble with the law. Others had come to him simply out of greed. But they all owed him, and because of this Kerns had made them a part of the Association.

Watching each of the men, Bob Kerns reveled in his control over the clandestine organization. As an esteemed lawyer in both Kansas and Missouri, Kerns had managed to manipulate records and witnesses until each of the men before him had been vindicated of wrongdoing and had benefitted from his power. However, the price he extracted in return was monumental in both dollars and devotion.

The announcement he'd just made had created a rather strained atmosphere among the members. He read skepticism in the eyes of some, fear in the eyes of others. He waited for someone to break the uneasy silence, but as usual the initiative would have to be his own. His gaze fell on Patrick Conrad. The man seemed to wilt.

"You're going to run for governor? Governor of Kansas?"

Conrad questioned nervously.

Bob smiled tolerantly and took his seat. Now the meeting could truly begin. He loosened his tie, slowly undid the top button of his shirt, and smiled. Anyone who knew him recognized it as his trademark courtroom smile. It was a smile that promised action. It was a smile that left no one doubting the force behind it.

"I suppose this seems rash to some of you," Bob began, much like a surgeon about to describe a delicate procedure, "but I'm sure you can realize the unlimited possibilities such a position could give this organization."

"Yeah, Bob, but . . ." Conrad interrupted. Kerns narrowed his eyes and turned a tight-lipped expression on the man. Silence once again filled the room.

"The Association has a great deal to gain from this," Kerns continued. "You are all well aware of the things I've done for you, and the risks I've taken on behalf of your concerns." He made eye contact with each man, knowing full well no one would look away. Patrick Conrad quickly lit another cigarette and puffed as though it were his last. The hazy noose seemed to lower around his neck.

Kerns made certain he had their full attention simply by tapping his well-manicured fingers against a thick legal dictionary. The smoke grew thicker as two more members lit up.

"As I was saying, the office of governor would allow us to accomplish quite a bit in our businesses. Wouldn't you agree, George?" he said, turning abruptly to the man on his right.

George Sheldon was a giant in the chemical world, but here he was Sheldon the Environmental Protection Agency violator. Kerns had more goods on him than the man would ever be able to shake or buy off. Right at the top of the list was a little chemical groundwater pollution problem that Sheldon had still not brought to Kerns for help. Bob smiled as George reached for a cigarette. It was only a matter of time before he would come crawling—until then it was important to give him decisive strokes of confidence.

"George has been an important part of this organization since the EPA thought to contradict his operating procedures." Kerns paused and reached out to give George a quick slap on the back. "But we showed them otherwise, didn't we, George?"

The man seemed to relax a bit and smiled weakly between long drags.

"And I don't know how we could possibly function without KANCO," Kerns continued. "Pat Conrad has given us an excellent source of information through this fine janitorial service. KANCO now holds a large percentage of government contracts and will no doubt continue to be of help to us in the future."

Conrad nodded with only the slightest hesitation.

"Of course without Cameron Hedley's help through ENTER DATA we'd be doing twice as much work in consulting and database areas." He paused. "I don't need to continue down a long list of what each of you has done for me or"—he folded his hands and leaned back in his chair—"what I've done for you."

Just then a young professional dressed in a three-piece suit and gold wire-frame glasses entered the room and handed Kerns a stack of papers.

"Ah, just the man." Kerns got to his feet, took the papers, and put an arm around the younger man's shoulders. "I'd like to introduce Russell Owens. Russell comes to us from a law firm in Kansas City. I managed to entice him to join me here in Topeka for both the law business and the campaign. Russell will be my campaign manager—which means he will be in touch with each of you on a day-to-day basis. Get to know him, and understand this"—Kerns paused for emphasis—"answering to Russell will be answering to me. I expect your full cooperation in every matter. Understood?"

A murmur of agreement rose above the hazy air, while Kerns and Owens exchanged a look of satisfaction.

"Good." Kerns motioned for Owens to take a seat before he handed the papers to George. "Pass these around and keep a copy. You'll see from this printout exactly what it will take for us to win this election. We're up against tough competition. The incumbent governor is well liked and greatly respected, but he's a pompous fool. Local news articles have shown him to be too much the do-gooder and now that's catching up with him. His weak areas are clearly pointed out on page two. With all of us working together, we can surely stop him before he bankrupts the state."

"That's a little dramatic, don't you think, Bob?" The question came from John Myers of Myers Architectural Services. Of all the men in the Association, Kerns had the least amount of dirt on him—which meant Myers was never afraid to voice an opinion.

"Are you a supporter of Governor Glencoe?" All eyes moved from Kerns to Myers in anticipation of an answer.

"Not particularly," the dark-haired architect replied. "I just think it will take more than mudslinging to beat him in this campaign. He is well liked, just as you've pointed out. He's got a strong following in the rural communities among the religious right. That's one group you could never hope to win over on your reputation alone. People don't have a high opinion of lawyers these days."

Kerns met Myers' steely eyes and felt a small amount of respect for the man. "True enough, John, and that's exactly the kind of input we'll need in order to iron out the rough places in this campaign. Kansas is an agricultural- and livestock-minded state. Even the major industries here take their cues from the barometric readings of the farming community. To ignore the outlying areas of Kansas would be to cut our own throats. However, as you all know, I've recently won two major cases for farming cooperatives. That gives me a stronghold with farmers—especially in light of the fact that both cases were against the federal government and very well publicized."

"But is that enough to make you a major contender for the office of governor?" Myers braved again.

"That, along with my favorable reputation in Topeka, Kansas City, and Wichita, will make a good start. If you'll read the printouts, you'll see where our weak points are and how you can help. As I said earlier, Russell will be contacting you in the near future to give you updates and see what assistance you might be willing to offer the campaign." Kerns glanced at his watch. It was nearly midnight, and the best thing to do now was to give each member of the Association time to consider the news.

"I motion we adjourn for the evening," Kerns said, knowing there would be no challenge. Conrad seconded the motion and the other members echoed their agreement.

As the room cleared of both smoke and men, Kerns signaled for Owens to stay behind. "Russell, I want you to get right to work on a list of possible running mates. The right person should strengthen my public appeal. We need some- one whose reputation is impeccable, someone to draw the more conservative skeptics who question my background. However . . ." Kerns turned to look out on the city from his ninth-floor vantage point. The light atop the Capitol building glowed in the darkness, drawing his attention. He wanted the position of governor more than he'd ever wanted anything in his life.

And he would have it.

"However?" Owens questioned from behind him.

Kerns turned back to the table. "However, I want someone I can control. A yes-man who will take orders without question. A man who will take the fall for me, if necessary, and who will smile while doing it."

Russell grinned and wrote in a black leather notebook. "Anything else?"

Kerns studied the man for a moment. His suit was expensive but certainly not GQ. Owens' hair was fashioned in the current rage of young professionals with a generous amount of mousse and hairspray to give it that "just styled" look. Overall, he represented the crisp no-nonsense image that Kerns desired for his campaign. If Owens were a little older and more widely recognized in the public eye, he'd make a great running mate.

"How old are you, Russell?" he asked, knowing full well the answer.

"Thirty, sir."

"You've done well for yourself," Kerns said with one final appraisal before picking up his briefcase. "Stick with me and you'll do even better."

Owens smiled and pushed up his gold-tone glasses. "I intend to, sir."

Kerns laughed, liking the man's confidence, but knowing his reputation for ruthlessness and double-crossing. These qualities, and not the fact that he'd graduated summa cum laude from law school, had made their coming together advantageous to Kerns. A man like Owens would get things done. And, at this stage of the game, he was smart enough to recognize just who was buttering his bread.

"Play the game right," Kerns stated as he headed to the door. "And never, ever forget who runs the board."

Three

Russell Owens pulled back the powder blue damask drapes from the sliding-glass window that led to his patio. Sunlight flooded the room, falling on stacks of unopened boxes and haphazardly placed furniture.

He grimaced at the sight.

His small west-side apartment was temporary election headquarters for Kerns, and boxes of campaign materials mingled with ones marked "FRAGILE" gave the apartment a warehouse appearance. Russell had barely set down his own things before Kerns had begun parading campaign necessities into his home. Given his upcoming schedule, Russell knew it would be a long time before everything got sorted out properly.

Switching on the television, Russell sat down to a Sunday afternoon of Kerns-focused work. He glanced at the TV, rolled up his shirt-sleeves, and picked up his notes. A large stack of newspapers covered his glass-topped coffee table, and beside these were clippings from magazines and business newsletters. All of the articles pertained to Kerns in one way or another, and it would be Owens' job to sort through the mess and deem the effects of each in regard to his candidate.

Sipping a hastily made cup of coffee, Owens grimaced at his ineptness in the kitchen and put the drink aside. First thing tomorrow, he would locate the coffee maker, no matter how many boxes he had to search through.

He listened to the TV news broadcaster give a sketchy

report on two legislative bills before turning his full attention to the task at hand. Jotting rough notes on a legal pad, he pored over one article after another. KERNS REPRESENTS FARMERS, read one headline. This was good, Owens decided. It would make for a good campaign quote at a later date. The next newspaper article was not as favorable: KERNS SEEKS TO COVER UP CHEMICAL SPILL. Owens read through the article and found the story of Sheldon Industries' battle with the EPA to be quite fascinating. Toward the middle of the story he circled a paragraph that he would use as a compaign slogan. *"Robert Kerns supports the needs of Kansas industries over the safety of local residents. . . ."* Of course the quote would be trimmed to end after the word "industries."

The game was beginning to be fun. Owens smiled and circled additional bits of information before turning his attention to a list of possible running mates for Kerns. The list was long and unreasonable. Owens immediately took to black lining any name that even mildly represented a problem. Having done his homework on the men listed, Owens saw the list diminish in size until only two possibilities held any real interest for him. And even those names conjured up the possibility of a political crisis. One man was well known for his support of the death penalty—an issue that Owens hoped to keep out of the public eye for as long as possible. The other man had created his own business in computers and had become an overnight phenomenon across the state. But he had a reputation for being a playboy. In and of itself, it wasn't necessarily all that damaging, but in conservative Kansas, it just might be the one thing to send voters running to the other side.

"And on the local scene," a female reporter was saying, "I had the opportunity to spend a day with Cara Kessler. Mrs.

Kessler is the co-founder of HEARTBEAT Ministries, a statewide youth ministry that seeks to give spiritual direction, job training, and education to Kansas young people."

Russell looked up, not really knowing why. He found an attractive brown-haired woman smiling back from the twenty-seven-inch screen. She looked like the stereotypical country sweetheart with her shoulder-length hair just turned under at the ends.

"Cara Kessler, you've been most notably described as a 'dynamo' and 'spiritual torchbearer.' Your ministry work with HEARTBEAT is nationally acclaimed, and HEART-BEAT's founding motto, 'Youth are the pulse points by which we monitor the heart of our nation,' has even been praised by the President of the United States. What can you tell us about your work?"

Russell put down the list and leaned forward for the remote. Quickly pressing the "record" button, he watched, completely mesmerized, as Cara Kessler eloquently explained.

"My husband, Jack, and I founded HEARTBEAT ministries almost ten years ago. We saw a desperation among the youth in our hometown, as well as in the cities around us. As youth ministers in our local church, we sought to answer why there was such deep despair among people who had so much for which to live."

"And what kind of answers did you get?" the reporter asked.

Cara Kessler smiled from the screen in innocent radiance. Russell liked her clean-cut girl-next-door image. She was petite and delicate, yet there was a strength in her dark blue eyes. Wearing a plaid wool dress, Cara Kessler looked as though she were about to bake cookies or drive the car pool, not lead a youth ministry to national acclaim.

". . . and so it seemed that lack of opportunity along with training, education, and spiritual guidance surfaced as the root cause of most problems. With so much social acceptability toward activities that only work to harm children, my husband and I felt the need to do something positive. We created HEARTBEAT to meet the needs of Kansas youth."

"But how does HEARTBEAT differ from other organizations that deal with the betterment of youth?"

Cara nodded as if anticipating the question. "HEARTBEAT seeks to train people to help their own community's children. Unlike national organizations that headquarter in places well removed from the people in need, each community is responsible to facilitate their own organization. HEARTBEAT stresses local people meeting local needs. Each chapter sets up their own organization, based on the anticipated goals of their community. Of course there is the office here in Topeka, but it's mainly a gathering place for information. If the local chapters need answers to questions or help finding assistance outside their community, the Topeka office is here to assist them."

"Does HEARTBEAT represent a particular church or religious affiliation?"

"No, we've sought to keep it interdenominational. We see great diversity across the state in regard to religious views, occupational focus, educational needs, and cultural attitudes. The problems that face a youth whose parents are farmers are different from the problems of the inner-city child whose mother is working two jobs to make ends meet. And while children have much in common, it seems to be the individual problems that create the significant complications. HEARTBEAT is designed to help find answers to any and all of these needs, because again, the local church and community are in charge of setting and achieving the goals of their particular chapter."

"So how does HEARTBEAT fund expenses?"

Cara's expression never changed as she demurely folded her hands in her lap. "HEARTBEAT is a nonprofit organization. As I said before, because the needs are met at a local level, each community is responsible for their own chapter and what they accomplish. Local businesses and community leaders generally seem more than willing to financially support the kids in their neighborhoods. They see it as an investment in the future good of all who live there. The office here has benefited from a network of support from all across the state. That money comes in the form of donations, and after paying small overhead costs and the salaries of my partner, Pastor Joe Milken, and myself, it is always turned back into the ministry."

"But how can you support a business without a steady stream of funding?" the reporter asked in disbelief.

"That's where faith comes in. God has yet to let me down when I've needed Him."

Promising some around-the-state footage of HEART-BEAT's progress after a commercial break, the reporter carefully steered away from the issue of God.

Russell looked down at the coffee table and picked up one of the newspapers. Dropping it in his lap, however, an idea began to formulate.

"I want someone I can control. A yes-man who will take orders and not question them," Kerns had told him. Was it possible he might settle for a yes-woman? And if Kerns was willing, could Cara Kessler be pressed into service as his running mate?

When the program resumed, Russell continued to consider the possibilities. Footage showed HEARTBEAT programs from all corners of the state, and in each area Cara was heartily applauded and praised.

"Mrs. Kessler was just what we needed," a representative from a small west-Kansas town said. "Our kids were dropping out of school, marrying early out of necessity, and generally finding themselves in dead-end situations. The community was concerned but had no real direction until HEART-BEAT helped us organize. Since then, we've added a community youth night, some local job-training programs complete with apprenticeships, and a Bible study aimed at addressing teen issues. Our drop-out and teen pregnancy rates are way down, and the number of kids going on to college is up forty-five percent."

That story seemed to be echoed throughout the remaining portions of the program. Russell considered the possibilities before him, his certainty growing with each new thought. Throwing his list in the trash, he turned off the VCR and television and picked up the telephone. There was no longer any doubt in his mind. Cara Kessler was exactly what he needed for Bob Kerns' campaign.

Four

Auburn billowed out behind Melissa Jordon as she ran down Main Street in Lindsborg, Kansas. Governor Glencoe would be making his speech in less than two minutes, but ever since she'd stopped to call Cara to postpone their interview, Melissa couldn't seem to catch up with the day.

Her editor had called at five-thirty that morning to announce he needed her in Lindsborg to represent *The Capital-Journal* when the governor announced his intentions to run for a second term. Melissa had tried to explain her obligations to Cara and to ask for someone else to cover the announcement, but it was no use. The photographer was already on his way to pick Melissa up. Cara's interview was put on indefinite hold.

She approached a black- and yellow-striped barricade and waved her press pass at the highway patrolman on duty. The uniformed man took her credentials, studied them for a moment, then let her through. Still panting, Melissa took her seat just in time to hear the master of ceremonies ask the crowd to join him in greeting the governor of Kansas. Throwing down her purse, Melissa got to her feet and opened her notebook.

"Ladies and gentlemen, it is my great pleasure to present the current and next governor of this state . . . The Honorable Edward R. Glencoe."

Cheers rose up in a deafening roar. It was hard to believe a crowd no bigger than this could produce that kind of noise.

Melissa did a mental head count and figured about two hundred people had come to hear the governor.

Like many candidates, Glencoe had chosen his hometown of Lindsborg to make his "intent to run" announcement. And Lindsborg had turned out in grand style to receive one of their own.

"Friends," Glencoe began, waving down the continued roar of applause. The governor waited for the fervor to quell, and Melissa jotted notes about the crowd before turning her attention back to Glencoe.

The man was a grandfatherly sort—medium height, with a softly rounded midsection that seemed appropriate for his sixty-five-year-old frame. His balding head sported a ring of snowy white hair, and he smiled in a broad open manner that Melissa had come to appreciate as sincere. He was more like a member of an extended family than the prestigious governor of the state—maybe that was why people liked him so much.

"Friends," Glencoe began again, "please join me in singing the national anthem."

A band began the familiar notes and Melissa put aside her notebook and placed her hand over her heart. She noticed that only a handful of other people mimicked her patriotic action. From her days as a Girl Scout, she had developed a deep sense of pride in her country. She still got goosebumps when she heard *The Star-Spangled Banner*. Thinking of Girl Scouts reminded her again of Cara. Why had she let their friendship slip away? Why had she been unable to deal with Jack's death in a way that would have allowed her to keep her relationship with Cara intact?

As all eyes focused on the color guard, Melissa joined in singing.

". . . and the home of the brave." The last notes of the national anthem faded away and a strange silence seemed to hold the audience captive.

Melissa watched Glencoe, wondering what he would do next. She wasn't surprised when he took out a pair of reading glasses and put them on. With typewritten notes in front of him, the governor began his speech. This had always been his no-nonsense style.

"Fellow citizens, friends, and loved ones, I come to you today in a spirit of gratitude and hope. Gratitude for the past four years we've shared together in this great state of Kansas . . ." Cheers interrupted his speech and Glencoe patiently waited, smiling benevolently from the podium. The noise died down and he continued. "And hope that we can share another four years. I take this opportunity to announce my intention to run for reelection as your governor." Again cheers.

Melissa took shorthand for the entire speech, underlining important points she'd want to draw out in her story and putting question marks by issues that needed a bit more clarity. As the speech wrapped up, Glencoe invited the crowd to meet him personally and to share with him their ideas for the betterment of their state.

People immediately began to swarm the podium area, and the press was soon engulfed in a massive wash of supporters for Governor Glencoe.

"Looks like we may be trampled underfoot," the man beside Melissa said. "I'm going to try to get to him for a few questions. You coming?"

Melissa shook her head. "No, I'll catch him later." She finished writing in her notebook and placed it in her purse. Then glancing around, she called across the crowd, "Darren!"

The man looked up and Melissa motioned him to join her. The clean-cut slender photographer from *The Capital-*

Journal looked hardly old enough to be out of high school. "I'd like you to get some good close-up shots. You might want to stand over there and use the zoom." She pointed and Darren nodded. "Get some good crowd shots and something that would tug at the heartstrings. You know, the governor and some kids . . . young and old blending for the good of tomorrow. Something like that."

"Got it, Melissa." The man loaded a new roll of film with graceful ease while juggling two other cameras, a bag of lenses, and a backpack crammed full of who-knew-what.

Melissa slipped in and out of the crowd, eavesdropping as she loved to do. There was more to be learned in the private little circles of politics than in the grand arena itself. People in the smaller groups forgot to guard their tongues. Melissa had gotten the scoop on more stories by riding around in elevators in state offices and the Capitol than anywhere else.

"I'm going to that little restaurant downtown," one of Glencoe's staff was telling another. "I think it's called The Swedish Crown. It's supposed to have authentic Swedish food, and since I've never eaten any, I thought I'd give it a try."

Melissa caught sight of Darren snapping pictures as the governor posed for a photo-op with the town's merchants.

"He's going to promote tourism this time around," a woman was saying to another reporter. "He promised this would be a top priority. There's a lot of money to be had in tourism, and Lindsborg has a great deal to offer."

"Such as?" the reporter questioned and Melissa hung on, waiting for the explanation.

"This community was settled primarily by our Swedish ancestors. We have a wonderful college here, and they put on first-class productions of Handel's *Messiah* twice a year. We have a beautifully restored Victorian mansion and a wonderful bed-and-breakfast called The Swedish Country Inn.

You can get some pretty good food here, too," the lady said with a laugh.

Melissa thought of laying hands on some of that "pretty good food" as she wandered down the street, continuing to take notes while her stomach growled in protest. Spotting Glencoe just ahead, Melissa pressed through the animated crowd and prepared to ask some of her own questions. Maybe she'd even address the tourism question. After all, the woman had a point, and the fierce pride of these people and their Swedish ancestry would make a great backdrop for the story.

She was less than an arm's length away from Glencoe now, standing directly in front of a shop that sported Swedish crafts and novelties. The window display portrayed a variety of candelabras. Most were bright red, painted with dainty white flowers and streaming greenery. This seemed to be one of the most popular items available. In the window opposite the door to the shop, a T-shirt blazed, "You can tell a Swede, but you can't tell him much." *Most politicians must be Swedes,* she thought with a smile.

"Ah, Mrs. Jordon, isn't it?" Governor Glencoe asked. "I see you're enjoying yourself."

Melissa turned around and nodded. "Very much. This is my first trip to Lindsborg." She was closer to Glencoe now than she'd been during the speech. It seemed to her that he looked a bit pale, maybe even sick. His eyes betrayed dark circles, although it was evident a makeup artist had tried to conceal them.

"And what do you think?" Glencoe asked in a voice that sounded almost pained.

"I think there's great potential here for tourism." There, she'd given him the ball to play with, now she'd wait and see if he'd take up the issue.

"Tourism can be a strong industry . . . ah," Glencoe stammered a bit and took out a handkerchief to wipe his forehead. "The state could benefit from additional tourism."

The uniformed highway patrolmen nearby seemed to take note of the situation.

"Are you okay?" Melissa asked, seeing the governor sway.

The ashen color of his skin spoke for him. Glencoe was obviously sick. Before he could take another step, the governor glanced almost pleadingly at Melissa, then collapsed on the ground.

"Help . . . somebody help!" Melissa yelled.

One patrolman grabbed a two-way radio, while another pushed back the crowd. "Have the plane standing by."

"What's wrong with him?" Melissa shouted above the din.

A dark-suited member of Glencoe's team came running. "Have you called ahead?"

"The plane's ready," the patrolman answered, then in a low voice he questioned, "Should I contact his oncologist?"

"Would someone tell us what's wrong with the governor?" Melissa shouted again.

Strong hands took hold of her shoulders. "I'm afraid you'll have to move back."

The handsome face of another patrolman looked down at her. The wide-brimmed hat he wore shaded his eyes, but Melissa thought he looked strangely familiar. "Is the governor all right?" she questioned him.

"Nothing serious. We're flying him back to Topeka," the man replied.

Melissa moved back and scribbled notes in a fury of ink smudges and illegible markings. She remembered the remark about an oncologist, and at the bottom of the page she wrote the word "Cancer," followed by a question mark. One way or another, Melissa was certain she was on to a much bigger story than the governor's intent to be reelected.

Five

"I'm so grateful you could take the time to reschedule our interview," Melissa said as she slid into the restaurant booth.

Cara smiled. "I'm just glad we could spend some time alone." It seemed a lifetime since she'd seen Melissa, and yet sitting here together melted away the years and brought back fond memories. "So tell me about this man you married and how life has been treating you."

Melissa snapped the burgundy linen napkin open and placed it on her lap. "Peter is positively wonderful. He's handsome and brave and, most importantly, faithful."

"That often seems a rarity in both men and women these days," Cara acknowledged, picking up her menu.

The waitress approached to take their order and Melissa immediately took charge. "I'm picking this one up," she announced.

"That isn't necessary, Melissa."

"I want to. My treat."

Melissa's chocolate brown eyes conveyed her sincerity, and Cara nodded in agreement. "This one time. Next time, my treat."

They ordered seafood salads and sipped iced tea while waiting for their meal. The room around them hummed with activity, but surprisingly enough the silence at their table seemed awkward and stilted. Cara wondered how to open the conversation, but Melissa settled the point by speaking.

"So did you mean it?"

"Mean what?" Cara asked, trying to remember what they'd been talking about before the waitress had interrupted them.

"Will there be a next time?"

Cara smiled. "Of course. I had no idea you were in Topeka, or we'd have done this long ago."

"I'm glad you feel that way." Melissa relaxed against the booth's back cushion. "I was afraid too much time had passed. . . ."

"And that we'd be changed, with nothing in common?" Cara added.

"Exactly."

Cara considered her longtime chum. Time had definitely been kind to her. She was the athletic sort who tanned easily under the Kansas sun. Whenever they'd gotten together as kids, Melissa was always the one to suggest some form of sport for entertainment. Tennis had always been a favorite among the "brat pack."

"Do you still play tennis?" Cara questioned, lost in her memories.

Melissa gave a puzzled frown. "Not as often as I'd like to. Peter travels a great deal and I go with him whenever I can. As for tennis, I still get in a game or two when the wind isn't blowing with galelike forces."

"That's Kansas for you. Well, I'd suggest a game, but I'm so out of shape that I'm sure it would be no challenge at all."

"You don't look out of shape. You look great. I almost didn't recognize you when I walked in. You always wore your hair down to your hips and I was certain you'd never cut it."

Cara sobered. "I cut it after Jack died," she said matter-of-factly. "I really only kept it long for him."

Melissa nodded. "I remember he was very fond of long hair. Does Brianna have long hair?"

"Yes," Cara replied. "Although she wears it that way because she likes it. I told her I wouldn't interfere as long as she takes care of it."

The tension of mentioning Jack seemed to pass. "And does she?" Melissa asked with a smile.

"Like a professional. She's one sweet kid."

Just then the waitress appeared with their salads, placing large platters in front of each woman.

"Thank you," Cara said and waited for the woman to leave. Melissa had her fork in hand when Cara asked, "Would you mind if we said grace?"

Melissa quickly put down her fork. "No, I . . . please, go ahead."

Cara knew Melissa was uncomfortable. She quickly bowed her head and offered the prayer aloud. "We thank you, Father, for this meal and for the fellowship of good friends, Amen."

She looked up to find Melissa rather surprised by the simplicity of the prayer and Cara shrugged with a smile. "Short and to the point. After all, I'm hungry."

They shared a smile as they dug into their salads, and for several minutes seafood was the focus of their interest.

Melissa broke the silence first. She dabbed at her mouth with the napkin, then took out a microrecorder from her purse. "Do you mind if I use this for the interview?"

Cara shook her head. "I think it'll be easier than you trying to take notes while eating."

Melissa switched it on. "I'll probably get home and find it full of munching and crunching sounds."

"Just leave that part out of the article," Cara chuckled.

"Well, if you're ready, here goes." Melissa picked up her fork again. "Why don't you tell me how you and Jack got HEARTBEAT started."

"Did you watch the television interview on Sunday?" Cara asked. Melissa nodded while downing more salad. "That's a pretty good explanation for the hows and whys of this ministry. Jack and I always wanted to get involved in youth work. We had an excellent youth pastor in our church when we were growing up. He inspired us to carry the torch for kids."

She found herself repeating a great deal of what the TV interview had covered, and soon the salads had disappeared and the waitress was offering dessert.

"Interested in splitting some cheesecake?" Melissa asked with a mischievous twinkle in her eyes.

Cara grinned and remembered the old days when they used to share dessert to avoid too many calories. "Nope, I want my own piece."

"Good. Make it two cheesecakes," Melissa told the waitress. "Now before she gets back, tell me about the future of HEARTBEAT and where you hope to go from here."

"Well," Cara said almost hesitantly, "I've been asked to consider advancing the ministry to other states. I've been approached by leaders in Colorado, Texas, Oklahoma, and Missouri. They want me to either oversee them in a managerial manner or offer seminars that would train their people and leave me as a kind of headquarter director." She knew Melissa would pick up on her less than enthusiastic attitude.

"And that's a bad thing?" Melissa responded just as the cheesecake arrived.

"Not in and of itself," Cara began, wondering if she could explain her misgivings to her old friend. "It's just that Jack and I always knew that in order for HEARTBEAT to work, it would have to stay at a very local, very personal level. I'm afraid if I expand to help other states, this ministry will grow into some kind of national monster. I don't mind if other people take our program as a basis for their own, but I worry about having a national headquarters."

"But kids in other states need help, too. Just think what this could do for large urban communities. If you could compel businesses in places like New York and Dallas to take an active hands-on interest in their kids, criminal and gang activities would likely drop."

"I've thought of all of that, Missy," Cara said, forgetting herself. "But I don't feel led to do any expanding. At least not yet."

"You mean led by God?"

Cara knew Melissa's skepticism where spiritual matters were concerned. "Yes, I mean led by God."

Melissa looked away uncomfortably. She tried to summon the waitress, but when that failed she turned back to Cara. "So in conclusion," she prompted, "HEARTBEAT is headed where?"

"I'm not sure at this point," Cara admitted. "It's been suggested we start a newsletter for the three hundred HEARTBEAT centers."

"Three hundred? Are there that many towns in Kansas?"

Melissa's disbelief made Cara smile. "Well, you're the news expert. I'd think you'd have all your facts and figures down. I have no idea how many little towns and communities there are in Kansas, but there are a bunch, let me tell you. Even so, some towns have more than one HEARTBEAT center. Remember this is localized—founded and funded by area businesses and churches. For instance, here in Topeka there are four HEARTBEAT branches. One is backed by a large Hispanic/Catholic community. One is interdenominational, another is heavily supported by a cooperative of local business leaders, while the fourth is thriving due to the combined efforts of a rather large evangelical church in the north area of town. So by and large, the bigger the city, the more

HEARTBEAT involvement."

"So will you put this newsletter out sometime soon?" Melissa asked. By now she was jotting a few notes on the back of a single sheet of paper.

"I don't think so. I am too busy, and again, I'm not sure it's the direction we want to go. I was just talking with my partner, Joe Milken, before lunch today. He reminded me that it's things just like this newsletter that consume massive amounts of time and energy and lead to an overall picture of organized business."

"But seriously," Melissa said, putting down her pen, "isn't HEARTBEAT an organized business?"

"I like to think we're a ministry for God—first, last, and always."

"So is it something you and Mr. Milken will be able to handle between just the two of you?"

"If we can keep people from forcing us to make HEART-BEAT something it was never intended to be. However, if you're interested in a job, I just might be able to hire you on," Cara said, wondering how Melissa would respond.

She didn't have long to wait.

"Oh no," Melissa laughed. "Not me. I'd never be good at that kind of job."

Cara decided to push. "We always worked well together, and now that we've crossed paths again, it would be a shame to go our separate ways. You'd make a great PR woman, and just think of your contacts from the newspaper business."

Melissa fidgeted with her napkin. "It would never be intriguing enough for my interests."

"You never know," Cara smiled. "Hanging out with me can be a real adventure."

"So are you headed off on an adventure after this interview?" Melissa asked, snapping off the recorder and putting it into her purse.

Cara recognized the wall Melissa had put up between them and let the subject drop. "I suppose you might say that. I'm due to pick up some materials from the secretary of state's office at the Capitol. They've been generous enough to provide some books and postcards of Kansas for HEART-BEAT to distribute throughout the state."

Melissa nodded. "I'll show you the way if you want to follow me over. I'm scheduled to see the governor at two o'clock."

"Sounds great." Cara looked at her watch and saw that it was already a quarter till two. "We'd better hurry."

At the Capitol, Cara parted company with Melissa and promised she'd be in touch soon. She watched Melissa walk through the second-floor doorway marked "Governor's Office." It was amazing to find Melissa all grown-up. Gone was the flighty girl who'd always kept them laughing from one joke to the next. This Melissa seemed quite serious, if not downright preoccupied. *Of course, I could have offended her by suggesting she join HEARTBEAT,* Cara worried. They had parted company more than once on the issue of religion.

Shrugging it off, Cara made her way around the rotunda to the secretary of state's office. She found a stack of supplies on the receptionist's desk marked with her name.

"I'm here to pick these up," Cara said, motioning to the stack in front of the young girl sitting at the desk.

The girl looked up from her computer keyboard. "Okay," she said, not asking for anything in the way of identification.

Cara picked up the materials and groaned. "They're heavier than they look."

The girl shrugged and went back to her work, seeming not

to notice that Cara had to juggle the armload in order to open the door.

To Cara's consternation she managed to walk right into someone coming in from the outside. Papers flew everywhere, postcards going one direction, coloring sheets and books slipping off in another.

"I'm so sorry," Cara announced to a pair of very shiny black shoes as she hurried to gather the things up.

A rich masculine voice replied, "It was all my fault. I'm the one who's sorry."

Her gaze traveled up dark blue slacks, with their perfect crease and French blue stripe on the side, to the lighter blue dress shirt bearing the badge and insignia of the Kansas Highway Patrol. The man was smiling at her with a sincere look of concern in his blue eyes.

Then he knelt down. "Here, let me help."

"Thanks."

Cara couldn't help stealing quick sidelong glances at the man. He was very handsome in his uniform. His broad shoulders tapered down to a trim waist, where a Sam Brown belt met the black holster holding his revolver.

"I really am sorry," she said, standing up as the man retrieved the last few pages.

He extended the papers to her with a broad grin. "I'm not. It gave us a chance to run into each other."

"Yes . . ." Cara murmured. "Literally." She liked the way his smile broadened and the way his salt-and-pepper hair fell down across his forehead.

"I'm Harry Oberlin," he said as she took the coloring sheets.

"Cara Kessler."

"Yes, I know. I recognized you from your television interview."

"Oh." She could think of nothing more to say.

"Do you get up this way often?" Harry asked.

"No, this is the first time in about two years," Cara admitted, feeling a strange warmth in her cheeks. She hadn't blushed in a long time and it was most embarrassing to find herself doing it just now. "Do you?" she asked, hoping to dispel the scrutinizing look he was giving her.

"I'm here quite a bit," he confessed. "I'm a pilot and bodyguard for the governor."

"I'm impressed."

Harry's eyes twinkled in amusement. "That should be my line."

Feeling a bit awkward, Cara smiled. "I guess I'd better go."

"Maybe I'll see you around."

"Maybe."

Six

Bob Kerns barely paid attention to the drone of the evening news. He had spent the better part of two days wading through the previous election's campaign materials. To his chagrin, most everything Ed Glencoe had promised to do, he had done. And he'd done it well enough to gain the favor of his constituents. Bob was just about to call it a night when the television flashed a picture of Glencoe. Kerns turned up the volume just as the scene moved to a local hospital.

"Governor Glencoe was released from the hospital today after a short observation stay. It was determined that a bout with the flu caused the governor's collapse while in Lindsborg last week."

Kerns perked up at this. *What a break,* he thought. This could work well to his advantage. If he could paint a picture of his opponent's physical inability to endure the pressures of public office, he might well knock Glencoe down a few notches.

With these thoughts in mind, Kerns switched off the television just as a knock sounded at the door.

"Bob, Russell Owens is here," his wife, Debra, announced. The bleach-blonde had once been a raving beauty, but now, after years of abusing herself with alcohol, yo-yo diets, and emotional turmoil, Debra Kerns looked a decade older than her forty-five years.

"Send him on back," Kerns commanded. "I've been expecting him."

40

In moments, Russell Owens appeared. His arms were laden with a variety of books, manila folders, and accordion files. "Have you heard the news about Glencoe?" he asked his boss.

"Just caught the story on the television. Is there more to it than they are reporting?" Kerns asked, taking a seat again on the black leather sofa.

Russell joined him, depositing his load on the already overflowing coffee table. "If there is, I haven't been able to get a scoop on it."

"We could use this to our advantage," Bob Kerns replied. "If the people of the state think there's something more to this than the flu, they might lose faith in him."

"They might, but I wouldn't bank on it for your campaign win."

"You have something better in mind, I take it?" Kerns eyed the younger man with great interest.

Russell smiled. "I think I do."

Kerns leaned back in the sofa and nodded. "Then by all means, fill me in on the details."

Russell pulled out one folder and held it up. "The facts in this folder show you to be a highly intelligent man. You were educated at some of the finest schools and have proven yourself over and over in the courtroom. You're a family man with a wife and children, which always suggests stability to the public, and you are even registered as a member of a prominent Topeka church, implying that you and God are like this." He intertwined his first two fingers.

Russell opened the thick folder and leafed through the papers. "You contribute heavily to a variety of well-known charities, as well as to your church. That kind of community involvement looks good to the lower-income families who recognize that they are helped by the good graces of the wealthy. However—"

"However?" Kerns interrupted, sitting up.

Russell put the folder down and picked up one of the two accordion files he'd brought. "You've made enemies."

"Is that all?" Kerns resumed his restful slouch.

"It's enough to cause you some real headaches. People aren't too fond of lawyers these days, and you have a reputation for being quite a cutthroat. You've made enemies in public places as well as in private enterprise, and all of them can hurt you if we give them the power."

"So we don't give it that kind of power," Kerns replied, sounding disinterested.

"Exactly," Owens stated. "The real question is how to render the situation powerless before it starts."

"That's why I brought you on board. You're the boy-genius, so you tell me. What do we do to disarm the public before they decide to run for their guns?"

"We leave no stone unturned," Russell answered. "We beat them to the punch, so to speak. It could be handled one of two ways. The first way would be to dissect your career from beginning to present. Look for any potential time bombs. You know, skeletons that won't stayed buried? Even little problems, real or imaginary, can flare up to cut your campaign to ribbons. For instance"—he pulled a folder from the accordion file—"this case is one you handled five years ago. It involved a chemical spill at Sheldon Industries. Three people were hospitalized with a variety of symptoms, all of which were supposedly related to the spill."

"That was proven to be false," Kerns interjected.

"Be that as it may, you were quoted as saying, 'The media has pushed the public into a frenzy of panic. The messages they send out appeal to the less-educated, less-informed general public. I'm not saying that the hospitalized individuals aren't truly suffering from something, but I would look more to the suggestive powers of the media than I would for an actual physical problem.' " Owens put the paper down. "Do you remember the fallout over that article and quote?"

Kerns grimaced. "I do."

"The media followed it for weeks, watching over each individual victim, scanning the area for others."

"But there weren't others," Kerns replied, narrowing his steely blue eyes. "And the doctors were unable to determine the physical problems of the three."

"Because you paid them handsomely to keep their diagnosis in a perpetual state of non-conclusion?" Owens asked matter-of-factly.

Kerns jumped up from the sofa and stared accusingly at Owens. "Whose side are you on anyway? I did what I had to do for the sake of my client. It wasn't George Sheldon's fault that someone was asleep on the job, but George was the one to pay the price. Why not pay that money to people who can get him off the hook rather than pad the pockets of the federal government in fines and cleanups?"

"I don't have a problem with the way you handled this, Bob." Gone was the boyish "yes, sir, no, sir." In its place, Russell Owens stared straight at his superior, refusing to back down. "But there are people out there who do have a problem with it, and they will remember what you did. The media would love to eat you for lunch because of the way you made them appear the fool. Don't underestimate their power to motivate the public."

"So what's the bottom line here?" Kerns' anger was apparent.

"Other than a handful of farmers and big businesses, you don't have wide public appeal. You're also relatively unknown in central and western Kansas, and while the bulk of the population hails from the areas where you are known, you can't pretend those people don't exist."

Kerns paced the bookshelf-lined room for several moments. His mind took him in at least twelve different directions, all leading back to one common goal: the governorship of Kansas. Owens was right. And that's what vexed him the most. He'd known all of this when he decided to run for office, but back then it hadn't seemed as important.

"So, are you telling me not to run?" Kerns finally stopped pacing and faced Owens for a showdown.

"Not at all."

"Then exactly where do we go with this? You've pointed out that people distrust and dislike the law profession. You've made it clear that I have insurmountable odds against me. . . ."

"I never said they were insurmountable, Bob. But they will need a powerful whitewash to keep people from dwelling on the past."

"And how do you propose such a whitewash be accomplished?"

Owens smiled in a way that suggested he now controlled the man before him. Kerns didn't like the smug expression, but he tolerated it because Russell Owens had proven to be good at what he did.

"I brought your can of whitewash right here," Owens said and pulled out an eight-by-ten glossy of a young woman. He threw it on top of the other papers and waited for Kerns to pick it up.

"Who is she?"

Owens' smile broadened. "She is your campaign salvation."

Still uncertain as to where Russell was leading him, Kerns took the photograph and sat back down. "How?" he asked, still studying the woman.

"Her name is Cara Kessler. She runs a religious youth ministry called HEARTBEAT. She is so well loved across the state, they've practically erected a monument to her. Given a few more months, she'll probably be canonized."

"Are you going to have her promote me in campaign ads?" Kerns asked, looking over the top of the picture.

"In a way." Owens picked up a computer-generated banner and unfolded it for Bob to read.

KERNS and KESSLER

"My running mate?" Bob asked in disbelief. Surely Owens didn't expect him to win the gubernatorial ticket with a sugary-sweet do-gooder at his side.

"I think Cara Kessler is the only hope you have of winning this election. She has everything you need. The most important of which is the trust of the people of Kansas." Russell pulled out a videotape from the accordion folder. "If you watch this, you'll see what I mean. The woman is not only admired and highly respected, she's practically a god to these people. She's managed to coordinate youth centers all across the state, and you should know by now that the people of Kansas think pretty highly of their children.

"Besides, her father, Augustus Brown, was once a district representative. He served eight years in the statehouse and was well liked in his community. Her husband, dead now for five years, was a popular youth minister. The name Kessler is held in high esteem in the Hays, Kansas, area."

"But a woman as lieutenant governor? We'd be having teas and fashion shows in the Capitol building."

"Don't be so sure," Owens replied. "Cara Kessler has the reputation for getting things done. She has a dynamic personality and she maintains a public appeal that you lack. If you want to be the next governor of Kansas, you're going to need Cara Kessler."

Kerns looked again at the photograph. The pixielike brunette gazed back at him with a wide-eyed look of naivet;aae. Purity and innocence were definitely this woman's calling card.

"And what makes you think Cara Kessler would be willing to play politics with me?" Kerns asked, throwing the picture back down.

Owens held up the second accordion folder and grinned confidently. "We'll just have to be very persuasive, won't we?"

Seven

Melissa Jordon stepped into the inner office of Governor Glencoe and closed the door behind her. "Thank you for seeing me."

"You said it was urgent," Glencoe replied from behind his massive mahogany desk.

The man looks decidedly tired, she thought. *A little thinner, too.* If her hunch was right and the real culprit was cancer and not just the flu, Melissa knew the battle was probably far from over.

"Yes, it is urgent."

"Well, have a seat and tell me what brings you here today, Mrs. Jordon."

Melissa smiled. Four years of covering the governor's office had given them a shared comfort level. She sat down on a chair opposite the desk and crossed her legs. Making a point to put her purse on the chair beside her, Melissa hoped the governor would see that she was not here to report or record.

Her actions raised his bushy white eyebrows. "Is this a personal visit?"

"At this point it is," Melissa offered. "I have something very personal to talk to you about."

Glencoe looked at her with a wary frown. "Go on."

Melissa wondered how he would take the intrusion of his privacy. There was no easy way to discuss a man's health without just plunging in headlong.

"I know that you're sick," she finally said in a very soft voice.

Glencoe paled. "It was public news."

Melissa shook her head. "I know that you have cancer."

The governor stared at her blankly for several silent minutes. "Who told you?"

"I was in Lindsborg when you collapsed. I overheard your aid mention to one of the highway patrolmen that he hadn't contacted your oncologist."

"If you overheard it, why didn't you say anything in your story? I read *The Capital-Journal*'s coverage of the reelection speech and my collapse." He acted as though he was waiting for Melissa to deny the truth.

"I thought I'd wait until I could talk to you about it. So here I am. I want to know the truth about your condition, and then, and only then, will I decide about a story."

Glencoe eased back against the thickly cushioned executive chair. "We've been talking to each other for four years now, am I right?"

"You are," Melissa answered almost like a child who was facing chastisement. A part of her wanted to focus her attention on the pearl buttons of her blue linen suit, while another part couldn't break away from the sincerely pained expression of her governor.

"You've always seemed an objective reporter, even though there were times when I was sure you disagreed with my solutions."

Melissa smiled, acknowledging the truth of his words.

"But," Glencoe continued, "you were one of the rare few in the media who kept her own convictions to herself and wrote the facts of the matter."

"I've tried to be fair," Melissa replied. "I'm trying to be fair now."

"I appreciate that, Mrs. Jordon. So I'm going to level with you, completely off the record, of course."

Melissa nodded and he continued. "I have a type of stomach cancer. I'm undergoing some experimental drug therapy, and it was the side effects of that therapy that caused my collapse in Lindsborg."

"I see. Is therapy controlling the cancer?"

"At this point it is difficult to say. The doctors have the highest hopes that the medicine will do the trick." He paused and slowly came around to where Melissa sat. "I can't begin to tell you what kind of harm it would do my reelection campaign if you were to announce I have cancer."

"But surely there are plenty of people who know the truth."

"Those who aren't bound by laws of confidentiality are extremely loyal and faithful to me."

"Then you're a lucky man," Melissa replied. "But it's only a matter of time before someone spills the story, and I think you and I both know the truth of that."

"It's something I live with every day," admitted Glencoe. "But the election is only months away, and if you were to announce this now it would put an end to my career." Beads of sweat were evident on his forehead.

"But don't you owe the people of Kansas the truth about your physical condition? As a servant of the people, don't they deserve to know exactly who they've elected to office?"

"Yes, of course," Glencoe replied. "But there isn't another person in my party with strong public appeal. The lieutenant governor isn't politically savvy enough to hold his own in a gubernatorial race, or I'd consider backing out in favor of him."

"So you plan to just keep going full-speed ahead?" Melissa felt her reporter's aggressive nature return. "What happens if the medication you're using causes your judgment to be less than sound? What if you endanger yourself or someone else, all because you didn't want to lose the election?"

Glencoe crossed his arms and leaned back against his desk. "I've considered all those possibilities."

"And?"

"And I'm training the lieutenant governor to do more than sit and look pretty."

Melissa smiled at the thought of the young man who held the second-in-command job for the state of Kansas. More than once she'd criticized him in the newspaper for doing little or nothing to aid the state. She had even suggested the position be audited and reevaluated to include additional responsibilities and accountability.

"I see you approve of that idea," Glencoe said, as though reading her mind. "But he's far from ready for the position of governor. He could never win an election on his own. I can. With reelection, I can give over more responsibility to him, and if the worst happens, he'll be set to fill my shoes."

"I see," Melissa responded, feeling that the governor had a good point. She liked Ed Glencoe, and it was her personal desire that he win reelection. But she was a news reporter and she was supposed to be objective.

"All I'm asking," Glencoe said with a look of pleading that instantly made Melissa feel guilty, "is that you say nothing until after the election. I, in turn, promise to keep you fully apprised of my condition, and I'll give you some important exclusives to make up for the one you aren't getting to share with the world."

Melissa's mind struggled with the fact that this story was big news. She held the power to possibly change the November election.

"I'll think it over and let you know," she said, getting to

her feet. She picked up her purse and walked to the door. "Thank you for your honesty. I won't say anything until I discuss it again with you."

"Thank you, Mrs. Jordon."

"Melissa. Call me Melissa."

Eight

Monday mornings were always hectic at HEARTBEAT. The weekend seemed to breed new problems and complications in a way that always promised excitement. Today looked to be no different. Cara had just settled down to a steaming cup of coffee and a large stack of letters when a knock sounded on her office door. Assuming it to be Joe, she pushed back the letters.

"Come in."

A man entered the office in a determined businesslike manner. He extended his arm to shake hands with Cara as he introduced himself.

"Russell Owens. I'm managing the Robert Kerns gubernatorial campaign."

The man wore an expensive gray suit and wire-rimmed glasses that gave him a studious look. Cara immediately pegged him as a little boy trying hard to appear grown-up.

"I'm Cara Kessler," she finally replied. "Won't you have a seat?"

Mr. Owens gave her a closed-mouth smile and a once-over with his eyes that made her feel as though she'd just been undressed. *Never mind with the little-boy appearance,* she thought. She began to feel increasingly nervous when the silence stretched to a full minute.

"What is it . . . what can I do . . . for you?" she asked hesitantly.

He appeared to be nearly leering as he replied, "Perhaps

it's what I can do for you."

"I'm sure I don't know what you mean." Cara decided to ignore the expression on his face.

"Are you familiar with Robert Kerns?"

"No, not really," she answered. "I heard the announcement a while back that he intended to run for governor, but otherwise I don't know the man."

"Let me enlighten you then," Owens began. "Bob is a tremendous man of talent with a background in law and a reputation for aiding the little man. He's a family man with a wife and two college-aged kids. He believes, as do I, that he would make a great governor for our fair state."

Russell drew a breath, and Cara utilized the moment to break in on his speech. "That sounds all very well and good, Mr. Owens, but I don't see what it has to do with me, or with HEARTBEAT."

Russell nodded. "I'm sure you don't, but that's why I'm here. We'd like to solicit your support for our campaign."

"I see," Cara said, getting to her feet. "I can assure you I have no interest in such a cooperation. My ministry is a nonprofit organization and we don't allow ourselves to become politically involved. I'm sure you can appreciate the implications and problems that can be created. . . ."

"And you can surely appreciate the possibility of support from the governor's office once Kerns is elected. If you are one of the avid supporters who help to see him elected, it could mean a great deal to your business."

"My business, as you put it, is just that—my business." Cara smoothed down her floral print skirt in a nervous gesture. "I have no desire to drag this ministry into an association that could suggest a political endorsement of any one person."

"Mrs. Kessler . . . Cara," Russell said without asking permission, "it is very important you hear me out." His voice seemed to drop an octave. "You're just the kind of person we're looking for, especially since you have political experience in your background."

Cara couldn't keep the surprise from registering on her face. "How would you know what is or isn't in my background?"

Owens got to his feet. "I've taken the time to study your profile. Your father was a district representative for over eight years."

"So?" She was growing more agitated by the minute. How dare this man research her background!

"You know what's involved in running for political office. You know the schedules and the demands."

"Yes, and that's exactly why I'm not interested in becoming involved in another campaign. Your Mr. Kerns may well be the very best candidate that this state has seen in years, and I still wouldn't want to play that game again. My father endured a great deal of suffering at the hands of the state political machine. It nearly cost him his health, and I have no desire to see it cost mine." She could feel her cheeks grow flushed.

Russell leaned across the desk. "You're very beautiful, even when you're uptight."

Cara hadn't believed Owens possible of more surprises, yet here he was stooping to flattery. "What has that got to do with anything?"

"I was hoping maybe if I couldn't interest you just yet in Kerns' campaign, I might get you to have dinner with me."

Cara gave him a hard look. "I'm sorry, no."

Russell shrugged. "Well, that's two strikes. I wonder if I dare brave a third time at bat."

"Mr. Owens, I'm very busy," Cara stated, crossing the

room to the door and opening it wide. "If you don't mind, I need to get back to work."

Russell came to her and stood so close that Cara backed up a step. "Would you at least agree to meet my boss? He's very impressed with the work you do here."

Cara felt her resolve crumble. It wasn't wise to make enemies out of powerful people—her father had taught her that much from his days as a representative. Perhaps if she met this man face-to-face, she could explain why she had no interest in politics.

"I suppose I could meet with Mr. Kerns for a short while."

"You won't be sorry," Russell replied. "I'll arrange the meeting and get back with you."

"Very well."

Cara watched him leave. She had a strange sense of foreboding, but knew it was probably just the way he'd started to come on to her. She wasn't used to men paying her such open attention.

Going back to her desk, Cara couldn't help but think of her chance encounter with Harry Oberlin.

"What a contrast," she murmured, thinking of the two men. Then her thoughts drifted to Jack.

Cara had often thought the pain of his death would never go away, but she had to admit she'd not really thought about Jack as often as before. It was just those early morning hours, when she had time to linger in bed, that the loneliness seemed to grip her afresh.

She picked up one of the framed photos on her desk. It was a family picture taken only weeks before Jack had died. Brianna shared so many of her father's features. She had his mouth and nose, and where Cara's features were more delicate and elfish, Brianna's and Jack's were rugged and boldly pronounced.

"I'm not doing you any favors, Bri," she said to her daughter's five-year-old image. "I've immersed myself too long in Jack and the memories we shared."

They had barely lived in Topeka for two months before the accident, and since that tragic day, Cara had changed relatively little in their lives. They lived in the same apartment Jack had chosen for them, and even the furniture was positioned just as he'd arranged it. She remembered with regret her reaction when Brianna had suggested they move to an apartment complex with a swimming pool. Bri couldn't understand her mother's reluctance to give up the last place she'd shared with Jack.

I've been stuck in the past, Cara admitted to herself. Somehow, meeting up with Melissa had allowed these thoughts to surface. Perhaps they were helped along by finding herself the focus of attraction by two very different men.

"Maybe it is time for a change." She traced Jack's outline with her finger. "I will always love you, and there will always be a part of me that belongs only to you. But I know it's wrong to live in the past." Tears came to her eyes and blurred the photo. Letting go was so much more than words and symbolic gestures.

Putting the picture in her drawer, Cara grabbed a tissue and wiped her face. *So much wasted time,* she thought. *Time I could have given Brianna. Time I could have spent among the living instead of the dead.* With new resolve, she picked up her Bible and found confirmation of her decision in the words of Philippians. *"But one thing I do. Forgetting what is behind and straining toward what is ahead, I press on toward the goal to win the prize for which God has called me heavenward in Christ Jesus."*

"God, give me strength," she whispered. "Give me the

ability to put aside the past and reach forward. Let me make a new start with my life, with Brianna—even with my work for You."

"Hey, Cara, you okay?"

She looked up to find Joe Milken peering into her office. She hadn't even heard him open the door. The sandy-haired youth pastor had an infectious smile and a perpetual tan that gave him the appearance of living outdoors year-round. Today he looked like a lumberjack in his red-and-black flannel shirt and blue jeans. Stepping into her office, Joe's rugged face held nothing but concern for her.

"Is something wrong?" he questioned. "You're crying."

"I'm just saying good-bye," she replied, trying hard to smile.

"Good-bye?" His voice held a note of concern. "To HEARTBEAT?"

"No, of course not. I've just been dealing with my fixation on the past. I know you understand, because you've been after me for a long time to make certain changes and do things differently. I've always held you up to Jack's standards, just as I've always held myself up to them. But . . ." She fell silent for a moment and gathered her strength. "Jack is gone and time marches forward instead of marching in place. I want you to put those ideas of yours on paper. We'll go over them together and see where they lead us. Are you game?"

Joe's expression was one of relief and satisfaction. "What in the world brought about this change?"

Cara grew thoughtful. "Little things. Brianna would mention doing something or buying something, and I'd find myself wondering what Jack would want. She also says things about wishing she had a daddy," Cara remembered in a wave of guilt. "Then there's my childhood friend from Hays, Melissa Jordon."

"Is she the one who wanted to write about HEARTBEAT?"

"Yes. Well, she got me to thinking. I mean, I listened to her talk about her life and where she'd gone with it in the last ten years. The last time we'd seen each other was at Jack's funeral, and I realized how much I'd closed myself away from the rest of the world. So little has changed for me since his death. HEARTBEAT and Brianna have been my entire domain and nothing else has existed."

Joe nodded. "And what about now?"

"Now we start fresh and new. I leave Jack with God and delegate my mourning period to the past."

Joe crossed the room. "May I be the first to welcome you back." He extended his arm and Cara surprised herself by getting up and hugging him.

"You've been a dear friend, Joe. You and Suzanne both have been so patient with me," Cara said, mentioning Joe's wife. "This ministry would have folded if I'd been left to my own devices. I'm glad God gave me the sense to bring you on board."

Joe gave her a brotherly pat on the back. "I'm just glad you are ready to take a fresh look at your life."

Cara's gaze drifted down to the drawer where Jack's image now resided. "I wonder why now, Joe? Why all of the sudden, after all this time?"

Joe held her at arm's length. "Because now is the right time. My guess is there's something important coming your way, and God is preparing you by taking care of old business first."

"I suppose I can see the logic in that," Cara admitted.

"Just don't be surprised when things start to happen."

For reasons beyond her understanding, Cara remembered the sense of foreboding she'd felt earlier. Maybe things were already starting to happen.

Nine

By Friday, Cara and Brianna had both exhausted themselves making new plans for their lives. With Brianna's desire to move to an apartment with a pool, Cara had made some calls and had managed to secure a three-bedroom townhouse in a complex called Misty Glen.

She and Brianna had immediately set out arranging each of the townhouse rooms on graph paper. Cara had never seen Brianna happier, and it gave her cause to pay closer attention to the child's emotional well-being. Cara could tell her daughter was thrilled at the new sense of purpose and direction in their lives. Years of mausoleum-like living had stifled her daughter's imagination and free spirit, but planning for their new home seemed to open them both up to life again.

Checking on the sleeping child, Cara stood for several minutes and watched Brianna's even breathing. Long hair wound its way around her angelic face and Cara reached out to smooth it back with a smile. Silently, she thanked God for giving her Brianna and for helping her to recognize her child's needs before it was too late.

A ringing telephone drew Cara's thoughts away from prayer. *Who could be calling at this hour?* she wondered, quickly closing Brianna's door behind her. She reached the phone in her bedroom but found no one on the line.

"Hello?" she repeated before hearing the distinct click that signaled disconnection.

Deciding it must have been a wrong number, Cara

shrugged off her clothes and pulled on pajamas and a robe. There was still time to look over some paper work before she went to bed, so Cara made her way to the dining room and spread out her work on the table.

She'd barely read through the first page when a knock sounded on her door. Another glance at her watch revealed that it was nearly ten o'clock. Immediately thinking of her elderly next-door neighbor, Cara opened the door expecting to see Mrs. Pritchard.

"Good evening, Mrs. Kessler." It was Russell Owens. Beside him stood a very distinguished-looking man.

Cara stared at them in open-mouthed surprise. "What are you doing here?"

"You agreed to meet with Mr. Kerns, and I thought perhaps your home would afford us an element of privacy," Owens answered.

Kerns waited no longer for his introduction. "I'm Bob Kerns, the next governor of Kansas."

He smiled in a way that immediately put Cara on her guard.

"May we come in?" Bob asked smoothly.

"Certainly not!" Cara exclaimed and pulled her robe together tightly. "It's after ten. Surely we can have this discussion in my office on Monday."

"It won't wait," said Kerns, pushing Cara aside to admit himself into the apartment.

"You can't just barge in here!"

Kerns eyed her for a moment, then shook his head and replied, "Calm down and hear me out. What I have to say could be quite profitable to you and your business."

By this time Russell had come into the apartment behind her and was quietly closing the door. Cara whirled around at the sound of the lock sliding into place. Her fears mounted with every second as she looked first at Owens and then to Kerns.

"This is uncalled for. Get out of my apartment." She tried hard to appear authoritative, but her voice sounded childlike even in her own ears.

"Calm down, Cara," Russell said, placing his hands on her shoulders.

Cara shuddered and pushed him away with her elbows. "Don't ever touch me again." Her voice held new power, and Russell backed away with his arms raised.

"Easy does it. I didn't mean anything by it. We aren't exactly the neighborhood boogeymen, you know."

Kerns chuckled. "I believe we've just taken this young woman off guard. Cara, why don't you come sit down and we'll tell you why we're here."

She realized they weren't going anywhere until she heard them out. "Very well, but I need to change my clothes first. Wait here."

Hurrying to her bedroom, Cara went immediately to the telephone. She started to dial 911, then put the receiver down. Robert Kerns was a gubernatorial candidate. She recognized him from numerous television interviews. Surely he was on the up and up. She drew a deep breath. There was really no reason to be afraid or to call the police. Was there?

Biting her lower lip, Cara hurried into a lavender sweat suit. She resented the way Owens and Kerns pushed her around, but perhaps she could get this over with and be rid of both of them for good.

She walked slowly back to the living room and assumed a defensive posture. Kerns and Owens looked up at her from where they sat on the sofa. Both were perfectly attired in business suits and striped red-and-blue ties. And both looked at her with the same self-satisfied smug expression.

Cara switched to the offensive. "If you're comfortable, I'd appreciate it if you would tell me what merits coming here in the middle of the night." She held a stony stare on Kerns, hoping the man would grow uncomfortable and apologetic. He didn't. Instead, he seemed only amused and smiled broadly, looking too much like a Cheshire cat.

"Please," Kerns motioned, "have a seat with us and we'll explain."

Cara noted the ease in which he commanded the situation. His square jaw was firmly set and the smile was frozen on his face, but it was eyes the color of steel that held her attention most. They were cold, lifeless, shark's eyes. Cara could see that Robert Kerns was the one in charge, and in that moment of revelation she could also see that he knew it as well.

Almost against her will, Cara sank into the nearest chair. "All right, I'm sitting. What is it that couldn't wait until Monday?"

Owens and Kerns exchanged a brief look of satisfaction before Kerns turned back to Cara. "As you know, I'm running for governor."

"Yes, both of you've made that abundantly clear," she replied dryly. "And you want the support of HEARTBEAT."

"In a way," Kerns said in a slow hypnotic manner. "In a way. You see, I'm very impressed with the work you've done in that organization. You have a great deal to offer this state, including a dynamic personality that will automatically draw people to you."

"I don't see why this has anything—" Cara began, but Kerns quickly silenced her.

"If you'll give me a chance to speak, I'll tell you what it has to do with you."

Cara crossed her arms against her chest and waited in obvious irritation.

"That's better," Kerns replied.

His manner and tone suggested he was a parent dealing with a child rather than a grown woman. His entire demeanor made Cara angry. How dare he come into her house late in the night and order her around! Cara had never felt so helpless, and without even realizing what she was doing, she found herself praying for God's protection.

". . . and that's why I want you to be my running mate."

Cara suddenly realized she hadn't been paying attention. "I'm sorry, what were you saying?" There was no way he could have said what she'd heard.

Kerns' eyes narrowed ever so slightly. "We will be here all night if I am to repeat everything I say. This is a matter of utmost importance, and I'd appreciate it if you would give me your undivided attention."

Cara held her temper in check and drew a deep breath. "You have exactly"—she looked at her watch—"ten minutes to wrap this thing up. I've had about as much as I'm going to take for one evening."

Kerns smiled in his patient annoying manner. "I'm certain this must be a surprise for you, but as I said, I've done my homework and you have a great deal to offer this state. You have a recognizable name out west with your father's terms in the statehouse. People respect his name, as well as that of Kessler for a variety of reasons. You know how the political scene works, at least from a small district approach. I can't imagine a stronger, more beneficial team for Kansas than Kerns and Kessler."

With perfect timing, Russell pulled out the makeshift banner and held it up for Cara to see.

"You can't be serious!" Cara gasped. "You want me to be your running mate?"

"That's the general idea here," Kerns said rather snidely.

"Forget it," Cara said, quickly getting to her feet. "Politics is a dirty nasty business and I want nothing to do with it. Being the district representative nearly killed my father. The work wasn't the hard part, either. It was the messiness of the game surrounding the job. I don't ever want to subject my loved ones to that kind of ordeal, and if you had made yourself clear the other day, I would have said no then, just as I'm saying no today."

Instead of making a move to leave Cara's apartment, Kerns eased back into the plush cushioning of the couch and crossed his legs defiantly. "I think you should hear me out."

Cara felt as though hands were around her throat strangling out any reply. Robert Kerns somehow made her feel helpless to deny his demands. Feeling like a trapped animal, Cara moved toward the front door.

"I want you both to leave. Now."

"Cara, just listen to us," Russell said in a soothing tone, coming to her side. "You have a chance here to reach a lot of kids. I thought your ministry was to better the youth of Kansas."

"Exactly," Cara replied, "and I can't do that from an office in the Capitol."

"You can't do it if HEARTBEAT folds, either," Kerns said flatly.

Cara turned. "What are you saying?" She felt her pulse speeding and her breath coming at a quickened pace. Everything in her told her to get as far away from this man as possible. Robert Kerns represented a very serious danger.

Perhaps Kerns sensed he was losing her with his railroading tactics. Perhaps he read the fear in her eyes and worried that the scene would become unpleasant. For whatever reason, he seemed to change his approach right before her eyes.

"I need you, Cara Kessler. You represent the traditional morals and family ethics that I value. People know you for those principles and they respect you. I want to do great things for this state, and I believe with the right partner we can make Kansas the best state in the union."

Cara relaxed a bit. "I want Kansas to be the best state in the union as well, but I'm no politician. I'm not even remotely interested in government, and I certainly have no desire to find myself answering to a legislative body, or to you. I answer to God and my direction comes from Him. Believe me, I'd know if He were leading me in this direction, and I would act on it. But He isn't, and therefore, I have no other recourse but to say no to you and your plans."

Kerns continued as though Cara had never spoken a word. "I'm a family man with two great kids and a beautiful wife. We're a close-knit group, but we aren't as widely recognizable as you are. Together, you and I would virtually reach every voting taxpayer in Kansas. We would—"

"You are not listening to me, Mr. Kerns!" Cara shouted above his speech. "I am not interested. End of subject. Period!"

Kerns motioned Owens. "I believe we have something here that might help you to change your mind."

Owens handed Kerns a briefcase. The snap of the latches echoed in the uneasy silence. Cara felt she was becoming an unwilling participant in a very bad theatrical production. What could he possibly have that would change her mind?

Bob Kerns held up a thick folder. "This might be of interest to you." Cara stared at him, uncertain what she should do. "Take it. You will find it self-explanatory."

Stepping forward hesitantly, Cara reached out for the papers. Her gaze never left his face. "Why don't you just tell me what's in here?" she asked.

"I'd rather you see for yourself. Go on, open the folder."

Kerns waited for her to obey, and Cara felt no other choice but to do exactly as he commanded. Opening the folder, she stared down at crisp white bond paper. Obviously typed in the legal jargon of which Kerns was most comfortable, Cara read, *"State of Kansas versus HEARTBEAT Ministries."*

"I don't understand," Cara said, looking back up to catch Kerns' stoic expression.

"It's really quite simple. You come on board as my running mate, willingly, happily, and of course, offering your utmost support for my candidacy, and HEARTBEAT will continue to thrive. In fact, it will probably blossom into everything you ever dreamed it could be. Reject my proposal, however, and HEARTBEAT Ministries will be tied up in lawsuits from now until that God of yours calls you to kingdom come."

"But HEARTBEAT has done nothing wrong," Cara said softly. She closed the folder, knowing even before Kerns answered that the truth didn't matter. She had attracted the attention of the very powerful, and now she was going to pay dearly.

"It will take years to prove otherwise, and by that time all of your resources will be exhausted and the ministry will die. And believe me, it won't be a quiet death. No, Cara, I will personally see to it that the battle is ugly and vicious and very, very public."

Cara felt as though someone had knocked the air out of her. Nearly stumbling, she fell into her chair again and hugged the folder to her chest. "Why are you doing this? I've done nothing to you. You don't even know me."

"I know enough," Kerns said with frightening certainty. "I know you don't need the money generated by HEARTBEAT for your living. Your husband's life insurance and the award from his wrongful death suit have left you and your daughter financially solid." Cara's mouth dropped open in shock. "But your friend Joe Milken is not as fortunate. He desperately needs this job to help subsidize his meager earnings as a youth pastor."

"And you don't care that an innocent man and his wife will be ruined if you carry out your plans?"

Kerns eyed her with contempt. "I leave caring about such things to big-hearted people like you, Mrs. Kessler. What Milken does with his future is of little interest to me, but you should know one other thing."

"And what's that?" Cara questioned warily. What more could he possibly throw her way?

"Milken's wife is expecting a baby. She just found out today."

Cara stared in disbelief. "Joe said nothing to me about it."

"It's my understanding they are keeping it to themselves. You see, Mrs. Milken has suffered through two miscarriages. I guess they're a little afraid to get their hopes up."

Cara looked at Russell Owens as if expecting him to deny the truth of Kerns' words.

"It's all true, Cara," he said, seeming to read her mind.

"How can you know these things?" Cara asked, turning her attention back to Kerns.

"I learn what I need to know when and where I need to know it most. Remember that. There will be no secrets between us."

Ten

Cara looked across her desk to find Joe Milken's puzzled expression most disturbing. She couldn't help but recall what Kerns had said in regard to Suzanne and the pregnancy, but because Joe hadn't volunteered any information, Cara hadn't brought up the subject. What she had brought up was her resignation.

"I don't understand," Joe said again. "Just a few days ago you assured me that leaving HEARTBEAT was the furthest thing from your mind. If you don't mind my asking, what changed?"

Cara bit her lip. There was no way to explain that she had to leave because an overbearing tyrant with secrets and power beyond her imagination was forcing her. She tried to smile at Joe, but it was a poor attempt. "I can't begin to give you all the details," she said, "but another project, of sorts, has come up."

"Something that means more to you than HEART-BEAT?"

"No, not really," Cara replied. She knew the conversation was headed in the wrong direction. If she continued along these lines, she'd soon be spilling the truth of Kerns' threats, and that was something she was determined not to do. She couldn't add stress to Joe's life. Especially not if Suzanne needed to remain calm in order to bring her child to term. Cara couldn't do anything that might risk that happiness. "It's just something I feel I must do," she said, knowing that it wasn't a lie.

"I see."

Joe sounded so dejected that Cara immediately pushed the conversation forward. "It will be a tremendous financial benefit for you, Joe. And as director of HEARTBEAT you will be able to take the ministry in the direction you have felt it should go."

"But we were going to decide those things together. You and me. This is your baby. I can't just take it over."

The word "baby" stabbed at Cara. She desperately tried to convince herself that she was doing the right thing. "The baby has grown up and needs a man with vision at the helm. I'm just starting to move forward in my life. You agreed that I needed a little change."

"A little change, yes," Joe admitted. "But you've already done more than a little with the plan to move to Misty Glen. Changing jobs is another matter entirely."

Cara nodded. "I know this comes as a shock to you, but it will be a good thing. I know you and Suzanne can use the extra money."

"Well, that's true enough. We've got a few extra bills coming our way in the future, but even so, I wouldn't want you to think you had to do this on my account."

Cara sighed. *If you only knew,* she thought. She was doing this on everyone's account. Everyone's but her own. No, that was a lie. She was doing this for herself as well. She didn't want to see HEARTBEAT ruined. She'd worked too hard at making it a great organization. It was her dream. It had been Jack's dream, too.

"I'm doing this because it's the right thing to do," Cara finally said in a sobering tone. "I've prayed and I just think it's the best way."

Joe leaned back in his seat. His face clearly showed he was

still stunned by the news. "I just can't imagine the place without you."

"Well, I won't be totally removed. I'll stay on for a while, and after that I'll still drop in from time to time to see how things are going. Besides, we'll always be friends, and you and Suzanne are welcome to come by the apartment anytime. Especially after—" She shut her mouth with an abruptness that caused Joe to raise his brows in question. She'd almost mentioned the baby.

"After what?"

Cara stammered, "Well . . . after . . . I mean—" She stopped to collect her thoughts. "After the November election."

Joe laughed. "What in the world does the November election have to do with anything?"

"It relates to my other project," Cara said, fidgeting with her pencil. "You see, Robert Kerns has asked me to be his running mate in the gubernatorial race."

Joe stopped laughing and his mouth formed a silent O. "This is a joke, right?"

"No, it's not," Cara answered very seriously. "I can do a lot of good for the kids in this state if I should become the next lieutenant governor. Just think of the influence I'll have and the opportunity to be a positive role model."

"But, Cara, you hate politics. You've said so a million times. Now you're telling me that you plan to run for lieutenant governor of Kansas?"

"That's about the long and the short of it. Do I get your vote?" asked Cara with a nervous grin.

"You're serious. You're really going to leave HEART-BEAT to get involved with politics. I can't believe this. Are you on some kind of publicity kick?"

Cara winced at the accusing tone. "I just think I can be of

more help to the ministry if I work with Kerns as lieutenant governor." It wasn't a lie, that was for sure. Cara bore the burden of knowing what would happen to HEARTBEAT—and Joe—if she didn't do exactly as Kerns wanted.

"Are you sure this is what God wants?"

Cara wondered that herself. She'd prayed and asked for a direction out, but God's silence was almost deafening in her ears. She had no peace in her heart when she thought about rejecting Kerns and battling through the threats. There was a chance he was bluffing about his lawsuits, but could she take that chance and risk everything? No, this was the only answer.

"I feel confident," Cara said softly, "that I'm doing the right thing."

Joe got up and stuffed his hands deep into his jeans pockets. "I guess this will take some getting used to."

"But you'll take the directorship, right? You'll see that HEARTBEAT makes the changes to keep it a strong ministry for God?"

Joe nodded. "I'll talk to Suzanne, but I'm pretty sure she'll agree with me. Running HEARTBEAT is a dream I've always had."

Cara could finally smile from the heart. "Good. Maybe you should bring Suzanne on board as your partner. After all, HEARTBEAT was always intended to be a husband and wife ministry."

Joe seemed to perk up at this thought. "She'd love it, and I know having her here would make me happy."

"Then it's settled. We'll draw up the papers tomorrow."

"If you're sure," Joe said, standing in the doorway. "It's not too late to tell me you've changed your mind."

"I'm sure about this, Joe."

Cara waited until she heard Joe close the door to his own

office before picking up the telephone. She could tell by the lighted second line that Joe was probably already calling Suzanne with the news. Dialing the number Kerns had given her, Cara wasn't surprised when Russell Owens answered the telephone.

"Kerns for governor, this is Russell Owens."

"Mr. Owens, this is Cara Kessler." She felt her mouth go dry and wondered if she could go through with it.

"Well, it's good to finally hear from you." He didn't sound at all surprised that she was calling. "What can I do for you?"

Cara hated playing the game but knew it would be only the first of many to come. "I'm calling to let you know that I'll run with Bob Kerns." She could imagine the smug smile of satisfaction on the man's face at that moment.

"Cara, that's great news. I know Bob will be pleased. Why don't you plan to come over to the office, say around four. We'll need to plan the press release."

"Very well," Cara said rather formally and hung up the phone without saying good-bye. She felt like a prisoner being led to the gallows. The finality of it all seemed to wash over her in waves of despair. What if Kerns actually won the election? What if she actually became the next lieutenant governor of Kansas? The entire thing was too much to consider as a possibility. From that moment on, it became Cara's fervent hope and prayer that Kerns would suffer a terrible defeat at the polls and she would be allowed to go about her business.

But after today, what would her business be? She was turning HEARTBEAT over to the Milkens. She couldn't just take it back when the election failed to put her into office. With a heavy sigh, she looked at the photograph of Brianna. It stood in the place of the old family photo and gave her a sense of encouragement. There were too many unanswered questions, but one thing was certain: Brianna needed her, and little else mattered. She would concern herself with the uncertain future when the time and place demanded it. To struggle with it before then seemed to deny that God was in control of her life.

To deny that would be giving in to utter despair.

Eleven

Making her way across the parking lot of the finest hotel in Topeka, Cara dreaded this evening like no other. Inside, the press and public waited for her to join Kerns in announcing her candidacy for lieutenant governor.

She looked down at her sedate blue suit and hoped she'd remember everything Kerns had told her to say. The only way Cara could make it through this nightmarish evening was to remember the ultimate goal. She had to protect HEART-BEAT and those she loved.

Entering through the glass doors, Cara was immediately besieged by reporters and bright lights. Camera crews from seven major television stations around the state shoved microphones in her face and attacked her with questions.

"Mrs. Kessler, will you tell us how you came to be Robert Kerns' running mate?"

"Mrs. Kessler, who will head up HEARTBEAT now that you're running for lieutenant governor?"

"Mrs. Kessler . . ."

The noise was overwhelming and Cara immediately began to look for some sign of Kerns or Owens. She didn't want this kind of attention. It was nothing like the quiet affairs of her ministry work. It wasn't even the mild pandemonium of her father's district campaigns. This was a hideous monster out of control.

"Ah, there you are," Bob Kerns said, coming to stand beside Cara. He took hold of her elbow with one hand and maneuvered her expertly through the crowd. "Are you ready?" he managed to whisper against her ear.

"No."

"You'll do just fine." His grip tightened on her arm as he led her toward the ballroom where they would make their formal announcement.

Kerns, too, wore a blue suit and made a striking match at Cara's side. His dark hair was combed straight back, while Cara's shoulder-length coif was parted on the side and delicately curled under at the ends. They appeared to be the all-American couple—polished and shined to perfection, no visible blemish to mar their image.

Cara allowed Kerns to take her through the onslaught of reporters to the ballroom where friends and supporters were gathered. Kerns had wanted her to bring Brianna, but Cara had flatly refused. There would be enough disruptions in her daughter's life later, especially if the election went their way. Cara could see no reason to put Brianna through any more than was absolutely necessary.

"This is my wife, Debra, and daughter Danielle," Kerns said, stopping in front of a pencil-thin blonde and a feminine version of himself.

Cara smiled at the women and felt a cold reception from Debra Kerns. "I'm pleased to meet you," Debra said, but there was no truth in the statement.

Danielle Kerns was also hesitant in her greeting, but obviously well-trained in public appearance. "I've heard great things about you, Mrs. Kessler," Danielle said, extending a hand. The two women shook hands and exchanged smiles, but Cara knew she was an unwelcome presence. *But why?*

Bob continued to move Cara through the room filled with well-wishers and a variety of "KERNS AND KESSLER" paraphernalia. Banners overhead in red, white, and blue declared the team in broad bold lettering. Across the podium where their announcement would be made, Cara found a huge rosette with "KERNS AND KESSLER" in gold lettering across the center. The sheer weight of her decision was beginning to settle upon her shoulders.

"And this is . . ." came the introduction to yet another of Robert Kerns' associates. Cara smiled politely and shook hand after hand. Both her face and hand ached from the abuse by the time Kerns led her to the podium. Would this night never end?

Searching the room, Cara felt a small amount of relief when she spotted Melissa Jordon. Although, her friend's expression told Cara that there would be plenty to discuss when the evening was over.

"Ladies and gentlemen, I would like to introduce to you a remarkable young woman who has taken the state by storm. She heads up HEARTBEAT Ministries, a business devoted to the promotion of our young people. She has given ten years of her life working to motivate our cities and towns into action on behalf of our youth. She has been awarded numerous community action awards from around the state and last year was voted Topeka's Woman of the Year. She is a widow and single mother who has broken the stereotypes to prove herself over and over again. I give you now my running mate and the next lieutenant governor of Kansas, Cara Kessler!"

Cameras clicked and flashed as the photo opportunity of Kerns and Kessler side-by-side became destined for front-page news in tomorrow's papers.

Cara remembered very little of her speech. It had been written for her by Russell and rehearsed by Kerns himself. She knew it was short and simple and kept the focus of the race on Kerns, but other than that she recalled few details. Suddenly, this was no game, and she was now stuck in a situation that seemed hopeless and frightening. She had relinquished the podium to Kerns amidst the applause of an enthusiastic crowd and forced herself to stand at his side until the conclusion.

With the speeches wrapped up, Kerns encouraged the crowd to mingle and enjoy the refreshments offered by the hotel caterers. Cara took that opportunity to slip away to the rest room before allowing the press to ask a single question. She had to find some peace and quiet, even if it was for only a few minutes. Purposefully finding a rest room as far removed from the ballroom as possible, Cara made her way inside and wished she could lock the door behind her.

She took deep breaths and felt a small amount of peace. If it was this hard just getting through the announcement, how would she ever be able to endure a grueling campaign trail?

"Cara?" Melissa called out as she entered the lounge.

Cara had just taken a seat on the floral print sofa. "I'm afraid so," she answered.

Melissa, dressed in a cream-colored suit that showed off her auburn hair, stood with hands on hips. "Well?"

Cara motioned to the sofa. "Have a seat and we'll talk, off the record."

Melissa smiled. "It's been a pretty trying evening, eh?"

"The worst in my life." Cara shook her head, remembering Jack. "Second worst."

Melissa seemed to understand. "You have to tell me how this all came about. I couldn't believe my ears when they announced you as Bob Kerns' running mate."

"Tell me about it," Cara said in a dejected manner. She pushed her hair back and tried to relax.

"No, that's *your* job. What's going on here?"

Cara cast a wary glance first toward the inner rest room door and then to the outer one. "Melissa, I was hoping we'd have some time to talk, but it has to be off the record. I mean, way, way off the record. Friend to friend."

"You've got it," she answered before dropping down beside Cara.

Cara envied the energy Melissa seemed to emit. "I don't know how you can stay so fresh and chipper through these things," Cara said, suddenly uneasy about confessing the truth for the first time.

"Because I'm not in the spotlight. Which brings us back to you."

Again Cara looked nervously at the doors. "Kerns forced me to join his campaign."

Melissa's eyes widened. "What do you mean?"

Cara drew a deep breath. "He threatened HEARTBEAT with lawsuits and inevitable collapse. He told me he'd see the whole thing tied up in court until kingdom come."

"I still don't think I understand. Why would Kerns put that kind of pressure on you? Are you two longtime enemies?"

"I'd never even heard of Robert Kerns until he announced his candidacy. He, on the other hand, was more than a little familiar with me, both my private life and my ministry work. He knew from his own research that I had wide public appeal across the state and"—she paused to looked quite seriously at Melissa—"he knew things about Brianna and me that he should never have known."

"Such as?"

"He knew we were financially secure due to the insurance and settlements I received after Jack's death."

"Some of that would have been public knowledge," Melissa offered.

"Maybe, but a person's medical condition isn't public knowledge."

"What do you mean, Cara?"

"Please keep this to yourself, but Bob knew something about the wife of my partner, Joe Milken. He had information about a private health condition that he used in the process of coercing me into running with him. Melissa, I don't understand how anyone gets that kind of information legally."

"Who said he obtained it legally?" Melissa replied, kicking her heels off and stretching her feet.

"Missy, I'm scared. Really scared. This man is a monster. What if he doesn't stop at forcing me in this campaign? What if he decides he wants me to do something else? I'm trapped." Tears came to Cara's eyes as the full implication of her situation suddenly became clear. Kerns could just go on threatening her forever, and there'd be nothing Cara could do to stop him.

Melissa took hold of Cara's hand. "I'm so sorry. I had no idea."

"What if he threatens Bri? I just don't know what to do." Cara's voice took on an edge of hysteria. "I don't belong here. I'm not like Bob Kerns and his friends. After what happened to Dad during his political career, I have nothing good to say about politics. And what happens if, God forbid, he should win the election and I'm stuck in the center ring of this circus?"

"I don't know, Cara. But I'll do whatever I can to help you. There must be some way out of this. We just have to think."

Cara dabbed at her eyes. "Do you really think there's a way out?"

"There was a way in," Melissa said softly. "There has to be a way out."

Cara nodded. "Help me find it then. Before it's too late."

"Look," Melissa began, "you have to go out there and at least pretend to be elated at Kerns' choice. We'll fix you up and mingle you around, and no one will know there's a problem. Peter and I will be out of town most of the week, but we'll be back on Saturday. I want you and Brianna to come to dinner, and together with Peter we'll figure something out."

"I can't talk about this in front of Bri. She just thinks it's a part of our new lifestyle changes. Her mind is full of how she'll decorate her room after we move and what kind of new furniture we'll buy. She actually thinks the idea of her mother being lieutenant governor is, as she put it, 'awesome.' "

"It'll be okay, you'll see. I've got a great computer set up with games, and Brianna will find herself so preoccupied that she'll never miss us. We'll set her up and then slip away to another part of the house."

"Okay," Cara said, squaring her shoulders. "We'll come to dinner Saturday."

"Seven sharp, okay?" Melissa said, slipping her shoes back on. "Then come along. We'll powder your nose and touch up your lipstick."

"And I'll play his game a little longer," Cara murmured, hating that she'd lost control of her life.

Twelve

Bob Kerns took a seat behind the desk in his den and began scanning the morning newspapers. The announcement of bringing Cara Kessler on board had gone better than he'd imagined. The papers and television reports were packed with high praise for the woman and for his insightfulness in choosing her.

Picking up the *Kansas City Star*, he read that Cara was an inspiration to other single mothers. The Wichita paper brought to light her childhood involvement in her father's campaigns, long background in administrating youth programs, and one-on-one approach to people. *The Capital-Journal* was surprisingly detached in its coverage of the event. The facts were there, but the story lacked a certain amount of enthusiasm that the other papers contained.

"Melissa Jordon," Kerns read the by-line. He remembered the redhead easily and had already been on the receiving end of her rapid-fire no-nonsense interrogations. Funny, but he'd expected something a bit stronger from Jordon. After all, she'd hung on Cara's skirts all night. Every time Kerns had looked up to see how Cara was handling herself, Melissa Jordon was there beside her.

Picking up the phone he dialed his right-hand man. "Russ?" he questioned at the sound of the groggy voice on the other end. "Look, I know it's early and all, but I need some information ASAP."

"What is it?"

Bob toyed with the paper. "I want to know the background on Melissa Jordon. She's the redheaded reporter for *The Capital-Journal*."

"The one that seemed to adopt Cara as her own pet project?"

"The very same. I need to know if there's something more between them. See what you can find out and have it in my office by noon."

"Okay," Russell answered, still sounding only half awake. "I'll do what I can."

Kerns hung up the phone just as his daughter entered the room. At nineteen, she was a striking young woman—not really beautiful, but definitely noticeable. Kerns liked the fact that she favored him in looks—tall and slender with well-defined features. The only thing she'd inherited from her mother were huge green eyes that seemed to absorb everything around her.

"Dad . . . are you . . . busy?" the girl asked hesitantly.

"Well on my way to it," Kerns replied. "What's up?"

Danielle tightened the belt on her robe. "I know you don't want to hear about this, but I can't stop worrying about Teri. Isn't there anything I can do to find her?"

Kerns' expression remained fixed, but his mind was racing at a rapid pace. Teri Davis was a longtime friend of his daughter, and for over six months now Danielle had been grief-stricken because of her disappearance. "Don't you think it's time to just let it go, Danielle?"

"But she could have been kidnapped or killed! Don't you care? She has no one in this world except her foster parents, and all they keep saying is, 'Teri's run away before.' But, Dad, Teri's almost nineteen and she was really excited about college. I can't see her running away unless something terrible happened."

"Look, Danielle, the girl obviously has her own agenda. You don't fit in it, so stop with the whining." He knew he was being heartless, but he had things of greater importance on his mind. "Everybody grows up and goes their own way. Teri's actions aren't all that surprising. She's never had any real reason to stick around Topeka, and she certainly doesn't owe you an explanation for her choices in life."

"But we were best friends," Danielle said, the hurt evident in her eyes and voice.

"Friends come and go. Obviously the friendship meant more to you than to her, so go make some new friends."

"That's a cruel thing to say," Debra Kerns snapped, coming into the room. "Friendships should be important. Dani and Teri were together for over twelve years."

"Everything runs its course in time," Kerns replied dryly. It certainly had with his marriage, so why not with mere friendship?

"What would you know about long-term relationships, anyway?" Debra quipped and reached out to embrace Danielle. "I know you miss her. Sometimes it's hard to deal with what life throws at you," she said, registering a glaring look on her husband.

"Yes, life sometimes gives you more than you can take, so you compensate for it the best way you can," Kerns said snidely. "Some people take up hobbies. Your mother is a good example of that."

Debra's face contorted in rage. "You're hardly around enough to know what I spend my time doing."

"The monthly bill for Scotch is enough to give me a good idea."

"Stop it, both of you!" Danielle exclaimed, pushing away from her mother. "I can't believe you have to turn everything into a fight. If you hate each other so much, why don't you get a divorce and just be done with it?"

"There's a novel idea, Bob. Why don't we get a divorce?" Debra questioned sarcastically.

Kerns got up from his chair, barely holding his temper in check. There was a deadly silence in the room as he moved to within arm's length of Debra.

"I would love nothing better, but a divorce wouldn't look good right now," he began in a very tight-lipped manner. "Any visible family tension would only cause me problems with the election, and that's why you are both going to hold your tongues and keep your thoughts to yourself. Do you understand me?"

Danielle nodded, but Debra defiantly refused to acknowledge his command. She stared at him silently, the hate quite evident in her green eyes. "Would visible family tension include very visible extramarital affairs?"

Kerns clenched his jaw. He could feel himself close to losing control and knew it was exactly what Debra wanted. Her only way to have even a small amount of influence over him was to anger him to the point of rage. Even now, she was smiling ever so slightly, waiting for him to explode.

Regaining his calm, he said, "I want you both to listen carefully to what I'm about to say. This election is only months away. Your job is to appear as the devoted family. It's that simple. If you fail at your job," he said, looking directly at Debra, "the repercussions will be severe. Don't test me on this and please don't imagine you can beat me at my own game."

"Come on, Mom." Danielle's voice hinged on desperation. "Let's go have breakfast."

"Yes, go pour your mother some breakfast," Kerns said, crossing his arms.

Debra said nothing, but her eyes were ablaze with accusation and hostility. Kerns was without remorse. For most of the time, she could drink herself into oblivion for all he cared. Just so long as she appeared the sober doting wife in public.

Danielle finally managed to lead her mother from the room, and Kerns quickly locked the door behind them. Picking up the first thing he could reach, Kerns hurled it across the room. The sound of shattering pottery echoed in the room and then died away to silence.

How dare they cause him this kind of trouble! They were an ungrateful duo, and Kerns was thankful his son, Gary, had already flown the nest, or it might have been a trio. Recklessly throwing papers into his briefcase, Kerns decided he'd find more peace at campaign headquarters. Let Debra stew in her own juices for a while. She'd settle her nerves with a drink or two, and after that, Kerns knew she'd no longer care whether he was a faithful husband or not.

Thirteen

"Melissa Jordon to see the governor."

The receptionist nodded. "He's expecting you. Go right in."

Melissa made her way to the inner office, wondering why Glencoe wanted to see her. She and Peter had flown in from New York only three hours earlier, and she'd barely made it through the door when the telephone rang and the governor's office summoned her.

"Governor Glencoe," she greeted from the doorway.

"Come in and close the door," the man replied from behind a thick legislative report.

The May afternoon had brought heat and humidity to the Capitol and the room was more than moderately stuffy. With the air-conditioning system on the blink, Glencoe worked rather casually without his jacket and tie.

"I'm glad you could come," he said, pushing aside the blue binder.

"I must say I was surprised to get your call. Is this official business?"

Glencoe shook his head. "Totally off the record."

"I see." Melissa took a seat, already feeling uncomfortable in the linen suit she'd worn. She could only hope the meeting would be a short one.

"I appreciate the way you've kept my condition to yourself," began Glencoe. "I know that as a reporter it couldn't have been easy to sit on a story of this proportion, but I'm glad you did. The doctor just gave me news this morning and I wanted to pass it on to you. The prognosis looks good—my cancer is under control!"

Melissa caught his enthusiasm. "That's great!"

"It's more than great. It means that we made the right decision in keeping silent. Now the election can go forward unhindered. There won't have to be any of those constant reminders of the cancer, and I won't appear compromised in anyone's eyes."

"So you've beat the cancer?" Melissa questioned, hoping he would affirm.

"Not exactly, but as I said, it looks good."

"I'm glad to hear it and I agree," Melissa said thoughtfully. "Keeping quiet was probably the best way to keep the gubernatorial race fair."

"Well, I want you to know my gratitude extends to a more productive vein for you. I will call you first on any news stories related to this office. How's that?"

Melissa was elated at the way this would help to boost her career. "It sounds wonderful." In the back of her mind she thought of Cara. News of Glencoe's cancer could have easily seen Kerns and Kessler as a front-runner for the November election. Remembering how desperate her friend was to escape from that possibility, Melissa was doubly glad she'd kept the story to herself.

Getting to her feet, Melissa extended a congratulatory hand. Glencoe shook it with great zest. "Thank you, Mrs. Jordon."

"Thank you, Governor, and may I wish you the best of health."

Anxious to contact Cara and coordinate their plans for dinner the following evening, Melissa made her way quickly from the office and headed down the stairs. To her surprise the handsome highway patrolman she'd seen in Lindsborg was on the landing below.

Strangely, she felt as if she should know the man, but Melissa presumed it was from the earlier encounter when the governor collapsed. Still, it nagged at her, and as the man approached, she planted herself in front of him.

"You look very familiar to me."

"Probably because you're in the Capitol about as much as I am," the man smiled back. "You're a reporter, right?"

"Yes," Melissa answered, not used to the open willingness of others to converse with a stranger. Usually people handled her frankness with a bit more hesitation. "Melissa Jordon."

"I'm Lieutenant Oberlin. Harry Oberlin. I pilot the governor's plane on occasion and work on his security team the rest of the time."

"Oberlin?" Melissa tried to put the name and face together and match it to something in her past.

"It's not a common one, that's for sure." The salt-and-pepper-haired man smiled broadly.

"I can't help but believe I know you from the past. Are you involved in writing or publishing?" she questioned, wondering if the connection had something to do with Peter instead of herself.

"Not since college and that was a long time ago," Harry assured her. "You said your name was Jordon?"

"Yes, Melissa Jordon. My husband is Peter Jordon."

Harry laughed. "Well, that explains it. Peter and I go way back. You've probably seen pictures of our notorious college days. That was before I settled down and made a few lifestyle changes. I haven't seen or heard from Peter in probably ten or twelve years. We lost touch after college."

Melissa was amazed. "Peter is with a publishing house out

of New York doing acquisition, and we live in Lawrence."

"We'll have to get together then," Harry replied. "I'd love to catch up on old and new times."

"Why don't you come to dinner tomorrow? I know Peter would love to see you," Melissa offered. "You could bring your wife, if you have one."

"I'm not married, but dinner sounds great. What time do you want me and where do I come?"

Melissa wrote down the address and time and handed the slip of paper to Harry. "It isn't hard to find."

"Seven o'clock, eh? Should I bring anything?" He put the paper in his wallet.

"Just yourself."

"Then I'll see you tomorrow," Harry replied. "Thanks."

"Thank me after you've eaten my cooking," Melissa said with a laugh.

It wasn't until Melissa was nearly to her car that she remembered Cara and Brianna were coming to dinner the same night as Harry.

She moaned and put the key in the ignition. *Cara will be absolutely beside herself if we can't talk privately,* Melissa thought. She had mentioned the problem to her husband, but Peter had been so preoccupied with business, he'd hardly said two words to her about anything.

Making her way to her next appointment, Melissa had the strangest notion that fate had just intervened. Maybe she could play cupid and take Cara's mind off her troubles. If Harry got interested in Cara, maybe he could even help her out of the campaign situation. *This mix-up may not be so tragic after all,* she mused to herself. Perhaps it was all intended to be this way.

Fourteen

"The place won't be the same without you," Joe told Cara as she packed the last of her things in a cardboard box.

"It'll probably be better in some ways," Cara replied. "After all, you'll get to have Suzanne here and that will give you more time together."

"For a while . . ." Joe replied hesitantly. "There's something I haven't told you. Actually, Suzanne wanted to keep it under wraps for a while, but I can't see not sharing it with you."

Cara felt a strange tightness in her chest. "Share what, Joe?"

"Suzanne is pregnant." His face beamed, but his eyes revealed his concern.

Cara tried to act surprised. "Congratulations! How wonderful!" Then remembering Kerns' words, she questioned, "Now why in the world wouldn't you want to share that news with the world?"

"Well, it's like this," Joe said, looking down at the floor. "Suzanne has had a couple of miscarriages in the past. We didn't want a lot of fanfare and such, in case she should happen to lose this baby, as well."

"Of course she won't lose this baby. What does the doctor say? Is everything going all right?"

"Yeah, she's doing great." Joe looked up with an expression of hopefulness. "In fact, she's already four months along. That's about three weeks longer than she carried the other babies."

Cara smiled and went to where Joe stood. "I just know it will work out," she said and hugged him. "You'll see. God has it all under control."

"I know," Joe replied, "but He had it under control the first two times, as well."

"True, but you can't stop trusting now. Suzanne's a healthy woman, and I feel confident things are going to be just fine."

"You'll be praying for her, won't you? For me, too?" Joe seemed years younger and very vulnerable.

"Of course. Now how about helping me carry these boxes to my car?"

"Nope, you sit tight and I'll take them all. Save your strength for unloading them at the other end."

Cara started to protest, but just then a ragged-looking young woman holding a baby appeared in the doorway. "Yes, may I help you?"

"Are you the lady who's running with Kerns?"

"Yes, I suppose I am," Cara replied, feeling less than enthusiastic. She eyed the woman, hardly more than a girl, and wondered what possible interest she could have in the gubernatorial race. "I'm Cara Kessler."

"I need to talk to you." Just then the baby started to cry.

"It's okay," Cara said, motioning the upset young woman to come in. There seemed to be a desperation in the girl's eyes. "Have a seat and we'll talk. Joe, if you'll excuse us, we can get these boxes later." Joe nodded and left the office with the one box he already held. Cara noticed that the girl had begun nursing the small baby and offered her a smile. "They do get hungry, don't they?"

"She seems to eat all the time."

"What's her name?" Cara asked softly.

"Jamie."

"And yours?" Cara wondered if the girl would tell her.

"Teri. Teri Davis."

Cara felt uncomfortable just standing, so she took a seat and studied the girl for a moment. She was in her mid-teens, Cara decided, and very tired. A look of exhaustion seemed to permeate everything about the girl. She was ragged in appearance, with unkempt dingy blond hair and old stained clothes that had definitely seen better days. But there was something more about Teri Davis. Cara thought she denoted an attitude of bitterness, maybe even hatred. This was one troubled young woman, and Cara's mind was scrambling to decide how she might help.

"So, what can I do for you?"

Teri looked up. "I've come to warn you about Bob Kerns."

This was an angle Cara had not expected. "Warn me?"

Teri's expression hardened. "Yes, warn you. Bob Kerns is scum, and you shouldn't be associated with the likes of him."

How true you are, Cara thought to herself. She couldn't help but wonder what contact this girl had with Kerns. "How do you know him?" she questioned.

Teri laughed in a cynical manner that suggested experience beyond her years. "Let's just say I know him on a very intimate level," the girl replied. "Jamie is his daughter."

Cara's mouth dropped open. It was impossible to hide her surprise, so she blurted out the first thing that came to mind. "But you're just a child."

"I was even more of one the first time he forced his attention on me," Teri replied.

"I don't understand," Cara said, sickened by the image coming to mind.

"It's not very complicated," Teri began. "I used to be best friends with Danielle. That's his daughter."

"Yes, I know her. Please go on."

Teri paused long enough to rearrange the now sleeping baby. "I used to spend a lot of time at the Kernses' house. Both of my parents are dead, so being with a family where everyone was related and lived all under the same roof held a lot of appeal. I didn't have many friends." Teri's voice dropped off and she seemed to consider Jamie for a moment.

"I'm sure you felt very lonely," Cara offered.

Teri nodded. "Danielle helped me to feel good about myself. She taught me how to use makeup and know what to wear to make myself look good. I used to borrow her clothes because we were about the same size, only I was shorter. Sometimes she'd even give me her clothes when she was through with them."

Cara looked at Teri's now slightly overweight form. She could imagine a slender and well-cared-for girl. "I had a good friend like that when I was younger," Cara said, thinking of Melissa.

"Danielle even helped me graduate from high school and get into college," Teri offered.

Cara was shocked to find that Teri was old enough for college. She looked to be no more than fifteen or sixteen. "How old are you, Teri?"

"I'm eighteen. I'll be nineteen in August."

"And how old is Jamie?"

"Three months."

Teri seemed at a loss for words past this, and Cara desperately wanted to know more. She had to know the truth of the matter. "What happened between you and Mr. Kerns?"

Teri's face contorted in rage. "He raped me, that's what happened. Oh, he says it was all my fault for hanging out at their pool in my bikini, but it didn't just happen once. It happened a bunch of times, and each time he threatened to make me miserable if I told anyone."

Cara felt sick inside. "How old were you when . . . the first time?"

"It was a week before my sixteenth birthday. I remember because he kept saying I looked so much older than sixteen."

Cara couldn't imagine any truth in his assessment. The girl sitting before her barely looked old enough to drive, much less be a mother. *Dear God,* she prayed, *how can I help?*

"Where was Danielle or her mother and brother?"

Teri shrugged. "Gary was already off to college and Debra was busy with one thing or another. She wasn't usually home in the afternoon, and that's when we went swimming."

"But surely Danielle would have had to know what was going on."

"She was usually changing her clothes or taking a shower. There was always some reason for why she was going to be away for more than just a couple of minutes. I think Bob usually planned it that way. Once he even locked her in her room and joked with her afterward that she'd accidently jammed the lock herself."

Cara shook her head. The whole thing was unreal. To imagine this young woman the victim of an animal like Robert Kerns left Cara angry, sick, and determined to help. Grimacing, Cara wasn't aware of the effect of her silence on Teri.

"I didn't want to hurt Danielle," Teri said, her voice growing ragged with emotion. Her eyes were spilling tears. "I was afraid she'd blame me for what had happened."

"But it wasn't your fault, Teri."

"He said it was."

"What he said isn't important. Tell me what happened. Tell me everything."

The young woman appraised Cara for a moment, as if

deciding whether or not she could trust her with the information. "The last time he . . . well, you know . . . the last time, I told him I wasn't going to let him do that to me again. I told him I was pregnant. I think it surprised him, but he didn't care."

"What did he say?"

Teri threw Cara a cynical look. "He asked me whose baby it was. I told him it was his and that I'd never been with anybody else."

"Then what happened?" Cara worked hard to keep her voice from even hinting at accusation.

"He said it wasn't a big deal. He grabbed his wallet, pulled out some money, and ordered me to go have an abortion. I got really mad. I started screaming and calling him names. I think I even hit him. I don't remember for sure. I was just so scared and upset."

"What did he do?" Cara asked, trying to visualize the scene. She'd worked with a great many distressed youths in her time, but the implications of Teri's situation made hers one of the worst.

"He told me to calm down and promised he'd take care of everything. He told me he'd even give me money to make up for the trouble."

"And what did he want in return?"

"My silence and Jamie's life. He absolutely insisted I have the abortion. He said I was too young to be a mother, and it was just going to mess up my future. He told me he'd give me two thousand dollars, and what I didn't need for the abortion, I could use to have fun and forget my problems."

Cara was growing more angry by the moment. She could imagine Bob Kerns thinking it a simple solution. Use the girl up and then throw her aside before things got too complicated. It was just one more example of the Bob Kerns method for getting what he wanted.

"What happened after that, Teri?"

"I told him I wanted five thousand dollars or I'd go to the papers. I'm still not sure why he agreed, but two days later he brought me the cash and the name of an abortion doctor in Wichita. He said the guy was a friend and would do the whole procedure without asking too many questions." Teri hugged Jamie closer to her. "I just couldn't kill my baby." Teri looked at Cara with a pleading expression that begged to know she'd done the right thing.

"You were very brave to bear Jamie alone. You did a wonderful thing giving her life," Cara confirmed.

"I took the money," Teri said, as though it made her an accomplice in a heinous crime. "I let him think I was agreeing to the abortion. I dropped out of college and disappeared. I never even called Danielle. I know she must have been worried, but I couldn't let her know what had happened. I was afraid she'd hate me for what had taken place between me and her dad."

"A good friend would have stood by you," Cara replied. "If Danielle was as close as you say she was, I think she would rather have known and helped you through it."

"But then he would have known I kept the baby," Teri explained. "I couldn't allow him to know or he might have tried to force the abortion issue."

"Yes, I could see that happening."

"You could?" Teri questioned.

"Yes. As a matter of fact, Bob Kerns has forced me into several unpleasant circumstances."

"Really?" Teri wiped her face with the cuff of her sleeve. "But you're famous. You have this HEARTBEAT thing and everybody knows you."

"It doesn't stop evil people from trying to hurt the innocent."

Teri's head snapped up at this. "You think he's evil, too?"

Cara nodded. "I know he's evil. But, Teri, God can protect us from the likes of Bob Kerns." She said the words even as she wondered how God might rescue them both. "I know it sounds simplistic, and maybe you won't believe me when I tell you this, but God is watching and He cares. He will see that Bob Kerns gets what he deserves."

"Well, I don't plan to wait around for God," Teri replied.

"What do you mean? What are you planning to do?" Cara asked, suddenly frightened for the young woman.

"I plan to get revenge!" Teri exclaimed, waking the baby. Jamie fussed only until Teri put her on her shoulder and patted her soothingly.

"Revenge is something best left to God," Cara advised. "You have a baby to worry about. What if your plans backfire and Jamie ends up in the middle? Kerns is a powerful lawyer with friends in high places. He could easily take Jamie away and cause you all kinds of costly battles in court."

"Not if he's dead," Teri said flatly.

"That's no answer," Cara replied, but even as the words left her mouth, she knew Teri wouldn't hear them.

Teri got to her feet. "I thought you could help me. I'd heard you were a fair-minded person and that you cared about kids."

"I do," Cara said, coming to Teri. She touched her gently on the shoulder. "I really do care, Teri. That's why I don't want you to try to take on Bob Kerns by yourself. Jamie needs you—your devotion, your love. Why don't you let me help you. I could get you into a protective shelter and see to it that you have a place to sleep and plenty of food to eat. Then maybe . . ."

"No!" Teri replied. "He'd find me at those places. Look, I'll do this my way. I just wanted you to know what kind of man he is. A nice lady like you shouldn't be working with him."

"I agree. But, like you, I found myself in a rather delicate situation. I'm working to figure a way out of my problem, but my problem doesn't involve a helpless baby." *Unless you count Brianna,* Cara thought grimly. Suddenly the answers seemed far from easy. Teri was probably right. If she went to a shelter, Bob would only hunt her down.

"I'm going to make him pay," Teri finally said. "I'll have my revenge and Bob Kerns won't be hurting any more kids."

"Please, at least let me help you find a place to stay."

"I'm still living off the five grand. I rented a place using a fake ID. Don't worry about us, Mrs. Kessler. I can take care of everything."

Cara felt a great sense of regret watching Teri leave with Jamie. She felt so sorry for the woman whose childhood had been cut short by the death of her parents and the viciousness of a manipulative man.

"Who was that?" Joe questioned, coming out of his office.

"A very messed-up kid," Cara replied. "Unfortunately, she's probably only one in a line of many."

Fifteen

"I'm really not sure I should leave her," Cara said to her next-door neighbor. Brianna was suffering the effects of a summer head cold, and Mrs. Pritchard had graciously volunteered to keep her while Cara went to Melissa's for supper. "I mean, the dinner is in Lawrence and after all—"

"Nonsense. The child isn't dying. She just has the sniffles. A good dose of hot chocolate and a board game or two and she'll be just fine. You go on to your dinner and enjoy yourself. After all, once you move next week, I won't have an opportunity to offer this again."

Cara smiled at the older woman. Mrs. Pritchard had been an angel on more than one occasion. "Thank you, I think I need it."

"Of course you do. You're a busy lady, especially with the campaign and all. You have a good time and we'll do likewise."

"Is that okay with you, Bri?" Cara asked her daughter. After a sneeze and a cough, Brianna nodded her approval.

Cara still wasn't convinced she'd done the right thing even when she stood at Melissa's door. Her mind was filled with images of Brianna growing gravely ill and needing her. Then, too, there were visions of another girl, not so very much older. Teri Davis and her baby still haunted Cara. Where would the girl go and what would she do with her life? Five thousand dollars wasn't going to go very far in this day and age. And what about her threats of revenge?

"Well, come on in," Melissa said, opening the door to Cara. "You look great!"

Cara looked down at her pastel print blouse tucked into beige slacks. "I was hoping you hadn't planned a formal affair," she smiled.

"No way, not this gal," Melissa laughed. She had chosen to wear jeans and a sporty top, so Cara felt quite at ease. "Come on in and let me get you something to drink. I have iced tea, cola, and fruit juice for Brianna. Say, where is Bri?"

"She has a cold, so I left her at home with a neighbor. I thought it might be easier to talk. I'm more anxious than ever to resolve this—"

"Well, hello again," a man interrupted from the doorway.

Cara turned to find the highway patrolman she'd run into at the Capitol. "Mr. Oberlin," she said in surprise.

"Please call me Harry."

"You two know each other?" Melissa asked.

"We ran into each other at the Capitol," Harry replied. "Literally."

"Cara, I hope you don't mind, but I kind of forgot about our dinner plans when I invited Harry. He's an old friend of Peter's."

Cara looked at him with a million questions on her mind. She wanted very much to discuss her political woes with Melissa, but she couldn't very well suggest Harry leave. Especially with him smiling at her that way. . . .

"—and I explained the situation to Harry."

"What?" Cara questioned, realizing she hadn't been paying attention.

Melissa laughed. "Look, you two go on out to the patio. Harry knows the way. I'll bring out some drinks. Iced tea for you, Cara?"

"Yes, that's fine," she murmured.

"That's good for me, too," Harry said before Melissa could ask. "Come along, Mrs. Kessler."

"Cara. Call me Cara."

He smiled down at her with a twinkle in his eyes. "I'd like that." He took hold of her arm and led her through the house to the sliding glass patio door. "Peter's got some steaks on the grill and potatoes in the coals. I'd say we're in for a great meal."

Melissa's husband glanced up from the barbecue. "You must be Cara," he said with a genuine smile of welcome. "I'm Peter."

"It's good to finally meet you. Melissa speaks very highly of you," Cara replied sweetly, liking Peter immediately. He was about her own height, unlike Harry, who stood at least another six inches taller than her five-foot-seven-inch frame. Peter, also unlike Harry, seemed quite plain and simple.

"She can say some unfavorable things at times," Peter said with a laugh. He seemed content behind his grill.

"But only when he deserves it," Melissa called out from the door. "Come and get it." She offered the tray up as if it were an award.

Harry reached out and took his and Cara's tea. He handed Cara one of the glasses and offered a toast as Peter and Melissa took theirs. "To new friends," he said, motioning Cara and Melissa's way, "and to old." He gave Peter a smile and Cara a sly wink. "I think the new friends may be ever so slightly more interesting than the old ones this time around."

Peter laughed and exchanged a conspiratorial look with Melissa. All at once, Cara felt manipulated, but decided it didn't matter. She rather liked the outcome.

". . . but the dean never caught us, so we were off the

101

hook," Peter concluded with yet another story of his escapades with Harry during their college years. Empty plates and scattered condiments were about all that was left of their barbecue dinner.

Cara tried to concentrate on the stories, but her mind wandered in too many different directions. Harry and his most obvious interest in her . . . the dilemma regarding the campaign . . . and not yet forgotten was Teri Davis and her baby.

"Let me help you," Cara offered as Melissa began picking up dishes.

"No, no. Peter and I can manage just fine. Why don't you and Harry walk on out to the back fence and see Peter's prize-winning roses."

Harry smiled and offered his hand to Cara. "I'm game."

Cara put her hand in his and hesitantly said, "Okay."

They walked several paces before Harry said, "Well, the last time I saw you, you were just Cara Kessler the wonder woman of HEARTBEAT Ministries. Now you're trying to kick my boss out of a job and take over the Capitol."

"Hardly that," Cara laughed nervously. She couldn't very well explain to Harry that running for lieutenant governor was far from her idea.

"I think you'd make a great addition to the state," Harry continued. "Maybe you'll even need a pilot to run you around."

"Maybe," Cara murmured, trying to think of a way to change the subject.

"What made you hook up with Kerns?" It was the one question Cara had sincerely hoped Harry wouldn't ask.

"It was a lot of things. A lot of little things." There was a definite sound of regret in her voice, and before Cara could cover it up, Harry had stopped to look at her.

"You don't sound too enthusiastic about it."

"Let's just say it wasn't my idea and I'm not at all enthusiastic, and leave it at that. Please?" She implored him with a look of misery.

"Sure, Cara." He tucked her arm more closely to his side. "What do you want to talk about?"

"How about you? You know all about me, but I know little about you."

"Fire away. I never could deny a pretty lady much of anything."

Cara felt herself blush. "Well, for starters, where are you from?"

"Topeka, and you?"

"I thought this was about you!"

Harry chuckled low in his chest, causing tiny goosebumps to form on Cara's arms. "I had hoped that maybe it could be about us."

"Us?"

"Sure." He stopped before one of Peter's rose bushes, pretending to study the blossoms. Refusing to look at her, Harry continued. "I've been thinking about you since that day in the Capitol."

"You have?"

"Yeah." He sounded so matter-of-fact. "I'd like for us to get better acquainted, you know, maybe spend some time together."

A part of Cara sensed that this would be a wonderful way to get back into the dating scene, while another part faced the moment accompanied by bittersweet memories of Jack. The first time he'd asked her out had been during a cousin's backyard birthday party. But Jack was gone and Harry was here.

"I think I'd like that, too," she finally whispered. "But . . ."

Harry turned abruptly. "But?"

"Well, like you said, we really need to get to know each other a little better."

"For instance?"

Cara smiled at his concern. He sounded like a boy afraid he might not get that new ball glove after all. "For instance, I have a ten-year-old daughter."

Harry seemed to relax a bit. "Yes, I know. What's her name?"

"Brianna."

"And what is Brianna like?"

Taking an interest in her child was possibly the best thing Harry could have done. Cara instantly warmed to his reception of Brianna and started to describe her child in detail. "Brianna's finishing fourth grade," she began. "She likes school a great deal, probably because she's gifted and it comes easily to her. She plays the piano, and her teacher has suggested she study it seriously. She loves strawberry ice cream and unicorns, and she's totally devoted to the idea of spending this summer at the swimming pool across from our townhouse."

Harry laughed and nodded. "Smart kid. Kansas summers can get a little unbearable."

"She's a good kid, too. She's been my mainstay, along with God."

"So is she pretty like her mother?"

Cara lowered her eyes and felt a wave of girlish delight wash over her. "Prettier. She's got long dark hair and huge eyes like her father." She mentioned Jack without feeling the usual twinge of regret.

"Well, I'll just have to see it to believe it."

"What do you mean?" Cara asked, looking up at Harry's amused expression.

"I mean I'd love to meet her."

"I think I'd like that."

The evening sky faded into a pallet of pastels on the western horizon, and the sweet scent of the roses wafted up to fill the air.

Harry took her hand in his, and Cara had to remind herself to avoid games. "Who are you, Harry Oberlin?"

This tactic seemed to take Harry by surprise. "Who am I? Nobody special. I work for the governor, fly a plane, live in a small west-side apartment in Topeka, and eat out most nights because I'm a terrible cook."

Cara shook her head. "No, who are you really?" The intensity of his eyes almost caused her to back down, but Cara held her ground. "Who are you?"

Harry grew thoughtful. "I'm a lonely Christian man, looking for someone to share my life. Honest enough?"

Cara nodded thoughtfully. "Exactly enough."

Cara considered Harry's words long after she'd returned home. Her heart was filled with the hope of possibilities as she looked in on Brianna and murmured a prayer over the sleeping child.

Kicking off her shoes, Cara realized that Bob Kerns had seemed a very distant problem in the wake of meeting Harry and agreeing to see him again. Now, however, with Harry far removed, Cara couldn't help but remember her frustrating situation. She tried to pray but found herself distracted. "Oh, Lord," she whispered, "please help me in this." It seemed to be all she could think to say. As if in response, thunder rumbled outside. A storm front had moved toward Topeka, even as Cara had driven home from Lawrence.

Remembering Teri and the baby, Cara made a quick check of the time and picked up the telephone to call Melissa.

She felt the need to share the situation with someone, and although she'd been gone from Melissa's home for less than an hour, Cara was sure her friend would understand.

"Hello?" Melissa said, answering on the first ring.

"It's Cara."

"Is something wrong? Did you forget something, or someone?" Melissa teased.

Cara laughed. "That remains to be seen." Again the storm made itself known.

"Hey, was that thunder?"

"Yes," Cara said, pulling back the edge of the drapes to look outside. "A storm's moving in."

"Looks like we finished our picnic just in time."

"Look, Missy, I have something on my mind—"

"I know, I'm sorry we couldn't work on your dilemma," Melissa interjected.

"Well, my dilemma took a strange twist yesterday, and I thought maybe you could help me figure out what to do."

"Okay, so what happened?" Melissa sounded genuinely concerned.

"I had a young woman come to see me at HEARTBEAT. It was late, and I was packing the last of my stuff. She came in and sat down with a tiny baby in her arms."

"What is the great problem in that?"

"She says the baby belongs to Robert Kerns."

"Oh," Melissa breathed, "I guess I see the great problem for myself."

"It seems this girl, Teri Davis, used to be a friend of the family, particularly of Kerns' daughter, Danielle."

"I'd say even more particularly of Kerns himself," Melissa said sarcastically.

"No, and that's part of the problem. She says he forced the relationship and that it happened on several occasions.

Apparently when she found out she was pregnant, Kerns tried to buy her off."

"But it didn't work?"

"No," Cara replied. "He wanted her to abort the baby, but Teri took the money and hid out instead. She gave birth about three months ago and now she wants revenge."

"Revenge? She said that?" Melissa asked in a voice of disbelief.

"She said exactly that. Melissa, I don't know what to think. I mean, I knew Kerns was scum because of what he did to me, but this is different. This is the life of a child, two children actually. Teri wasn't quite sixteen when Kerns raped her the first time."

"And you're absolutely sure it was rape?"

"It doesn't matter even if Teri encouraged him. She was a minor, and Kerns was fully aware of the laws. Teri says he manipulated her whenever he could and that her baby is the result of that coercion. I want to help her, Melissa, but I don't know how. I can't expose her to Kerns or he might do something horrible to her."

"On the other hand," Melissa began, "you could give him just enough information to make him realize there's a problem. Maybe this is your ticket out of the campaign. You go to him and tell him you know what he did to Teri. You don't have to explain that she didn't have an abortion and that he has an illegitimate child."

"He'd want more than words."

"But you could make a good threat on words alone. If you did it right, Kerns would know you weren't playing games and that you would expose his infidelity and illegal activities. Was anybody else around when Teri made her confession?"

"No. Joe saw her when she first came in, but he went to his office so we could talk privately."

"So bring a photograph of her with you, just something to help Kerns understand the serious nature of the situation and that you aren't bluffing."

Cara thought on the possibilities for a long hard moment. "I can't use someone else to avoid my responsibilities," she finally said. "If I can't get out of the campaign on my own, that's my problem, but if I drag a helpless young woman and her baby into it . . ."

"But the threat would be enough to put him off. Tell him I'm prepared to run a full front-page story on the situation," Melissa suggested. "Tell him whatever you want regarding the content and I'll put it together."

"We can't go public yet. Teri and the baby would be endangered."

"I suppose you're right, but you can't sit around and do nothing."

Cara sighed. "I know, and that's the part eating me alive." Despair seemed to wrap a band around her heart.

C-R-A-S-H! The windows rattled from the force of the thunder. And then it started to rain.

Sixteen

"You'll want to hear this, Bob," Russell Owens said, coming into campaign headquarters dripping wet. It had begun raining Saturday night and was still raining on Monday morning.

"What is it? I'm kind of busy." Kerns sat studying his agenda for the day and felt a distinctly bored disregard for his sidekick.

"I wouldn't have bothered you if it weren't important," Russell replied, stripping off his wet trench coat. He produced a tape recorder from the pocket.

Just then an attractive brunette with a steaming mug of coffee appeared in the office doorway. "Here, I think you're going to like this," she announced in a voice full of seductive promise. "I made it especially for you."

Russell glared at the woman and tossed the recorder onto a nearby chair. Kerns thought Russell's reaction amusing. "Serena Perez, this is Russell Owens. Russell is my campaign manager and a very good one, at that. He's come here in the midst of this deluge to bring me important information." An evident look of tense acceptance passed between Russell and Serena.

"Dedication is an important virtue," Serena replied, flashing dark eyes at Russell.

Kerns liked the way she commanded attention with her exotic Hispanic looks. The very short peach-colored suit made an artistic contrast to her *café au lait* skin.

"Serena is my new press secretary," Kerns announced.

"She's worked in public relations for years and can give us her time until November. Personally, I hope to keep her on even after the election." He eyed her with open lust.

"I see," Russell replied, picking up the tape recorder. "If you don't mind, this will be a private meeting."

Serena gave him a catlike look of indifference and left the room.

"Well?" Kerns questioned as Russell secured the door. "What is it that couldn't wait?"

"I was out of town yesterday, as you know, otherwise I would have called you at home." The tone of his voice left little doubt in Kerns' mind that this was a very serious matter.

"That bad, eh?" Kerns eased back in his chair.

"That and more. Where's Cara?"

Kerns smiled. "Shaking hands and kissing babies at Westridge Mall. Why?"

Russell held up the recorder. "I have no idea what this is all about, but you may have cost yourself the campaign. This needs immediate action, or I guarantee being governor of this state will be totally off limits to you."

Kerns assumed his stoic stare. "Play it."

Kerns wasn't prepared for the contents of the tape. He erupted in anger, pounding his fists against the desk and jumping to his feet. "I can't believe this is happening. I gave that conniving little . . ." He fell silent and tried to contain his anger. "I gave her five thousand dollars to have an abortion and what does she do? She stabs me in the back."

"So it is true?" Russell braved the question.

Kerns turned on him. "Yes," he hissed the word. "For whatever good it does to tell you."

"Bob, when I asked you if there were any skeletons from the past that wouldn't stay buried, you assured me there weren't. I'd say this is a pretty big skeleton, and from the sounds of it, this Teri Davis isn't going to let things just drop." Water from his rain-drenched hair dripped down the side of his face. "You'd better tell me everything," stated Russell. "We'll judge from that what kind of damage control is necessary."

"I don't want damage control. I want that girl dealt with! This is outrageous. I run grown men like a drill sergeant, but you're telling me that one teenage girl is going to make me lose an election? That doesn't call for mere damage control, Owens, I can tell you that much!"

"So what do you suggest? Hire her on as another press secretary?"

Kerns tried not to react to Russell's sarcasm. He knew the man's attitude was born out of fear that the election was over before it had truly started. Still, no one could talk to him like that and get away with it.

"Maybe she'd make a better campaign manager," Kerns said in a low threatening voice.

"At least she knows all of your secrets," Owens replied, sounding almost as angry as Kerns felt.

Bob started to answer, then stopped abruptly. He realized the futility of arguing with Owens. He needed this man more than ever now. "All right, truce," he called and took his seat at the desk. "What's happened is over and done. What I need is a permanent solution."

Russell pulled a chair closer to the desk and took a seat. "What do you mean by permanent?"

Kerns eyed the younger man. "I mean, I want this taken care of once and for all before Cara and her devoted buddy take this any further. I can't very well force Mrs. Kessler to continue the election if she holds a bigger trump card over my head than I hold over hers, now can I?"

"No, I suppose not, but she already knows about Teri and

nothing is going to change that fact."

"She knows about Teri, but Cara is easy to intimidate."

"You've already threatened her ministry and she's since turned that over to her partner."

"She has a daughter," Kerns said, not breaking eye contact with Owens for even a moment.

"What about Jordan? She may not be so quick to shut up."

Kerns smiled. "If she starts digging in the wrong places, I'll take care of her myself. Besides, when Cara and Melissa see what befalls Teri Davis and her child, they'll be less inclined to interfere."

"And what is it you suggest happen to Teri and her child?"

Kerns folded his hands. "I don't much care so long as it's permanent. The more *eternal* the solution, the better. Do you understand what I'm saying here, Russell?"

Owens paled. "I think so. You don't care how I handle the situation or what happens to the people involved, as long as this whole thing goes away."

"Exactly right."

"But what about the baby? After all, the child is your own flesh and blood."

Kerns eyed Russell with contempt for the reminder. "The child is dead as far as I'm concerned. I paid for the abortion, remember?"

"Yeah," Owens answered.

Kerns could tell the light of understanding was just beginning to dawn in Russell's mind.

"How do you want it—"

Kerns interrupted. "I don't want to know anything. The less I know, the less I can confess. As far as I'm concerned, Teri Davis was a poor orphaned teen who ended up in one foster home after another. My family tried to befriend her and she robbed us blind. If I'm questioned beyond that,

I'll have nothing to say."

Russell nodded. "As unpleasant as the job is, I'll take care of it right away."

"Good," Kerns replied, seeing that Owens had reconciled himself to the situation. "I leave tomorrow on our statewide campaign tour, and of course Debra and Danielle are going to accompany me. By the time you join us in Wichita, I'll expect the matter to be resolved."

"Consider it done."

Russell Owens smiled to himself as he walked to the car. It was still raining, but nothing could daunt his spirits in light of what he'd just managed to do. Pressing the rewind button on the microrecorder, he waited for a moment, then pressed play.

"The child is dead as far as I'm concerned. . . ." Kerns' voice was clear. Russell hit the stop button and popped out the tape. This was going to be his insurance policy for controlling Kerns in the years to come. He'd do the man's dirty work, but it would come at a considerable price.

Seventeen

When September rolled around, Danielle Kerns had left the campaign trail to return rather reluctantly to college in Topeka. She wasn't the least bit scholarly minded and wished instead to open a dress boutique that would specialize in designer fashions. Her father refused to listen to her idea, however, and so hoping to win his elusive approval, she headed back to school.

Danielle walked from room to room, feeling the emptiness. An uncomfortable silence held the fashionable house captive. Mrs. Gleason, their housekeeper, was on vacation visiting her daughter in Canada. Staring out of the kitchen window, Danielle missed the companionship of friends and family more than ever. Her brother, Gary, now newly graduated from the University of Kansas, had moved to Dallas in an effort to distance himself as far as possible from his father. They'd never gotten along, and often Danielle had found herself playing mediator between the two. The fights always stemmed from her father's desire to control them without investing any real part of himself in their lives. That much Danielle had learned from her brother. Gary was a good friend to her. He always listened to her dreams and encouraged her to break free from their father's stranglehold and live her own life. Unfortunately, Danielle knew she wasn't made of strong enough stuff.

On this particular September morning, Danielle couldn't help but think of Teri Davis. They'd been friends for such a long time, and it seemed so out of character for Teri to just pull out of college and leave without a word to anyone. Danielle shuddered to think of what might have happened to her.

Noting the hour, Danielle realized there was little time for daydreams and regrets. Grabbing her books and purse, she headed for the door just as the telephone rang. It was probably her mother, Danielle decided and deposited her things on the hallway table. Debra Kerns was possibly the only person who understood Danielle's plight, and because of that, Danielle loved her mother more than anyone else in the world.

"Hello!" Danielle greeted with a warm eager voice.

"Dani?"

Danielle nearly dropped the receiver. "Teri, is that you?"

"Yeah, surprise," the girl responded in a voice that sounded less than enthusiastic.

"Teri, I can't believe I'm talking to you. I was just thinking about you and how it's been almost a year—"

"I know," interrupted Teri. "Look, Dani, I called because I wanted to explain about that year."

"Are you all right? Where are you?" Danielle asked quickly. Suddenly nothing mattered as much as seeing Teri again.

"I'm okay. I'm living here in Topeka . . . well . . . actually outside of town," she said, hesitating. "I'm going to give you the address, but you've got to swear you won't give it out to anyone else. Not even your family."

"But Mom and Dad have been worried about you, too," Danielle stated.

"You can't let them know you've even talked to me. Not yet. Look, I'm living in an out-of-the-way place off of west Highway 24. You go south on Hodges Road until it dead-ends. I live in the old white house near the river levee. It's on the left and easy to spot. Can you come?"

"Sure, but I still don't understand."

"It doesn't matter," Teri insisted. "I'll explain it all to you when you get here. How about tonight? Say around eight?"

"Can't I see you sooner?"

"No, I need to take care of some other business, and I'm not sure I can be back here before then."

Just then, Danielle heard a baby's cry from the other end of the line. "Teri, who's crying?"

"I'll tell you all about it when you come tonight. Look, I can't hang on. Please don't tell anyone you've talked to me. It's really important, okay?"

"Sure, Teri. I'll see you tonight."

The phone call to Danielle was exactly the break Russell Owens needed. After weeks of detective work and failed leads, he was finally going to be able to take care of their little problem with Bob's past. Kerns hadn't been too kind when Russell had showed up in Wichita shortly before the Fourth of July, only to announce that Teri Davis was nowhere to be found.

As Kerns had put it, this wasn't an optional job. It was something that had to be ended quickly. The closer it got to the election, the more trouble it could be. Now with the election only weeks away, Russell was running out of time.

The girl was smart, he had to give her that. She apparently hadn't given birth in any Kansas or Missouri hospital and wasn't signed up to receive welfare. Russell had turned the Vital Statistics and Social and Rehabilitation Services upside down trying to find even a single piece of paper that would evidence Teri's existence. There was none to be found.

Looking at the notes he'd made, Russell gave the audio

surveillance equipment a pat. *I should call Kerns and give him the good news,* he thought. He picked up the telephone, then put it back down. No, he'd wait until the job was done and Teri Davis was no more of a threat to the campaign. Then, once the problem was eliminated, Russell could join up with Kerns on the campaign trail and see about getting rid of Serena Perez.

But eliminating Teri Davis and her child was the one thing that truly bothered Russell. He didn't mind the thought of erasing a potential threat, he was just hard-pressed to trust anyone to get the job done. He had gone through a list of people that Kerns had supplied, but every time he started to consider one of them, Russell could only think of the guy as a future witness against him.

"I'll do it myself," he said, making his final decision aloud. There was far less risk that way. He went to his desk drawer and reached into the far back. Slowly, almost ceremonially, he pulled the .45 semiautomatic from the drawer. The stainless steel barrel caught the light from his desk lamp, causing the gun to glow in his hands.

"If you want a job done right . . . do it yourself," he muttered as he pulled back the slide.

Eighteen

Teri had just placed Jamie in the bathtub when a knock sounded at her door. She glanced at her watch. It was only seven-thirty, but no doubt Danielle was anxious to find out what was going on. She wrapped Jamie in a rough worn towel and snuggled her close for warmth.

"You're early," she said, pulling the door open, the chain still in place. Expecting to find Danielle staring back at her, Teri wasn't prepared for the sight of the dark-clad man. "Who are you?"

"I'm a friend," he announced.

"I don't have any friends," Teri replied.

"What about Cara Kessler and Danielle Kerns?" the man called back.

Teri's heart stopped beating for a moment, then she fumbled with the door chain and opened the door. The man pushed up gold wire-framed glasses. "I know them, but I don't know you," she said suspiciously.

"You went to see Cara Kessler today, right?" the man said in a hopeful tone.

"Yeah, so what?"

"So, Cara was real worried about you. She found out that Kerns is cutting his campaign trip short, and she's afraid he'll manage to locate you when he returns."

"But unless Cara has said something to him about me, Kerns doesn't even know I'm here in Topeka."

The man shrugged. "Cara just sent me to get you to a safe

118

place. She says it's important you come see her right away. She has to discuss this situation with you and decide what's to be done."

Teri eyed him for a moment longer. It was true she'd gone to see Cara Kessler. In fact, that was what had taken her away from home most of the day. She'd been keeping in touch, usually by phone, with Cara. But she was always careful to use a pay phone in town. She even used a different pay phone each time, just in case someone tried to trace the call. Now here was a complete stranger standing in her doorway, expecting her to go with him.

"I can't leave. I'm expecting company."

"Cara said it was a matter of life and death," the man replied. "Why don't you dress the baby and I'll wait here to drive you into town."

Jamie was starting to fuss from her uncomfortable position, and Teri couldn't argue the point of dressing the child. "Okay. Just give me a minute."

She went to the well-worn couch, where a package of diapers and change of clothes were already waiting. Unwrapping Jamie, she placed the diaper on the baby and was just pulling open the sticky tabs when it suddenly dawned on her. She hadn't given her address to Cara. The hair on the back of her neck began to prickle. Cara couldn't have sent this man.

Whirling around, Teri noticed beads of perspiration on the man's forehead. "I think I'd like to call Cara first."

Pulling out a gun, the man motioned to the couch. "Get that brat dressed and hurry up."

Teri felt the color drain from her face. Her hands shook so badly she couldn't do up the little buttons on Jamie's pajamas.

"Come on." He yanked her arm and threw her a bag. "Get

what you need for the baby. You're going on a little trip."

"Who are you?" Teri finally managed to say.

The man smiled at her with cold indifference. "Let's just say I'm a close friend of Jamie's father."

Danielle was more than a little disgusted by the evening's turn of events. A flat tire had rendered her without transportation while she waited for over an hour for the repair service to come to her rescue. Then, when the serviceman had announced the tire had been slashed and was beyond repair, Danielle was further delayed by getting the car towed to the service station for a new tire.

Finally on the road and heading north on Highway 75, Danielle heard the disc jockey announce the time as nine-thirty. Smacking the flat of her palm on the steering wheel, Danielle winced in pain. She'd desperately wanted to call and explain the delay to her friend, but she didn't have the telephone number.

"By the time I get there, I'll be almost two hours late," she muttered to no one. Taking the cloverleaf exchange to Highway 24, Danielle couldn't shake the feeling that she already knew what Teri was going to tell her. It all seemed to make sense now. The fact that Teri had just disappeared without a word and the baby crying in the background. She must have gotten pregnant, Danielle decided, but she saw no reason why Teri had to run away from their friendship.

Nearly nine miles west of town, Danielle had to rely on her headlights to locate Hodges Road. It was the kind of night that seemed to snuff out the light from every source, and even her car lights didn't seem to reach far into the thick blackness.

Finally the sign appeared and Danielle breathed a sigh of relief. Her relief, however, was short-lived. The gravel road was darker still, and the only light around was a pinpoint porch light in the distance.

Pulling into Teri's narrow dirt drive, Danielle couldn't find a sign of anyone. The porch light, which had belonged to another house far to the north, offered her nothing in the way of help.

Cautiously she got out of the car. The rushing sound of the river just beyond the levee and the wind in the trees gave Danielle an eerie feeling of isolation. She lost little time making her way to the house.

"Teri!" she called out and knocked loudly on the door. "Teri!"

There was no reply.

Looking in the darkened window, Danielle felt a shiver of apprehension. A dog barked in the distance and something flew overhead in the moonless sky.

"Teri, it's me, Danielle. Open up!"

Still, there was no answer.

Getting up her courage, Danielle walked around the house. Finding no sign of Teri, Danielle made her way back to the car. She was scared through and through, but her apprehension had more to do with Teri than with the frightening darkness. Tripping, she reached down to find that she'd put her foot into a small empty box. She yanked it off and held it up to her face.

"Baby cereal," she read, barely able to make out the words.

She moved to where the outline of a trash barrel caught her eye and threw the box in. White lumpy forms caught her attention and Danielle gingerly lifted one out to find a disposable diaper.

"Teri has a baby," she whispered. It confirmed her earlier beliefs. "Oh, Teri. I would have understood." She dropped the diaper and went to her car.

If Teri had a baby, then she'd need as much help and emotional support as Danielle could possibly give. The only question was, where was Teri?

Nineteen

Cara sat trying to have a normal conversation with Melissa. From the moment her friend had arrived at the apartment, Cara's mind had been too preoccupied with Teri Davis to give Melissa much consideration. Even after Brianna had pestered them to come outside and watch her skate, Cara had found it impossible to turn off her thoughts.

"All right, I give up," Melissa finally said, shifting in the lawn chair. "You're a million miles away."

Cara offered a weak smile. "I'm poor company, huh?"

Brianna whirled by them and waved.

"She certainly is growing up fast," Melissa remarked.

"Yes, I'm amazed at it myself," Cara murmured.

"But that's not what's bothering you, and I happen to know that you and Harry have had several very nice dates, despite your campaign schedule. So what gives?"

"Teri Davis," Cara replied flatly. "She promised to call me last night. She's been pretty faithful about checking in. I'm worried something has happened to her, Melissa."

"Well, we could go look for her."

Cara shook her head. "Where? Where in all of Topeka would we start?"

"It would have to be a low-income area if what she told you about living off the five thousand is true." Just then Melissa's beeper went off. "Hey, can I use your phone?"

"Sure, go ahead. I'll round up Brianna."

"I've got to run," Melissa announced as Cara came back

123

into the living room. Already she was grabbing up her things. "Some big story is breaking and I have to cover it because the regular feature writer is sick."

Cara walked her to the front door. "I promise to be better company next time."

Melissa smiled. "You'd better be! Hey, this is timing," she added and waved at the man coming up the sidewalk. "How's it going, Harry?"

Harry Oberlin flashed a smile at the two women. Dressed comfortably in jeans and a polo shirt, he looked ready for a day of play.

"My day is almost perfect," he replied.

"Well mine just got a bit busier," Melissa announced and rushed past him. "I'm on my way to cover up-to-the-minute breaking news."

Harry laughed at the vivacious woman's words, but his eyes were for Cara only. "Hi, there. I thought maybe we could take Brianna to Gage Park and have a picnic. Interested?"

"It sounds great. I love this warm weather," Cara managed to say without sounding too nervous. "The only problem is I have to be back by five. I'm doing a campaign dinner tonight."

"No problem." Harry seemed genuinely at ease with her nonstop schedule. "I already have everything in the car." He grinned infectiously. "You know, just in case you said yes."

Harry watched Cara with undisguised interest. "So will you let me fly you around Kansas if Kerns is elected governor?" he questioned. He studied her for a moment, then added, "Better yet, I could take you out flying now, just for the fun of it."

Cara laughed and continued pulling out food from the

picnic basket. "I'll just be glad when all of this is over. You know, for the first time I think it will work out all right. Governor Glencoe is so popular, I don't see how Bob Kerns can hold a candle to him."

"I don't know, Cara. I may be telling tales out of school, but Glencoe is worried. He said you and Bob represent something he hasn't got."

"What's that?"

"A visual focus on the future. He's an old man and he knows it, and his lieutenant governor isn't well liked or prepared to take on more responsibility. Glencoe's been called a stagnating parasite, and worse."

"I find that so hard to believe," Cara replied, sitting down across from Harry at the cement picnic table.

"Kerns' campaign ads have hit him harder than he's likely to let on. Normally, I wouldn't be saying anything to you about it, but I already know how you feel about Kerns and this campaign."

"I don't want to be the lieutenant governor," Cara stated matter-of-factly. "I'm tired of the whole game already. What's it going to be like if Kerns actually wins this thing and I have to sit in the Capitol day after day?"

"Hey, cheer up, the last few lieutenant governors have been living in Wichita."

"Great, that's just what I need. Another major change in our lives."

"Change can be good," Harry said with a wink. He reached out his hand and covered hers. "I like the change you've brought into my life." He thought it pretty the way she blushed and lowered her eyes, charmingly embarrassed by her feelings.

Cara Kessler is one incredibly special lady, he'd decided long before this day. He'd thanked God on more than one occasion for the chance to get to know her better, and always after they'd shared the day or evening together, Harry went home with a better sense of accomplishment. Cara had changed his life in so many ways—giving him perspective, direction, purpose. He wasn't just spinning his wheels anymore. Now he had his eyes on the future and knew that he wanted that future to include Cara and her daughter.

"Come on, Harry," Brianna called from the swings. "You promised to push me really high."

Harry laughed and got to his feet. "So I did. I guess lunch will have to wait a few more minutes," he added apologetically to Cara.

Pushing Brianna gave him time to consider the situation without fear that Cara would read the emotions in his expression. He liked playing father to Brianna, and he felt, too, that she was eager for him to assume that role. Still, was it fair to let the young girl draw so close to him when there was no certainty as to what would happen down the road? Cara always steered clear of talking about the future with Harry, and he knew full well the reason for her evasiveness: the campaign.

But a life with Cara and Brianna was exactly what he wanted.

Twenty

Bob Kerns felt the mounting tension of the moment. Russell Owens had telephoned earlier and left a message with the hotel switchboard that he would call back at nine o'clock that evening. With his own watch reading two minutes after the hour, Kerns began to pace.

Serena Perez eyed him from where she sat at the small table. She had been rewriting speeches for him all evening, and now with the November election so close, Kerns found himself relying on her heavily for support.

"Don't worry," she fairly purred the words. "Russell will call." As if on cue, the bedside phone rang. "See, I told you." She smiled up at him with warm red lips.

"Hello?" Kerns said, picking up the telephone.

"I see you got my message," Russell said from the other end.

"What's the news?"

"I just wanted you to know that our little problem has been eliminated."

"Eliminated?" Kerns questioned, feeling perspiration begin to form at his temples.

"That's right. It's clear sailing from here, boss. I'll give you the details when you get back to Topeka."

Kerns took a deep breath. "You're sure about this?"

"Of course. How's it going at your end?"

"Same as can be expected. Debra's passed out in the room down the hall, and Serena and I are working overtime on speeches you should have written for me."

"I'll be joining you tomorrow," Owens said, seeming to ignore Kerns' tone. "When is Cara coming out?"

"She'll join us on Saturday and we'll make one grand whistle-stop tour back to Topeka. Is she behaving herself?"

"She's reacting perfectly to the demands of her role," Owens replied. "I think she finally sees the merit of doing things our way."

"You mean my way," Kerns said rather snidely. "Don't forget who's in charge here."

"I wouldn't dream of it," Owens replied. "Look, I've got a million things to do before I can leave. I'll see you sometime tomorrow."

Kerns hung up the telephone, still uncertain as to whether he was truly rid of the Teri Davis situation. Russell sounded confident and that was a good sign, but there was always the possibility that somehow things could be linked back to him and ruin his chances for the governorship.

Watching Serena as she bent over the stacks of papers, he questioned, "Are you finished yet?"

Her brunette head shook from side to side.

"Well, I'm starving and I'm going downstairs to get a bite to eat. You want to come along?"

Serena glanced up with an expression of question on her face. "And who would finish these?"

Kerns ran a finger down the side of her cheek. "There's still time to do them later."

"No," Serena said with a flash of a smile. "I never procrastinate. You go ahead and eat. By the time you get back from supper, I should have these done."

Glancing at his watch, Kerns nodded. "I suppose I'd better check on Debra first. There's no telling what she might do if I don't."

"Didn't you put a couple of guys at her door?"

"Yeah, but if she thinks I'm with you, things could get ugly and noisy. I'll be back as soon as I can." With one final glance at the shapely woman, Kerns left the room and made his way down the hall. Sooner or later he'd have to do something about Debra and her drinking, but for the sake of the campaign, he hoped it might wait a little longer.

Cara went over her agenda one final time. Spending a week on the road with Bob Kerns and Russell Owens hardly held any appeal. This was to be their final push. They'd head out from Salina with two days devoted to the Wichita area. After Wichita, they'd take the turnpike north to Emporia, then include another series of token visits to Ottawa and Olathe before finally coming to rest in the Overland Park/ Kansas City area. It was going to be a grueling ride by hired bus, with long hours and tight close quarters.

With a heavy sigh, Cara folded the agenda and put it in her purse. The only good part about the trip was that it would only last a week. Melissa had agreed to stay nights in Topeka with Brianna, while Mrs. Pritchard had volunteered to drive over and get her off to school and wait for her bus in the afternoons.

Looking around the cramped quarters of her office, Cara knew she'd be happy when the campaign was finally over. Kerns had chosen the 6th Street headquarters for two reasons: One, because it was close to the Capitol; and two, because it was cheap. Given the fact that the small three-room suite was roach infested and without proper heating, Cara thought they should have been paid to stay there instead of the other way around.

Hearing the doorbell, Cara was happy to find Melissa and Harry being ushered into her campaign office. The young receptionist nodded at something Harry was saying and pulled the door closed behind her.

"Well, I must say this is a treat. I was just going over—" Cara stopped in midsentence. The look of grim despair on Melissa's face and stark concern on Harry's screamed that something was desperately wrong. "What is it?"

"Remember when my beeper went off yesterday and I had to leave to cover a story?" Melissa asked softly.

"Sure. What about it?" A quick glance at Harry did nothing to calm Cara's nerves.

"A body was found in the river," Melissa replied.

"A body?" Cara shook her head. "I don't understand."

Melissa swallowed hard and looked at Harry as if seeking council. Cara felt a spreading dread consume her.

"It was Teri Davis," Melissa said, her expression full of sympathy.

"Teri? But how?" Cara felt her mouth go dry and her hands grow clammy.

"The autopsy hasn't been performed yet, but for now it's being listed as a drowning."

Cara sat in shock, the grave news slowly forming thoughts in her head. Teri Davis was dead. The child so harmed by Bob Kerns would be harmed by him no more. *Bob Kerns!* The name came unbidden to her mind and without warning she flew up from the chair in a rage.

She considered Harry and Melissa for only a moment. "Kerns! I'll see him hanged for this!" She pushed past Melissa and headed for the door. Already blinded by her tears, Cara gave little thought as to where she would go.

Harry moved with lightning speed and took hold of Cara's upper arm. "You can't go after Kerns. We don't have any proof that he's involved."

Cara tried in vain to pull away from Harry. "Let me go! I

know what I'm doing. Kerns has to pay for this."

"We don't have any proof," Melissa repeated.

Cara turned accusing eyes on her friend. "I have all the proof I need. I have Teri's story and that beautiful baby." *The baby!* "Where's the baby?" she asked, looking up at Harry. "Where's Jamie?"

"I don't know," Melissa replied.

"What do you mean?" Cara was strangely calm.

Melissa nervously bit at her lower lip. "The press was directed as to where Teri lived. We reviewed the premises and were allowed to photograph her place. There was a lot of damaging evidence to suggest Teri was involved in dealing drugs."

"That's ludicrous. It must have been planted there. Teri was a good decent kid. She couldn't help what had happened to her in the past."

"No, she couldn't," Melissa said, coming to where Harry still held Cara tightly. "She also had to find some way to support herself."

"Selling drugs wouldn't have been an option," Cara protested.

"How can you be so sure?" Harry asked her softly. "People do what they think they have to, even when it isn't very pleasant. I have friends in the sheriff's department, and they didn't have anything too complimentary to say about the situation. They found a great deal of heroin on the site."

"No! I refuse to believe that Teri was dealing drugs. She had Jamie to worry about. She knew Jamie had no one else to rely on. Teri wouldn't have risked that."

"Honey, you didn't really know Teri."

Cara bristled at the term of endearment. "How dare you patronize me at a time like this! I can't believe you two are taking this so calmly." She tried to wrench away from

Harry, but it was no use.

"You're the one who needs to calm down. Without your help, we may never find Jamie Davis," Harry said sternly. Cara immediately quieted.

"That's right," Melissa joined in. "For all the world knows, Jamie has never existed. There was no sign of her at the house. Not one bottle or diaper or even a crib to suggest that a baby had once lived there."

"But maybe it wasn't Teri's house," Cara protested.

"The car outside was the same dilapidated Ford she drove to your office. It was registered to the name on her fake ID and driver's license."

"Which was?"

"Lonna Jessup. That was also the name under which the house was rented," Melissa replied. "Look, I've been at this all night. I found papers with both Teri's name and the Lonna Jessup name. What I can't find is a record of Jamie's birth. For all purposes, that baby doesn't exist."

Cara felt what little calm she'd managed to obtain fade in light of this news. "Do either one of you need more proof than this? I'm telling you, Kerns was involved. Somehow he found out about Teri and he took care of the problem. He knew—better than anyone else—what he stood to lose because of her."

"Cara," Harry said, putting a hand to her chin and gently lifting her face to his. "We have to handle this carefully. I don't doubt for a minute that your suspicions are true. What I can't stress enough is that Kerns is going to be on his guard more than ever, especially if he arranged for this."

"He needs to pay," Cara said in a voice that broke into a whimper. "He has to pay."

"I know." Harry's voice held the hope that Cara so desperately needed to hear.

"We're not going to let this rest," Melissa promised her.

Cara drew a deep breath and let it out slowly, collecting herself, and Harry dropped his hold. "Okay," she said, looking up at Harry first and then Melissa, "what do we do first?"

Twenty-One

Cara was glad for Melissa's suggestion that she spend the night with Cara and Brianna. Harry, too, seemed quite relieved to know Cara wouldn't be alone.

Cara found it impossible to unwind from the news of the day. Tomorrow she would join Bob Kerns on the campaign trail. How could she spend a week under his close scrutiny and not break? It was the first time she truly felt capable of hating another human being and she didn't like feeling this way. Even the drunk who'd killed Jack had incited more pity than disgust.

With Brianna in bed for the night, Cara returned to the living room to find Melissa holding two hot mugs of coffee.

"I thought maybe a little something warm would help. It's decaf so it shouldn't keep us up all night."

"As if I'd need something else to stimulate me into staying awake all night," Cara said, taking the extended cup. "I don't think I'll ever sleep again."

"I know. I feel the same way after my time in the morgue and at Teri's house. It just seemed so . . ."

"What?" Cara prodded, leaning on the edge of the seat she'd just taken. "Anything you think of might help us."

"Now that I think about it," Melissa replied, "it just seemed too perfect. The house didn't look right, you know what I mean?"

"I'm not sure."

"Well, it just seemed like a stage set with props. It didn't have the feel of being natural. Everything was in perfect order, even in the midst of the mess and clutter. The heroin was in plain sight. The scales and paraphernalia were lined up in meticulous order. It just didn't feel right."

"What did Harry say about it?"

Melissa smiled. "Harry says very little about anything except you."

Cara felt her face grow hot. Another time she might have welcomed this conversation. "But he said he had friends with the sheriff's department. Did he say what they were concluding?"

"A drug deal gone bad." Melissa offered the explanation, then took a long drink from the mug.

"That's it? A nineteen-year-old girl is dead, her baby is missing, and the police are chalking it up to a drug deal gone bad?"

"What do you expect?"

Cara stared at her friend for a moment. What did she expect? She had prayed and pleaded with God for an answer to her dilemma. She had begged for a pathway that would lead her away from Kerns and his control.

"I don't know," she finally answered. "I'm just so tired of all of this."

"I know."

The words were simple and matter-of-fact, but Cara felt her friend's sympathy and understanding.

"I don't think I can deal with next week." Cara put her cup down and stared blankly at the wall above Melissa's head. "I mean, it was one thing to have to support this campaign. I grit my teeth every time I have to tell people how great Bob Kerns is. I'm living a lie, Melissa. How can that be right?"

"Maybe it isn't. Hey, you're the one with the religious

beliefs, not me. Harry said, 'God doesn't always explain His purposes, but He always rewards the faithful.' I guess that's what a religious person would say to you just now."

Cara smiled and thought of Harry's words. "Yes, I suppose you're right. Faith seems like such a simple thing until you see children dead at the hands of madmen."

Melissa said nothing, and Cara felt the silence weigh down upon her like a millstone. Teri Davis was truly dead. Jamie Davis was missing and most likely just as dead as her mother. And though she cared deeply about the girl and had hoped to help her, Cara couldn't stop the heinous act from happening. Through the darkest moment in her life, Teri Davis had faced death alone.

No, not alone, Cara thought. *A God who sees a sparrow fall surely stood beside Teri in her hour of need.*

"You really should try to get some sleep," Melissa said, breaking the stillness. "Harry will be here at five-thirty to take you to the airport. That's going to come around awfully early."

Cara knew the truth of her words. "I can't imagine being able to sleep with what I know."

"But what do you really know? We may be all wrong about this."

"No," Cara said, meeting Melissa's gaze. "I know Robert Kerns is responsible, and I won't rest until that baby is found and he answers for Teri's death."

By the time Harry knocked on the door the next morning, he'd given Teri's death more than a little thought. He'd spent hours talking to friends in the sheriff and police departments, but answers were scarce.

"Ready?" he asked as Cara opened the door to him. She was dressed smartly in a dark green woolen suit, but her sleepy expression and puffy eyes told him she'd not had a very restful night.

"I guess so." She picked up a suitcase, which Harry immediately took from her.

Melissa came to stand behind Cara. Resting her hands on Cara's shoulders, she said, "I suppose it's no good telling you to have a nice trip."

"And completely futile telling me not to worry," Cara said, patting Melissa's hand. "But I'll do my best anyway. Thanks for being here for Brianna and me."

"Anytime."

Cara looked at Harry with eyes that seemed to plead for him to tell her it was all a mistake—Teri's death had never happened and Bob Kerns had never forced her into the campaign. How he wished he could ease her worry.

"Here, don't forget this," Melissa called out. She brought Cara's purse and overnight case. "You'd be hard-pressed without these."

"True, and I'd look worse than I do now without my makeup."

"You look just fine," Harry said.

Cara tried to laugh. "Are you sure you can see well enough to drive? I caught my reflection in the mirror this morning and even I was frightened."

Harry put the suitcase in the trunk of his car and came around to open the door for Cara. "I happen to like what I see, beyond the lack of sleep."

"Spoken like a true knight in shining armor," Cara whispered in reply.

Harry grinned. "My steed awaits," he said and motioned to the car with a sweeping bow.

Cara took her seat with a smile.

Harry thought she looked so much younger than her years.

He worried about what the campaign trail would do to her that it hadn't already done. There was a high price to pay for public exposure, and he hated to think of it wiping away Cara's innocence and joy.

Taking his place behind the wheel, Harry was halfway to the airport before he spoke. Cara seemed immersed in her thoughts, and he wondered if she'd even hear him.

"Cara, if you need me this week, I want you to call me. I'll take vacation time if necessary. I've already explained to the governor that I have a strong connection to the opposition. There's another pilot who'll fly him around the state this week, and I'll be in Topeka. You have my work and beeper numbers, right?"

Cara nodded affirmation, still seeming to Harry to be in a world all her own. When the light turned red, Harry stopped the car and reached to take hold of her hand.

"Cara, I care a great deal about you and Brianna. I don't want to see either of you hurt."

Cara looked down at the hand engulfing hers and with slow deliberate action took her free hand and placed it on top. "I'm glad you care."

The light turned green, but Harry refused to go. He felt a desperation to suspend the moment. He looked deep into Cara's eyes and found an unnamed fear that he wished he could take from her.

"God is still in control, Cara. He knows what happened, and no matter who is responsible, they will answer to Him for their actions."

"I know," Cara whispered. "I guess the human side of me wants them to answer to me as well."

Harry smiled. "But the human side isn't in charge, is it?"

Cara averted her eyes and looked out the window, noting that the traffic light had turned red again. "I'm trying not to let it be, but it's very hard."

"I know and I'll be praying for you," answered Harry. There seemed to be little else he could say. He wanted to tell her that it would be all right and that God would bring Kerns to justice. He wanted to assure her that nothing would harm her or Brianna. He wanted to kiss her and hold her close until all fear melted away. Instead, he took his hand from hers and waited for the light to turn green again.

Twenty-Two

Danielle Kerns buttoned her jacket against the blustery October breeze and hurried toward the student union building. The weather had taken a sudden wintry turn, leaving Danielle rather unprepared. Tomorrow she'd remember her coat.

Sometime in the night, her mother and father had returned from their week-long campaign trip. She'd heard them arguing in the hall and then again later from behind their closed bedroom door. There was little doubt in her mind that her parents would have liked to divorce. Her father wouldn't allow it, however, because his political career would be complicated by such an action. Sometimes Danielle thought he simply enjoyed inflicting pain too much to let her mother go.

Nearly tripping up the steps to the building, Danielle hurried through the doors and down the stairs to the bookstore. She hoped to find a newspaper in order to pull together a last-minute current events assignment. She had it all planned in her mind. She'd get the paper then go upstairs for some coffee and spend her short break between classes searching for an appropriate article.

"Do you have today's paper?" she asked the first clerk she saw.

"Right over there. You can choose from local or otherwise," a girl about Danielle's own age replied.

"Thanks."

Danielle saw the stack and immediately fingered through them. *USA Today*, *The Wall Street Journal*, and *The Topeka Capital-Journal* were all the choices left to her. She started to reach for the last copy of *USA Today* when something from the local paper caught her eye.

"Autopsy Reveals Heroin Overdose," she read. Scanning the article, Danielle nearly dropped the paper at the sight of Teri's name. *"Cause of death has been concluded to be an overdose of heroin. Teri Davis, 19, was found dead Friday afternoon. Law enforcement officers discovered her body floating in the Kaw River. The coroner put the time of death to be between the hours of eight o'clock Thursday evening and six o'clock Friday morning."* The article continued with irrelevant information that blurred before Danielle's tear-filled eyes.

Danielle began to shake so fiercely that the paper rattled in her hands. Teri was dead, and if the paper had reported it correctly, she had died the same night they were to have met. Barely able to get her breath, Danielle paid for the paper and ran to the nearest pay phone.

Awkwardly she dialed her home number and hoped her father would have slept long enough to bear up with her interruption.

"Kerns residence, Mrs. Gleason speaking."

"Grace, I need to talk to Dad. Is he awake?" Danielle questioned in a near-frantic voice.

"He's in the study with Mr. Owens, and I don't believe he wanted to be disturbed."

"Grace, this is life and death. I have to talk to him now!"

"Are you all right, Danielle?"

"Yes . . . no, not totally. I just found out Teri Davis is dead."

"Oh, my." The housekeeper sounded quite shaken. "I'll go see if your father will take the call."

Danielle waited the painfully long moments until her father's voice sounded on the telephone. "What is it, Danielle?" He sounded irritated.

"Dad, I just read the newspaper. Teri Davis is dead."

"I heard about that. I guess that answers your questions about her disappearance."

Danielle ignored his lack of compassion. "Dad, I was supposed to meet Teri the same night she died. I was at her house by the river, but she was gone."

"What are you talking about?" Her father seemed suddenly interested.

"She called me and told me that she wanted to explain about our year apart. She said she had something very important to say and that I should come to her house at eight o'clock that night."

"And did you go?"

"Yeah, but I didn't get there until nearly ten. That was the night someone slashed my tire and I had to go to the service station with the tow truck driver."

"I seem to recall your mother saying something about it," her father replied.

"Dad, this is horrible. I can't believe Teri is dead. I know she wouldn't use drugs, but the paper says it was a heroin overdose that killed her."

"Well, we can't always know what a person will or won't do. Teri was out of your life for a long time, Danielle. She could have been robbing banks for all you know."

"No, Dad," Danielle insisted. "I know she wasn't like that. She'd been hurt too much by things in the past that involved drugs and alcohol. She wouldn't have used heroin. Besides that, I think she had a baby."

"A baby?"

Danielle thought her father sounded even more upset.

"Yes. When she called me, a baby was crying in the background, and when I went to her house, I found an empty baby cereal box and disposable diapers in the trash can."

"I see. What makes you think it was her baby? Maybe she had a roommate."

"Don't you see, Dad? It makes so much sense. She disappeared because she must have found out she was pregnant. For some reason, she was ashamed and afraid of what we would think. I think she ran to keep us from finding out about the baby."

"I think you've seen one too many movies, Danielle. Teri obviously had more problems than we realized. Just mark it down to experience and forget about it."

Danielle was hurt by her father's indifference. "Forget about it? Forget that Teri is dead? What about her baby?"

"As I understand it, there was no baby."

"I don't believe that and I'm going to find out the truth about it."

"Look, you've got too much studying to do and the election is next week. We can't cause anything to get in the way of that, can we?"

"I guess not," Danielle replied half-heartedly, knowing that if she didn't agree with what her father said, she'd face his wrath at home.

"That's a good girl. Look, if it makes you feel better, I'll have the thing privately investigated."

"Really? You'd do that for me?" Danielle was stunned by his generosity.

"Sure. You just leave it alone and I'll get Russell Owens on it right away."

"Okay, Dad. Thanks."

Kerns hung up the phone and turned to face the questioning expression of Russell Owens.

"It seems you were a bit sloppy in your duties. Did you know Danielle was to meet with Teri Thursday evening?"

Russell nodded. "That's how I found her in the first place. I had your phone wired in case she tried to make contact with Danielle."

"Well, it seems Danielle went to meet her friend and found evidence of a baby that doesn't exist."

Russell swallowed hard. "I combed the place as best I could, but it was pitch black."

"The trash can is the first place investigators look for signature evidence of a character's lifestyle. How could you be so stupid?"

"I went back for the trash. I just didn't get there before Danielle did. That's all. Look, she doesn't have any proof."

"No, but she has me and she expects me to answer her questions. She's determined to prove Teri innocent of drug-related activities and to find her child." Kerns' voice was a deadly mixture of anger and disgust.

"I'll take care of it," Russell assured him.

"You'd better, and you'd better do it in a way that ensures no one ever finds even a single bit of evidence to suggest a baby ever existed."

Russell nodded.

"I think, too," Kerns said with very little emotion, "you'd better talk to the people who have the kid. I want to ensure absolute silence in the matter. Since you were stupid enough to leave the child alive, you'll have to be responsible for the outcome."

Russell nodded again.

Kerns eyed him with contempt. "Make sure all your bridges are burned and the evidence with them. If Cara gets wind of this, there'll be no stopping her from ruining us both."

Twenty-Three

Harry Oberlin ran down the preflight checklist and prepared the governor's plane for the trip back to Topeka. They'd pushed hard these last few days and Harry's mind was held captive with thoughts of Cara and the governor's failing health. One thing or the other would have been more than enough on which to focus, but Harry couldn't seem to balance the two without giving more attention to Cara. *You have a job to do,* he kept reminding himself, but his heart failed to heed the message.

Glencoe relied on him for safe transportation and sometimes even for advice. Harry thought of it as Glencoe's man-on-the-street opinion, but he always seemed to listen and sometimes to even act on the things Harry mentioned. Cara, on the other hand, didn't really seem to rely on Harry for anything—but he wished she would.

He knew he was falling in love, but he was torn as to how he should handle it. Cara already had a full slate of problems. If he suddenly announced his intentions and declared his love, she might feel the pressure was too much and push him away. Then, too, Harry wasn't exactly sure Cara returned his feelings. He thought she cared a great deal for him. He'd seen her looking at him when she thought he was otherwise preoccupied. She seemed to assess him with the same interest that he held for her, but she never said so. She went places with him eagerly enough, and Brianna was always pleased to make it a threesome. They'd gone to the park and out to eat, and once they'd even managed to drive all the way to Kansas City to take a riverboat ride. The campaign limited them on just how much time either Harry or Cara could spare, but Harry was always determined to give them every available moment.

Now on pilot and personal security detail for the week preceding the election, Harry barely had time to telephone Cara. And even when he did call, Cara was usually unavailable. It left him feeling a great deal of frustration. How was Cara holding up to the last-minute pressures? Was she able to conceal her fears about Kerns and deal with the stress?

"Sign here for the fuel," a voice said from behind him.

Harry turned to take a clipboard from the man. He reviewed the totals and signed his name. The man gave him a copy of the receipt. "Weather is clear with unlimited visibility. You shouldn't have any trouble getting back to Topeka."

"Thanks," Harry replied and continued to check the rudder. He knew he was dangerously preoccupied with Cara and tried hard to keep his mind focused on the aircraft. Had he checked the ailerons? Better do it again and this time pay attention to the plane.

"Lieutenant Oberlin, the governor has just arrived. He's giving a last-minute speech inside the terminal, but our estimated time of departure is 1400 hours." The man who'd appeared to bring this announcement was Jeff Mitchell, Governor Glencoe's assistant.

"We're ready, Jeff," Harry said, trying to sound confident and lighthearted. "And how did the people of Salina receive our governor?"

Jeff grinned. "He's got it in the bag. These folks are close enough to his native Lindsborg, and they know what he'll do for them. I'd say that Kerns isn't a real threat. He may pull some of the bigwigs in Kansas City and Wichita, but the common people will swing the vote. And they belong to Glencoe."

Just then Jeff and Harry noticed a procession of people moving across the tarmac to the plane. "Well," Harry said, finishing his walk-around, "this plane is fit and ready for flight."

"I'm glad this is nearly finished," Jeff replied. "Another week of campaigning and my family would have reported me missing in action."

Harry laughed and followed Jeff to greet the passengers.

It was apparent to Harry that Glencoe was suffering from his latest bout with chemotherapy. His cancer had taken a turn for the worse. How the man kept on the campaign trail and dealt with life-threatening cancer was beyond Harry. But Glencoe had managed to pull it off, and as far as Harry knew, the media was clueless as to the governor's condition.

"Ed, we're right on schedule," Jeff said, crowding in to speak with the governor. The accompanying members of the governor's campaign team moved aside to give him time with Jeff.

Harry looked up just in time to see a strange expression consume Glencoe's features. It was a look that almost suggested wonder, maybe even of a sudden revelation. For a brief moment Glencoe's eyes locked with Harry's, then without warning, the governor's knees buckled and he sank to the tarmac.

Harry pushed the campaign aids aside. "Give the man some air and block him from the reporters." The men and women quickly complied, forming a semicircle around the fallen governor. "Anderson!" Harry yelled to another highway patrolman. "Give me a hand."

The young officer joined Harry and helped to loosen Ed Glencoe's tie as Harry searched for a pulse.

"Harry," Glencoe whispered. "Harry, this is it. I'm not going to make it."

Harry grimaced and counted the barely perceivable pulse beat. "Save your strength, Ed."

"No strength to save," Glencoe managed to say and then fell silent.

"Get an ambulance!" Harry ordered, putting his ear to the governor's chest. "He's gone into cardiac arrest." Harry ripped open the front of Glencoe's dress shirt.

"He's not breathing!" the shaken Klark Anderson announced.

"Keep your voice down," Harry growled. "We'll have to do CPR. You breathe for him, ready?"

Anderson nodded.

They went to work, but in the back of Harry's mind he knew it was futile.

"Ambulance is on its way!" Jeff announced, putting his hand over the cellular phone. "I'll go deal with the public."

Minutes seemed to become hours. Harry kept pumping the older man's chest, hoping, praying that resuscitation was possible. *Dear God,* he prayed, *help me to do what's right.*

The ambulance, already standing by at the airport because of Glencoe's dignitary status, screamed its way across the flight line. Harry and Klark gave way to the on-call doctor and his team, but it was clear that Glencoe was gone. Everyone knew it, but no one wanted to admit it.

After desperate attempts to revive the governor, the doctor finally declared Glencoe dead at 2:45 P.M. Harry was stunned, but no more so than the people around him. The election was in two days, but now there was no incumbent to run against Robert Kerns.

Jeff was already on the phone to the lieutenant governor, while what seemed an entire army of highway patrolmen had assembled on the tarmac to offer crowd control and protection to the governor's team.

"We'll tell the public that Glencoe is very sick. Put him on a stretcher, but for pity sakes don't pull the sheet over his face," Jeff announced after concluding with the lieutenant governor. "Harry, you'll fly him back to Topeka, but not to Forbes Field. The press will catch wind of this by then, and everybody and his brother will be there. Go to the municipal airport."

"They'll be there, too," Harry replied. "Say, I know a little field up north of town. It's called Mesa Verde. It's just a grass and dirt strip, mostly used for crop dusters, but I know we could get in and out of there easily. Why don't I land there and you could have the funeral home waiting to receive the body."

"Good thinking," Jeff replied. "I don't want a lot of pictures splashed across the paper until all the family is notified and the lieutenant governor has a chance to make the announcement."

Without further delay, Glencoe was loaded onto a stretcher and then into the plane.

The whole thing seemed unreal, and to his surprise, all Harry could think about was getting home to Cara. He needed her. He needed to put his arms around her and hear her say that God would make everything all right. He needed to immerse himself in life and set aside the months of watching a friend die.

"Lieutenant Governor Campbell will tell the first lady," Jeff said from the seat opposite Harry's.

"She won't be surprised," Harry replied. "When will you go public?"

"Well," Jeff answered, still sounding quite shaken, "Lieutenant Governor . . . no, make that Governor Campbell will make the announcement at 1700 hours from the Capitol. His office is already setting it up."

"No doubt news of the collapse is already out," Harry said, knowing how the media worked. "Hopefully our landing at Mesa will make the difference and buy us time."

"Yeah," Jeff murmured. "Time."

Cara sat across from Bob Kerns at their campaign headquarters. His office was slightly bigger than hers. Even so, it would never be big enough to put the kind of distance between them she would have liked. But duty called and Cara had to endure his company. There was a massive reception planned that night, and support was running high for the event. Kerns was concluding instructions to the very attentive Serena Perez while Cara awaited her own list of do's and don'ts.

"Well," he announced as Serena took her leave, "we've nearly won this thing."

"You think so?" replied Cara dryly. "I heard the polls have Glencoe way out in front."

Kerns' eyes narrowed. "We're going to win. You might try to sound enthusiastic."

"You mean lie?" Cara questioned bitterly. "You know I don't want this. I hate the fact that I've had anything to do with this race. And once the election is over, my part in it is over as well. I've decided I'll resign as lieutenant governor if we win."

"I don't think so, Cara." Kerns said the words so matter-of-factly that Cara's mouth dropped open in surprise. "You see, there is a great deal to be done and you can help me. Your image is something I need, and I intend to benefit greatly from your puritanical right-winged facade."

"You can't be serious. Take Russell on board as lieutenant

governor, but leave me alone. I've had it with campaigns and politics. I told you from the start—"

"I don't care," interjected Kerns. "You seem to forget who is in charge." He waited a moment, lacing and unlacing his fingers. "You leave when I tell you to leave. Not before and not after."

Cara felt genuine fear as she looked into his eyes. They were cold and indifferent, but the tone of his voice made his intentions clear. "And if I don't?" she dared the question.

Kerns smiled maliciously. "Then you'll pay the price for double-crossing me."

"Sorry to interrupt," Serena Perez said, coming unannounced into the office. "But you need to come see the television."

"What in the world for?" Kerns asked rather indignantly.

"I don't know. Russell just said to get you in there now," Serena replied.

"Come along, Cara. Let's see what's so important."

Reluctantly, Cara followed Kerns into the windowed front room. Here and there volunteers worked at making last-minute phone calls, but in one corner most of the staff gathered around the TV, and a definite hush had overcome them all.

"Governor Glencoe will be sorely missed by the people of this state. We extend our deepest sympathies to his family members and friends." The announcement was coming from the new acting governor, James Campbell. "I can take a few questions at this time."

A mad rush of clamoring reporters filled the television screen as Cara exchanged a look of surprise with Bob Kerns.

"What time did the governor pass away?" the first question came.

"The time of death is given as 2:45 P.M."

"Has cause of death been determined?" This question came from Melissa Jordon.

"It was not well known, but the governor had been ill for some time. He had a form of stomach cancer, and it was hoped that with chemotherapy and other treatments, he might recover. Cause of death is presumed to be related to that cancer."

"Can you give us more details on the disease itself? How long had the governor been sick, and why didn't he allow the public to have knowledge of his condition?" a reporter from the *Kansas City Star* questioned.

"I can't give you any more information about the form of cancer, at least not at this time." Great beads of perspiration formed on Campbell's brow. "The governor chose to remain silent on his condition and I respected his wishes."

"The election is less than forty-eight hours away," another reported commented. "How will this affect you, and what outcome do you see for the election?"

Campbell was fading fast, Cara thought. He looked incapable of dealing with the strain. He glanced nervously from side to side, as if in doing so he might summon help.

"I'm . . . well . . . it is . . ." he stammered, then stopped all together. He seemed to take a deep breath, and Cara noticed that he gripped the podium more tightly. "The campaign will move ahead as planned. I'm uncertain as to how the actual event will be handled."

Kerns began laughing, and to Cara's surprise, so did a great many of the staff members. "This is it!" Kerns announced. "This is our ticket to victory."

"Campbell is hardly any competition. The man is completely incompetent," Owens said, shaking his head. "Who could have known it would be this easy."

"What if he wins out of sympathy votes?" Cara suddenly voiced aloud.

Every face in the room turned to stare at her. Feeling very out of place and stupid for such a suggestion, Cara lowered her gaze to the floor.

"A very good point, my dear running mate," Kerns replied calmly. "We will have to call in some last-minute favors, Russ. Get ahold of your people at the papers in Wichita, Kansas City, and of course, *The Capital-Journal*. We're going to need a strong stab at the secrecy and deception practiced by the current administration. No matter what it costs us, we have to instill doubt in the minds of the Glencoe/Campbell supporters."

Owens nodded and was already headed to his desk. Cara met Kerns' smug expression. "How could you?"

"It's nothing personal, Cara. It's just politics."

"Obviously," Cara replied in a voice that betrayed her anger.

Twenty-Four

A hush had fallen over the gathering of wall-to-wall Kerns supporters. The hotel ballroom, in its festive red, white, and blue decor, was designed to promote the victory of Kerns and Kessler. Among the people assembled were press representatives and wealthy friends and family who had paid plenty to see Kerns elected.

"And with the majority of precincts reporting in, it's now clear that Robert Kerns will be the next governor of Kansas," the commentator on the projection screen announced.

The cheers around the room were deafening. These people had gathered en masse to celebrate victory or, if necessary, share defeat with their man. Now it became clear the party was to be a celebration, and they were all more than ready.

News reporters from every major paper and television station were gathered there as well, and only when the current governor came on the television did the cheers die down again.

". . . and so I offer my congratulations to the new governor-elect and pledge this administration's support and assistance to make a smooth transitional period." Campbell continued, mentioning the deceased Governor Glencoe, but Cara couldn't make out anything else. The crowd of well-wishers was cheering again and chanting, "KERNS AND KESSLER! KERNS AND KESSLER!" Finally it fell away to just, "KERNS! KERNS! KERNS!"

I'm the new lieutenant governor, she thought. Looking around the room, Cara felt as though she might be in the middle of a dream. Better yet, a nightmare. People were clamoring around Bob and his family, and those who couldn't reach him seemed content to merely push toward him. All at once, someone spied Cara from where she stood half hidden behind a huge potted tree.

"There's Mrs. Kessler!" a voice shouted, and soon Cara was engulfed in an overwhelming sea of people. Microphones were shoved in her face, although not as many as Kerns had in his.

Suddenly Russell Owens appeared at her side. "Come on, you're going to stand beside the new governor and make your statements with him."

As strange as it seemed, Cara was actually glad for Russell's possessive hold on her arm. He pushed his way through the exuberant mass and helped Cara up the platform steps.

"Take your lead from Bob," Russell reminded. "Offer nothing on your own, and whenever pressed for a personal opinion, defer to Bob. Understand?" Cara could barely hear him, but she nodded in affirmation and took her place beside Governor Robert Kerns.

Kerns immediately noticed her presence and grabbed her hand, raising their arms high in a victorious salute to the crowd. This would be the front-page photograph for tomorrow's various state papers, and Cara knew Kerns would play it for all he was worth.

Bulbs flashed nonstop for nearly five minutes, and combined with the television camera lights, Cara's eyes began to hurt. The noise and lights gave birth to a throbbing sensation that started at the base of her skull and worked its way up and over her forehead. All Cara could do was smile and pray that the night would pass quickly.

Kerns signaled for his supporters to quiet, and Cara was amazed at how quickly they complied. As always, Kerns was in control.

"Thank you!" he called out as the clapping and cheers faded. "Thank you so very much!"

Cara glanced around, noting that Debra and Danielle had been brought onto the platform to stand on the other side of Kerns. Debra looked smashing in a Christian Dior suit of fire engine red, and Danielle, although rather serious in expression, was all feminine charm in a navy-colored angora sweater dress. Looking at her own well-tailored suit of navy blue with a red-and-white print blouse, Cara could see how careful the planning of this moment had been. Choreographed down to the last detail, the people surrounding Robert Kerns in his victory were true patriots in their red, white, and blue.

"Well, we did it!" Kerns announced, and the cheers rose up again in deafening waves of support. "Without you, none of this would have been possible. My thanks go out to each and every one of you who have seen us through this process and who voted their support to our new administration." Like an actor confident of his part, Kerns put an arm around Debra and flashed her a loving smile. "And of course," he began again, "none of this would be possible without my dear wife, Debra, and our daughter, Danielle. They both worked long hours to give me the kind of extra support that always spells victory!"

Again, applause and cheers.

Kerns then turned to Cara, and she thought for a moment her heart might stop beating. The look he gave her was almost threatening, though to the crowd below them, Cara was certain it appeared nothing of the kind. She detected in his eyes, however, a menacing underlying threat that made her blood run cold.

"And to this young woman, my running mate—" Cheers interrupted the speech and Kerns allowed it for a moment. "Cara Kessler, our next lieutenant governor, has worked as hard as anyone. She has devoted herself to the campaign and has made herself available to assist me whenever and wherever I needed her. She is a fine young woman and she will make a tremendous lieutenant governor."

Applause and five hundred faces turned to acknowledge her. More bulbs flashed, and Cara didn't know what else to do but smile and wave at the crowd.

Kerns continued his speech, but Cara heard very little of it. Staring down at the audience, she became more aware than ever before that these people expected something of her that she might not be able to give. What would they think of her if they really knew her heart? Would they be so supportive six months from now—or even six weeks?

Politics was such a fickle business, and no one knew this better than Cara, who had borne a good share of stress during her father's political career. Now she was the one in the limelight. Well, not exactly. She reasoned with herself that the lieutenant governor was just a show position. A second runner-up who would assume the duties of office should the governor be otherwise unable to fulfill his obligations. She'd attend funerals and dinners on behalf of Kerns, and she'd sit behind a fancy desk in the Capitol building. She'd share in meetings with the chief of staff, who would no doubt be Russell Owens, and pretend to agree with whatever fate Kerns had slated for the state. Or would she? What kind of power could she have in this position?

Suddenly her thoughts were running rampant. *I may have had to bow and stoop to Kerns during the election process,* she thought, *but now that I am duly elected, I should have some say as to what I do on behalf of the position.*

She thought of HEARTBEAT Ministries and all the children she'd known through the years. Worried kids without futures, frightened kids without hope, desperate kids seeking answers. She wondered how she might benefit them from her position as lieutenant governor.

Cara tried to force herself to concentrate on what Kerns was saying, but it was no use. When she looked out on the precisely assembled mass, it was the faces of nameless children who haunted her. Children who needed her voice to be heard. Children like Teri and Jamie.

Kerns had opened the floor to reporters, and Cara wasn't surprised when Melissa Jordon asked him point-blank what the focus of his administration would be.

"There are a great many projects and interests on which this administration plans to focus. The concerns of the people are my concerns, and their needs will be my uppermost consideration," he replied in political mumbo jumbo while reporters hurried to scrawl notes.

"And you, Mrs. Kessler," Melissa questioned with a look that went straight through Cara. "What will your focus be?"

Cara hesitated a moment and saw Russell motioning her back to Kerns. Realizing her forum, Cara squared her shoulders and smiled at Melissa. "My focus will be much as it has always been. I want to give a voice to those who have no voice. I want to bring justice to those who can't seek it for themselves."

Later that evening Kerns followed his wife and daughter into a black limousine, with Russell bringing up the rear and waving reporters away from the vehicle.

His family was greatly subdued by the events of the evening, and although others might have found this strange, Bob Kerns welcomed it. Ripping his tie away from his neck, Kerns turned to Russell.

"Just what did she mean by setting her own agenda? 'Justice for those who can't seek it for themselves'?" His voice revealed barely controlled rage.

"I told her not to step out of line. I specifically told her to defer to you on any personal opinion item. Frankly, Bob, I think you're going to have your hands full with Cara Kessler."

Kerns caught the expression on his wife's face. The slightest smirk lined her lips. "I'll bring her under control," Kerns promised aloud. "No one is going to ruin this for me—certainly not a do-gooder with a private agenda."

Debra crossed her legs in a slow deliberate manner and smiled. "This should be more fun than I'd imagined. I'm going to enjoy watching Cara make a monkey out of you."

Kerns flashed her a warning with the narrowing of his eyes, but it was Owens who spoke. "Cara will do what she's told to do, or she'll pay the price. Since there's only one thing she possesses that really and truly matters to her, I think she'll be happy to fall into line."

"And just what is it you think will make Cara Kessler dance to your tune?" Debra asked sarcastically.

Owens and Kerns exchanged a smile.

"She has a daughter," Kerns stated matter-of-factly.

With the look of an animal about to corner its prey, Owens nodded. "Her name is Brianna."

Twenty-Five

"I saw you on TV, Mommy!" Brianna declared, crashing into Cara's bedroom. "That party looked like a lot of fun. Tell me all about it!"

With a moan, Cara rolled over and saw that it was only eight o'clock. She'd barely had five hours of sleep. "Oh, Brianna, it's too early. Let me rest a little longer."

The ten-year-old giggled and jumped on top of the bed. "You looked beautiful, and now you're going to be the governor."

"Lieutenant governor," Cara corrected and tried to rub the sleep from her eyes.

"What's the difference?"

"A great many things, Bri. For one, I won't have all those responsibilities, and for another, we won't have to move to Cedar Crest."

"What's that?" questioned her daughter.

"That's where the Kansas governor and his family live. It's the beautiful house out west of town. Remember the one that sits way back off the interstate on the way to the museum?"

"Oh, wow!" Brianna exclaimed. "I want to live there!"

"Well, you can forget about that," Cara said, easing herself into a sitting position. "We'll no doubt visit there on many occasions, so you should get your fill that way."

"What else is different about your job?" By now, Brianna was bouncing up and down on her knees.

"My job is to support the governor's office and to help

wherever he needs me most. I have some things I can do on my own, but not many. Most of the time I guess I'll just be working at the Capitol building, and it will be like most any other job."

"Can I call you at work?" Bri had stopped bouncing and was now scooting off the bed.

"Sure. In fact, I'll probably even take you to work with me a few times and let you see what I have to do."

Brianna's face brightened at this prospect. "I'm going to call my friends!" She hurried from the room, leaving Cara to stare after her.

She is so young and naive, thought Cara. Like any mother, Cara wanted to protect her child from the evils of the world. But unlike other mothers, Cara felt she was walking right into the middle of a battle. A battle that could well cost them the peaceful world they'd known.

Slipping into a satin robe, Cara was surprised when the telephone rang. Brianna must have gotten herself side-tracked.

"Hello?"

"Hi there, lieutenant governor. Need a pilot to fly you around the state?"

Cara smiled. "Good morning, Harry."

"You actually looked like you were enjoying yourself last night. Have you given in to the position and decided to accept your lot in life?"

"Hardly." Cara sat down on the edge of her bed. "I'm just trying to figure out what my role in this entire situation is going to be."

"Well, how about if I pick up you and Brianna, and we go out for a celebration breakfast? We can discuss your role over eggs and bacon."

"That sounds wonderful. I suppose being the lieutenant

governor-elect has its perks."

"Maybe I'll bribe you and be able to keep my job."

"Hmmm, better make it a good bribe."

Harry laughed, and the sound warmed her. She could get used to that laugh.

"So, how about if I pick you up in ten minutes?"

"Ten minutes! There's absolutely no way I can be ready in ten minutes. Give me at least half an hour," Cara demanded.

"I'll be there in ten. If you aren't ready, Brianna and I will go by ourselves."

"Okay, but you asked for it. I can't vouch for what I'll look like."

"You'll look perfect," Harry said with a sudden seriousness to his voice. "You always do."

Cara hung up the phone, looking forward to the date. "Brianna!" she called, hurrying to her closet. "Harry's coming to take us to breakfast. He said he'd be here in ten minutes and we'd better be ready!" Cara was pulling out jeans and a white cable knit sweater.

Brianna came running in, clapping her hands. "Harry's coming!"

The declaration was so positively filled with delight that Cara paused to consider her daughter for a moment.

"You really like Harry, don't you?" she finally asked.

"Don't you?" Brianna threw back the question with such matter-of-fact ease that Cara had to laugh.

"Of course. He's a good friend."

Brianna was already dancing out the door. "He'd make a good daddy, too. I can tell, 'cause when he laughs his eyes crinkle up."

Cara was stunned by this revelation. She'd not anticipated Brianna's astute contemplation of Harry, nor her daughter's dreams for him.

Ten minutes later to the second, Harry rang the doorbell.

"Well, I must say, you are a man of your word." Cara offered a beaming smile and stepped back from the door.

Harry was dressed in a heavy denim jacket, plaid flannel shirt, and blue jeans. In what little time they'd actually managed to spend together, Cara couldn't remember him wearing anything but jeans or his patrolman uniform.

"What?" Harry questioned, looking down at his shirt. "Did I spill something on me? Did my buttons pop off?"

Brianna's laughter filled the air. "She looks at me like that before she lets me go to school or church."

Cara blushed, feeling her cheeks grow red-hot.

"I like it when she looks at me that way," Harry confided conspiratorially to Brianna.

"I don't," the girl admitted. "It usually means I have to go wash my face again."

"Well?" he asked Cara, lifting his chin in first one direction and then the other. "Should I go wash my face?"

Cara couldn't contain the laughter that rose up in her throat. "I give up. Didn't someone promise me breakfast? I believe I've kept my end of the deal. I've never dressed so fast in my life."

"I guess we'd better head over to Cracker Barrel then," Harry agreed. "I wouldn't want to go back on my word." He smiled, and when he did, Cara couldn't help but notice the laugh lines around his eyes.

As if reading her mother's mind, Brianna reached out and took hold of Harry's hand. "I told you his eyes crinkled."

"So you did," Cara replied, noticing that Harry's expression had changed to one of confusion. "Don't worry about it," she told him. "I'll explain it later."

When they walked into the restaurant, Cara was immediately recognized, and two people even came forward with their newspapers and asked for her autograph.

"People around here are starved for celebrities," she muttered as they were led to a table in the corner. "I'd better sit on the inside. Maybe that will discourage interruptions."

"Don't bet on it," Harry said. "I've worked at this for four years, remember? But I tell you what. This will be my chance to prove what a great asset I could be to the new administration. I'll play bodyguard and keep the crowd away."

"Are you really a celebrity now, Mom?"

Cara shook her head. "I don't think so, Brianna."

"Hey, congratulations," a petite redheaded waitress said. She put down three glasses of water as she introduced herself. "I voted for you and that Kerns fellow. I figured it was time to get more women in government."

Cara smiled politely, while Harry took control. "We'll have coffee and orange juice." He looked to Cara for confirmation.

Nodding her head, she felt herself relax a bit. Harry seemed quite capable of taking charge, but his way was so much more desirable than Kerns'.

"I'll give you a chance to look over the menus and bring your drinks right out."

After the waitress had disappeared, Harry turned to Cara. "How'd I do? Did I keep the crowds back?"

"Okay, you're hired," Cara said in mock exasperation. "But only on a trial basis."

"Can I go look in the store?" Brianna interrupted. Cracker Barrel was divided into two parts, a store filled with craft items and a restaurant with old-fashioned meals.

"Sure, honey, but don't be surprised if someone asks you for your autograph."

"Cool! I'll sign, Brianna Rachelle Kessler." She pretended to write the letters in the air.

"That'll keep 'em happy," Harry joined in.

Brianna suddenly stopped writing and stared at Harry intensely. "What's your last name?"

Harry looked at her seriously, as if he was considering whether her question merited an answer. Then without warning, he whipped out a leather billfold and flashed his badge in Brianna's face. "What's it say on my identification?"

"Harold T. Oberlin," Brianna read. "What's the T stand for?"

"Thomas."

"Like the guy in the Bible? The one who doubted Jesus was alive?"

"Guilty as charged. Only I believe Jesus is very much alive."

Brianna smiled. "Me too." She leaned closer to Harry. "I like the name Oberlin. I think it would make a great last name. Don't you, Mom?" She grinned at her mother and hurried off to the store.

"What was that all about?" Harry asked, putting his wallet away and opening the menu.

"Oh, just Brianna being a funny little girl."

The waitress reappeared with the beverages, and Cara allowed Harry to order for all of them. Once the waitress had gone her way, Harry surprised her by asking about Teri Davis. "Have you been coping all right with the news of her death?"

"I think the business of the campaign has kept my mind from being too consumed. But I do plan to get to the bottom of it."

Cara paused for a moment, her thoughts drifting to the young woman. "I hardly knew her at all, but I keep reminding myself her situation could be the same for a hundred other girls. It could even happen to Brianna."

"No." Harry shook his head. "Brianna has a stable home and a mother who loves her very much. As I recall from the paper's article, Teri was an orphan and had been in no less than ten different foster homes."

"I know," Cara replied. The subject caused her to grow quite thoughtful. "I can't help but believe there are other kids out there just like her. There's a lot I want to do with my new-found power." She laughed a bit. "Well, whatever power there really is playing second fiddle to Kerns. Anyway, I want to help as many people as possible, and I think I'll need strong people like you to help me out."

"Your wish is my command," Harry whispered.

Cara sighed. "If only that were true."

"What would you wish for first?" questioned Harry. His eyes seemed to search the depths of hers for answers she couldn't give.

"I'd wish for all this to go away."

Twenty-Six

The months of November and December passed quickly, and before Cara knew it the new year had begun. She'd tried to give Brianna as much of her free time as possible, while in the back of her mind were visions of the handsome patrolman who had shared Christmas with them.

The transitional period of changing one governor for another was running more smoothly than anyone had expected. For Cara, there was very little to do. Kerns kept her busy with insignificant tasks while he appointed his staff and ordered changes for his office. The big surprise came when Kerns announced that he was buying a palatial new home in Clarion Estates. It would be this home, and not Cedar Crest, in which he and his family would reside. Cedar Crest would be used as a public house, with meetings, tours, and special events allowed to take place there.

"It's an ancient monstrosity," Kerns told Cara when she'd questioned his decision. "I have no desire to spend the next eight years sitting in that Victorian dump."

"It's hardly a dump," she protested, trying to ignore his reference to eight years. "It's a very elegant and graceful home. Plus, the people of Kansas might take offense at you rejecting the governor's mansion. You might be limited to the four years you were lucky enough to get."

Kerns hadn't cared for her attitude, and Cara hadn't concerned herself with his. However, as punishment for her outburst, Kerns put her in charge of issuing pink slips to most of the former governor's staff. This was a job Cara didn't relish at all.

Government employees, at least those appointed by new administrations, knew that their jobs were temporary. They weren't protected by civil service rules and regulations. Even so, it didn't make Cara's job any easier. She felt a personal responsibility to these people.

"Hey, got time for lunch?" Melissa Jordon stood in the doorway still decked out in her navy wool coat.

Cara looked around at the disheveled mess her office had become. "I think lunch sounds like a wonderful idea."

"Good. I've got a few things I want to discuss with you."

"Regarding?"

Melissa glanced around before mouthing, "Teri."

Cara nodded and went to the coatrack where her khaki trench coat awaited duty. "Let's go."

"Where?" Melissa asked as Cara grabbed her purse and joined her.

"Well, they'll never miss me here, so why don't we go all out and head for someplace nice. Say Paisano's? I have a craving for Italian."

"That does sound good."

"Janey, I'm going to lunch," Cara told a gray-haired woman who had just come into the outer office. "I'm not sure when I'll be back, but I have my beeper, so if you need me just call."

The woman flashed a smile. "Running out on us, eh?"

"As far away as possible," Cara said with a laugh. She liked the older woman and was sorry to see her go. Fortunately, Janey was retiring and would not face one of the ominous pink slips.

"So you have a beeper now?" Melissa questioned. They took the stairs to avoid the long wait at the archaic main elevator.

"Kerns insisted, and the next thing I knew Russell was handing them out like candy."

Melissa laughed and led the way. A brisk January wind blew steadily against their faces and Cara shivered. "It feels like snow," she murmured and happily jumped into Melissa's compact car. "Brrr!"

"The weatherman didn't say snow, but he did promise cold and lots of it. I hope you have clear weather for the inauguration. They do it on the south steps of the Capitol building, you know." It was more a statement than a question.

"Yes, I've been apprised of that very thing. I was told to dress warm but not too flashy. I should appear poised and refined, but not overly elegant."

"I'm surprised they don't show up with a rack of costumes and let Russell Owens pick out your dress," Melissa said dryly.

"Oh, he does give final approval," Cara replied, and Melissa rolled her eyes. "But enough of Russell and this nightmare. What have you found out about Teri and Jamie?"

"Not much. I managed to get back into her house," Melissa said with a coy smile. "I have a friend in the sheriff's department. Anyway, I scoured that house from one end to the other and didn't find so much as a pacifier. I've researched hospital and clinic records, at least those I could bribe someone to let me see, and I went through *The Capital-Journal* notices of birth for the last year."

"But?" Cara questioned, knowing the answer before Melissa gave it.

"But there is no record of Teri giving birth to Jamie."

"Did you look under her assumed name?"

"Sure, but again, there was nothing. My guess is Teri had the baby at home or in the care of a midwife who kept her mouth shut."

"But the baby would have to have a birth certificate."

Melissa shrugged and pulled into the restaurant parking lot. "Apparently, this baby didn't. I have an appointment to talk privately with the coroner. He's been on vacation for three weeks, and before that he was tied up in some kind of criminal trial and wouldn't grant interviews to anyone."

"What do you hope to find out from him?" Cara asked. "I mean, he's already established the cause of death as a drug overdose."

Melissa shut off the engine and turned to explain. "He didn't say what condition the body was in. He can tell me whether there were multiple track marks on Teri's body. That would show us if she was a regular drug user. He could also say whether there were signs of foul play—strange bruising or broken bones. He can probably even establish whether or not Teri had ever given birth."

"I never thought of that! Melissa, that's great thinking. I wish I had someone like you around on a full-time basis." As soon as the words were out of Cara's mouth she formed a plan. "Why not?"

Melissa stared at her. "Why not what?"

"I've just issued all those termination notices, so why don't you come to work for me? I know you like your job at the paper, but working for me would allow you to get into places a regular reporter couldn't go. You know what to look for, and you could keep me up to speed on what Kerns is planning and how I should respond."

"I don't know about that. You're talking a major lifestyle change. Long hours and low pay. Hey," she declared with a grin, "sounds like working for the paper!"

"Oh, please say you'll at least consider it," Cara pleaded. "I'll see to it that you get a decent salary and the hours will be up to you."

"Are you sure Kerns is going to approve of my joining the team?"

"He'll have nothing to say about it," Cara replied. "I'm entitled to chose my own staff. Will you think about it?"

"Okay. I'll talk to Peter and see what he thinks. I know you're right about getting into places that normally would have closed their doors to me, and it makes a lot of sense. However, you and I both know that Kerns will have someone watching both of us. He may very well not realize we know the connection to him and Teri Davis, but he does know that you aren't a willing party to this gubernatorial affair."

Bob Kerns was enjoying his newfound attention. He was exactly where he wanted to be, and the power rush was incredible. Spread out on his desk were the plans for his new home in Clarion Estates. The three-story brick palace was perfect. Located at the end of a cul-de-sac, Kerns gave strong consideration to buying up the lots surrounding the circle in order to keep the home isolated and even more commanding.

"Danielle's here," Serena announced, coming into his office.

"Send her in and call Russell. Tell him to bring the results of our investigation on Teri Davis."

Serena nodded. "I've also set up your next Association meeting. The men will be here at nine." Serena had turned to leave but stopped rather abruptly. "Oh, and your inaugural committee called with some problem about entertainment, but I referred them to Russell."

"Good girl. That's one mess I don't need. The parties can be someone else's baby, but I want them elaborate and very, very public."

"You've got it," Serena promised and left in search of Russell Owens.

Danielle came into the office as though sharing a revolving door with Serena. "Hi, Dad. Serena said there was news?"

"That's right. Russ will be here shortly and we can go over what the private investigator found out." Kerns motioned her to a seat.

"So what did they discover?" Danielle asked, not even taking off her coat before sitting down.

"I'd rather you hear the entire matter from the reports. I might forget something. Ah, here's Russell now."

"Sorry, I was tied up with the inaugural committee. I've brought the papers given to me by the investigator." He put the folder on the desk in front of Kerns.

"Good. Close the door and you can explain them to Danielle."

Russell appeared to grimace a bit, but he did as Kerns directed. Taking the chair beside Danielle, he reached across the desk and took the file up once more. "Well, it seems that after a thorough investigation," he began, "the cause of death by heroin overdose cannot be disputed."

"But Teri was never into drugs!" Danielle protested.

"Maybe you just never knew about it," Kerns replied. "It seems, from our records, that Teri had a long history of trouble with drugs. It's probably why she dropped out of college."

"That doesn't make sense. What about the baby?" Danielle questioned.

Russell thumbed through the papers, all the while shaking his head. He pushed up the gold wire-framed glasses and spoke, "There's nothing here about Teri having a baby. However, she did share the house with a woman who did have a small infant. Ah, here." He pulled out a typewritten sheet of paper and handed it to Danielle.

"The woman has disappeared from sight. It's thought that

perhaps she had something to do with Teri's death. The authorities are still seeking her," Russell concluded.

"Why haven't I read about this in the papers?" Danielle asked in disbelief.

Kerns gave her a tolerant smile. "They can't very well carry on an undercover investigation if they announce to the world exactly what it is they are investigating, now can they?"

"That's right, Danielle." Russell picked up the torch and ran. "They certainly don't want to alert Teri's roommate to the fact that they know of her existence or her presumed involvement."

"I guess that makes sense," Danielle replied reluctantly. "And that woman had a baby?"

"Yes," Russell answered. "A six-month-old girl. That accounts for why you found diapers and cereal boxes in Teri's trash."

"I don't understand, though. If Teri died from heroin, and you say she had a history of drug problems, why would there be any concern about someone else being responsible for her death?"

She's a smart one, Kerns thought, eyeing her with a misplaced sense of pride. "Perhaps Teri didn't take an overdose. Maybe she had just shot up, and while she was high this woman shot her up again. Who knows? We do know that somehow she got in the river. Maybe she overdosed and then this roommate of hers disposed of her body. There's no way to tell until we find the woman."

Danielle drew a heavy breath and sighed. Slowly she handed the paper back to Russell. "I guess this explains everything, but I still find it hard to believe Teri was involved with drugs."

"I wasn't going to do this," Kerns said, reaching into his desk drawer, "but I can see you need the extra proof." He took out fanfolded computer paper nearly an inch thick. "This is a report of all Teri's run-ins with the law. Most of them are drug related. Minor possession charges. Even possession with intent to sell."

Danielle's eyes widened in disbelief. "I can't believe it!"

"Believe it, Danielle. I'm about to take office as the governor of this state. I don't have time for games, and I don't want controversy clinging to my term. Russell has very graciously spent a tremendous amount of time gathering this information for you and assisting the private investigator. If you're going to sit here and tell me you don't believe our proof, then how can I help you?" His voice was edged with anger and unspoken accusation. He wanted to belittle her and make her feel like the helpless child she'd always been. By the look on her face, Kerns could tell his plan was working.

She swallowed hard and got to her feet. "I believe you," she muttered. "It's just hard to realize I was such a poor judge of character."

Kerns nodded and put the papers down. "At least the matter is settled."

"Until they find that woman," Danielle added.

Russell coughed nervously, but Kerns wasn't in the least bit shaken. "That's right," he agreed. "And I know the law enforcement agencies will do their level best to locate her."

Danielle nodded, appearing years younger. In her eyes, Kerns could read reluctant acceptance of the facts, along with a great deal of pain. At least she wouldn't be pestering him for answers as to why Teri had gone away without a word. This would be the end of it.

At the door, Danielle turned and faced the two men. "Dad, thanks for doing this for me. Teri was a good friend, and it was important for me to know."

Kerns got to his feet and fixed a stern expression on his

youngest child. "Good friends don't use people. Teri used you and our family for whatever good it could bring her."

There were tears in Danielle's eyes by now, but Kerns had no feeling for the pain she was suffering. No, it was better to bring her to her knees on this Teri Davis issue. That way, the cut would be clean and permanent.

He continued, "I am sorry she endangered you with her lifestyle. She obviously had no regard for your safety. Her illegal activities could have caused you a lot of problems, Danielle. Don't ever forget that."

Danielle hurried from the room, clearly unable to deal with one more word on the matter. Kerns crossed the room and closed the door. Turning a satisfied smile on Russell, he retrieved the computer printouts and handed them to his new chief of staff. "File these and thank your friends for making them look real."

Twenty-Seven

Trademark blue smoke saturated the conference room in the law offices of Kerns and Dubray. Another meeting of the Association was about to convene.

Kerns walked into the room with Owens at his side. It was easy to see that no one was fond of being called to this meeting. *George Sheldon has lost a great deal of weight,* Kerns thought. Probably because that toxic waste spill was about to go public. Sheldon had still not come to him, and the EPA was breathing down his neck in a major way. Kerns supposed he'd have to take the initiative and approach George on the matter before it got completely out of hand.

"Well, we did it," Kerns said, echoing his acceptance speech the night he'd won the election. "Now the real work begins."

He took his seat at the head of the table and Owens took the placc at his right. "I've called you here tonight to announce position placement and to reward you for your support in the past."

Their faces seemed to relax a bit.

"I've kept apprised of your situations, contributions, and desired placement for future service."

Taking a folder that Owens already held in preparation, Bob began to sort through the pages. "Gary Daggett," he announced. The man straightened in his seat and raised questioning brows. "As you all know, Gary is the owner of Consumers Natural Gas Company. He has provided the maximum amount of campaign contributions and has never failed to meet my expectations in service. Gary, I am appointing you to the position of secretary of administration. This critical job will put you in charge of a variety of other agencies within the administration. I'm confident you can handle the position and that you will be confirmed by the legislature without issue."

Gary smiled and made a nervous attempt at thanks. "I'm grateful . . . for the . . . for the chance to serve you and the state."

Kerns nodded and continued. "Cameron, I'm appointing you director of purchases. Hopefully Enter Data can bear up without you at the helm for a while. You know what purchasing is all about, and in the future we will need you to help us with a variety of things."

Cameron nodded.

Kerns turned to George, noting that not only had he lost weight, but he was balding as well. Nerves had a way of taking their toll. "I think it would be wise for us to schedule a private appointment, George." The man nodded and lit another cigarette. Kerns smiled, noting the two that already smoldered in the ashtray in front of Sheldon. George was in a bad way.

"Pat, with Cameron heading up purchases, you should have little trouble in sewing up any janitorial contracts. We're going to rely heavily on those contracts to get us inside all of the state agencies. Agencies are good at keeping their own little secrets. It'll be your job to ferret those secrets out, and you will be rewarded well for it."

"But those contracts are established by sealed bid. They even time-stamp them prior to the closing date. How are you going to manage to see my bid is the low one meeting specs?"

Kerns looked to Russell for the answer. "It's a fairly simple process," Owens stated. "Your bid will be so low that no one can possibly underbid you. You'll be compensated in other ways to ensure you can cover expenses. The janitorial contracts are generally for five-year periods and this will cover our first term."

"But you can't possibly know what each person's going to bid ahead of time," Patrick Conrad protested.

"With Cameron as director of purchases, we can see to it that it's a very close call in most situations," Russell replied. "Janitorial bid openings, though public, don't always have a large turnout. For those times when no one shows up to observe the bid opening, we simply fill the numbers in after reviewing the other sealed bids. For those times when we have people in attendance, we can have a prepared bid ready and waiting. Not only that, but there's always some way to disqualify the competition. It's really quite a simple procedure. This is Kansas, and the purchasing office is very low-tech, low-security. All we have to do is get a few of our own people in place, or buy those we need."

Pat seemed satisfied by this explanation.

The meeting continued for several hours. By this time, the air was barely breathable and the coffeepot at the end of the table was empty.

"Let's call it a night," Kerns finally announced, handing the folder to Owens. Russell stifled a yawn and straightened in the chair while the others quickly got to their feet. "I trust all of you have your inaugural ball and dinner tickets?" Nods made marginal ripples in the smoke.

"Keep in mind," Kerns said in parting, "if you keep my back covered, I'll mind yours. Understood?" All but George nodded in unison.

"I just don't understand," Cara said, bringing Melissa a cup of coffee. They'd decided to get together and hash out what little Melissa had learned from the coroner's office. "What do they have to lose in allowing you the information?"

"I don't know." Melissa took the coffee and sighed. "Mind if I kick off my shoes? I think I've been on the run for forty-eight hours."

"Be my guest," Cara said, pointing to her own bare feet. Brianna bounded down the stairs at that precise moment. With coat in one hand and backpack in the other, she announced, "I'm going to my piano lesson. I'll be back at five."

"Be sure to wear your hat and gloves. Do you have all your books?"

"Yup, they're all here," Brianna said, taking the books from the piano bench and shoving them into her backpack. "I'm going to ride my bike over to the school."

"It's pretty icy outside. Do you want me to drive you over?"

"No way!" Brianna exclaimed. "It's really neat outside, and I can slide on my bike all the way down the big hill."

Melissa and Cara both laughed at this. "Oh, to be ten again!" Melissa said with a salute of her coffee mug.

"I'm almost eleven," Brianna reminded them. "January thirtieth is my birthday."

"We'll have to plan a big party," Melissa said enthusiastically.

"I wanted to have it at Cedar Crest," Brianna replied, "but Mom said that was overdoing it a bit."

"Maybe just a bit," Melissa agreed.

Brianna took off for the door and surprised both Melissa and Cara by calling over her shoulder, "Harry's here!"

"Harry?" Melissa questioned with a teasing smile. "Now why in the world would the pilot of the governor's plane be here?"

"Stop it," Cara said, going to the door.

"Where are you headed, sport?" Harry was asking Brianna.

She pushed up the kickstand and pushed off into the snow-packed street. "Piano lessons!"

Cara waited for the uniformed patrolman to come up the walk. "Is this official business, Lieutenant Oberlin?"

He followed her into the house. "As official as any. I missed you. How about we go . . . hey, Melissa. I didn't know you were here. How's Peter?"

"Busy. How are you?"

"The same." Harry took a seat, and Cara brought him a cup of steaming coffee.

"Here, warm up a bit." She picked her mug back up and resumed the conversation. "Melissa and I were just discussing the lack of cooperation at the coroner's office. It seems the coroner is too busy to meet with Melissa, so one of the assistants talked with her instead."

"And from the look on your face it was far from satisfying."

"You can say that again. No one there knew anything. I tried to reschedule my appointment for next week"—Melissa shifted to slip her shoes back on—"but the coroner will be tied up indefinitely."

"I guess what I still don't understand," Cara said, putting her cup down, "is how Kerns found Teri in the first place."

"Presuming that he did, you mean?" Harry interjected.

Cara frowned. "There's no other logical explanation. The kid who came to me was no drug abuser. She was clear-eyed and sensible, albeit a bit dirty and unkempt. She had a genuine concern for that baby, and I've no doubt in my mind she was a good mother."

"So like you said," remarked Melissa, "how could Kerns

have found out Teri was here in Topeka? You were the only one she talked to, and she was always very careful to meet you when no one else was around. Her house was well out of town, almost in Silver Lake, and located in such a remote place that she could easily keep from drawing attention to herself."

"She told me she didn't even shop in Topeka," Cara murmured.

"So how did he find her?" Harry questioned. "My friends at the police and sheriff's department have had no trouble closing this case. Another troubled kid bites the dust."

"Harry! What a terrible thing to say!" Cara exclaimed.

"True, but it's just the way things are." Harry's countenance was apologetic. "The truth of the matter is, you're the only one who's trying to keep this thing alive. And you have no proof."

"There has to be an answer." Cara grew thoughtful and turned to Melissa. "Did you say anything to anyone after I told you about Teri?"

"No. I know how to keep my mouth shut. In fact, I knew Glencoe was dying of cancer for months before he actually died."

Both Cara and Harry looked at Melissa in surprise. The redhead shrugged and grinned. "I'm a good reporter."

"I guess so," Harry replied. "Glencoe kept that so secret, most of the staff didn't even know the truth. How did you find out?"

"I was in Lindsborg when he collapsed. I saw you there, but I didn't know who you were. I overhead someone say something about calling ahead to the oncologist and I put two and two together."

"I wish you were having that kind of luck now," Cara said with a heavy sigh. "There just doesn't seem to be any answers."

"Are you sure you didn't tell anyone else about Teri? What about Joe Milken?" Harry asked.

"Joe knew she'd come to see me, but he didn't know who she was or why she'd come."

"And why had she come?"

Melissa and Cara looked at each other and then at Harry. It dawned on Cara that Harry knew very little about the Teri Davis situation.

"Teri came to warn me about Bob. She was molested by him as a young girl, and the baby she had brought with her was his."

"No wonder you think Kerns was out to get her," Harry answered with a grim expression. Suddenly he sat straight up, nearly spilling his coffee. "How did you tell Melissa?"

"What?" Cara questioned, not following his train of thought.

"How did you tell her? Did you call her or tell her in person?"

"Let's see . . . I called her. I had planned to talk to her at the picnic we had, but you were there and it didn't seem private enough," Cara replied. "But what has that got to do with anything?"

Harry was on his feet. "Where did you call her from?"

"My old apartment?" It sounded like a question, and in truth Cara had a million of them on her mind.

"Did you bring the same telephone with you here?"

"Sure, it's that one." Cara's gaze turned to the cream-colored telephone not two feet from where Harry stood.

Harry lifted the receiver and unscrewed the mouthpiece very slowly. With a quick inspection, he nodded to Cara and put the receiver back together. Motioning Cara and Melissa into the front yard, Harry faced them with a grave expression. "Your phone is bugged, maybe even your apartment. Obviously Kerns learned the news about Teri when you telephoned Melissa."

Tears came to Cara eyes. "Then I'm the reason she's dead."

"You can't blame yourself, Cara," Melissa said, taking her arm.

"No, you certainly can't," Harry agreed. "Kerns is obviously more than two steps ahead of us. Somehow he bugged your phone and has probably managed to keep tabs on you in one way or another ever since he decided to force you into the election campaign."

Cara wiped her cheeks with the sleeve of her sweater. "This is just too much. He won't stop at anything, not even murder. Before, I'd hoped to be wrong about my suspicions, but now there's no doubt about the truth."

"And the truth will set you free," Harry reminded her. "Knowing the truth and realizing just where you stand is an act of freedom. Now you know exactly what Kerns is capable of, and that knowledge will enable you to be on your guard."

"Some freedom."

"We should plan our strategies," Melissa announced.

"What do you mean we?" Cara questioned, tearing her gaze away from Harry.

"I mean, I accept the job you offered me, and I think we'd better decide how we're going to deal with Kerns and his rowdies."

Cara smiled. Melissa had always been the adventuresome one, and now she was lending support just when Cara needed it the most.

"Count me in on this, too," Harry replied. "I want to be assigned to your security detail. That way I can keep both eyes on you."

And I do like those eyes, Cara thought and offered him a

smile as well. " 'A cord of three strands is not quickly broken,' " she quoted from Ecclesiastes.

"Exactly," Harry replied, taking hold of her hand.

"So if one of us falls, the other two can pick him up, eh?" Cara said, feeling the warmth of Harry's hand against the cold January air.

"The only one going down is Kerns," Harry stated matter-of-factly.

"Agreed?" questioned Melissa.

Both Harry and Melissa waited for Cara to speak. She nodded. "Agreed."

Twenty-Eight

Inauguration day dawned bright and clear. The cold January temperatures had warmed from the twenties into the upper thirties, giving everyone a sense of enthusiasm. The Capitol building and grounds had been meticulously cleaned in preparation, and now, less than twenty minutes before the ceremonies would take place, hundreds of people stood in anticipation at the south steps of the building.

Cara caught a glimpse of the crowd from the second-floor window. She wasn't sure she could go through with this. Her stomach churned nervously, and only the presence of Brianna kept her from running in the opposite direction.

"My friends are so jealous," Brianna announced, twirling in her new white dress.

"It was kind of your teacher to arrange for your class to be here today." Cara opened her arms and pulled Brianna close for a hug. She needed her daughter's strength and support, and it suddenly seemed an unfair burden to place upon a child. "I love you, you know that?"

Brianna nodded enthusiastically. "Of course. I love you, too."

"Bob wants to speak with you for a minute," Serena Perez announced from the door.

Cara looked up and gave a halfhearted smile. Serena was immaculately dressed in a winter white suit, trimmed with large colorful rhinestone buttons. She made Cara feel rather shabby in her mauve wool dress. Her own patent leather black belt and heels were far more sedate than Serena's colorful accessories.

"I'll be back in a minute, Bri. You stay right here and count the people for me."

"I think there are about a million," her daughter replied, running over to the window.

Cara followed Serena into the governor's office. Bob Kerns was issuing his final orders to Russell, and at the sight of Cara he grew silent.

"You wanted to see me?"

"Yes," Kerns said. "Russell, you and Serena can wait in the outer office for us. Oh, and make sure Debra's still sober."

Russell nodded and closed the door on his way out.

"This is an important day for us. I know we haven't had much of a chance to talk, but things are going well, and I'm prepared to offer you and your daughter whatever help you need to get resettled."

"Resettled?"

"Of course, I thought you knew. I plan for you to work out of Wichita. There are far too many people in the Sedgwick County area to have them inadequately represented. They need to feel in touch with their governor, and what better way than to put the lieutenant governor in their midst."

"But I don't want to move to Wichita. Brianna and I are happy here. We have a new apartment and Brianna is in the middle of a school year."

"Sorry, Cara, but that's the way it's going to be. Other governors have done it that way and it has worked quite well."

"Other governors have allowed their lieutenant governors to serve right here in Topeka. There's an office in the Capitol marked for that very purpose."

Kerns frowned, and Cara could tell she was pushing too hard. She remembered Harry's warning to play along with Kerns.

"Five minutes!" Owens announced from outside the door.

"Can we discuss this later?" Cara suggested. "It's such a shock right now, and with everything else on today's agenda . . ."

"Sure," Kerns relented. "I'll give you a full rundown at the end of the inaugural activities."

Reluctantly, Cara followed Kerns from the room. Her mind flooded with concerns. Kerns could make her move to Wichita. There was no doubt about it. If he insisted on the transfer, she'd have to comply to avoid blowing her chances at finding Jamie Davis and Teri's true killer.

"Are you ready?" Cara asked Bri. She helped her daughter slip into her powder blue coat before taking her own gray dress coat from Serena.

"Ready!" Brianna announced. Her long brown hair had been curled and styled, giving her a much older appearance.

Cara noted the look of sheer delight and anticipation in her daughter's expression. Brianna enjoyed the fanfare and the fact that her mother was suddenly somebody important. No matter what, she had to keep Brianna safe and happy. Nothing else mattered as much.

The swearing-in ceremony came off without a hitch. From the first cheers of the crowd to the final Air Force jet flyby, Cara was lost in a surrealistic world. All of the newly elected officials took turns receiving the oath of office. Among these were the secretary of state, attorney general, insurance commissioner, a variety of justices and others, and of course the lieutenant governor and governor.

Cara had taken her oath with Brianna beaming at her side,

but the entire affair seemed to be happening to someone else. A sea of people swarmed the grounds below her, and she could only imagine their unspoken questions. Would she be able to help them or would she be a party to their demise?

Cara couldn't even remember Kerns' swearing in. She knew Debra and Danielle were at his side, but beyond that, little else registered. There were parties that followed inside the Capitol, and of course, there was to be a week of parties throughout the state, all in honor of the newly elected governor. For the first time in her life, Cara gave serious consideration to running away.

"Brianna seems to be enjoying herself," a voice whispered in Cara's ear.

"Dad?" Cara turned, not believing the voice she'd recognized.

A gray-headed man with a bulbous nose and thick bushy brows grinned at her. "Surprise!"

"But you said you couldn't make it," Cara protested. "Is Mom here, too?"

"Sure. You think I could leave her back in Hays?"

Cara glanced around the ballroom. "Where is she?"

"Over at the door, giving your new governor instructions."

Cara moaned. "I should have known."

"Don't worry about your mom," Augustus Brown replied. "She can hold her own with politicians."

Cara saw her mother move away from Kerns and look in their direction. With a little wave, Cara held open her arms and went to greet her. "Mom! This is such a nice surprise."

Hazel Brown held her only child at arm's length. "You've lost weight again," she chided. Her mother's softly rounded figure was a comfortable reminder of home to Cara.

Cara wrapped her arms around her mother. "I've missed

you guys so much. When did you decide to come?"

"Oh, you know your father," Hazel said, giving Cara an extra tight squeeze. "I said, 'Gus, are you sure you can live with yourself if we don't go?' "

"Yeah, and I said, 'I thought you didn't want to travel five hours on a snow-packed interstate and take a chance of being stranded in a blizzard,' " her father joined in.

"So then I said—"

"Okay, okay," Cara interrupted, laughing. "I get the picture. I'm so glad you came. I just wish I'd have known in time to have you up on the steps with me. Brianna would have loved that." Just then Brianna caught sight of her grandparents and came at a full run.

"Grandpa! Grandma!"

"Hey, munchkin!" Gus said, lifting her in the air. "Hazel, I know where Cara's lost weight went. What are you feeding this kid?"

Cara smiled and Brianna wrapped her arms around her grandfather's neck. "I didn't know you were coming," she told him and added, "but I'm sure glad you did. This is a boring place."

"Don't I know it," Gus said with a wink. "What say we get out of here and go someplace more exciting?"

"Can we, Mom?"

Cara shook her head. "I'm afraid I'm stuck. But if you guys want to take Brianna over to the apartment, that would be fine by me."

"I can show you the way," Brianna offered.

"Sounds like a good arrangement to me," Gus answered.

Hazel turned to her daughter. "Are you sure you don't need us here?"

Cara glanced around the room. There wasn't a close personal friend in sight. Sending away her family was difficult, but she knew how her father detested these things. "I'm sure. You go on ahead, and I'll be there when I can get away. Brianna will give you the grand tour."

After they'd gone, Cara listened to more idle well-wishing and shook hands with what she calculated to be over a hundred people. This was meant to be a rather private gathering, but it seemed to be turning into a free-for-all.

Spotting a uniformed patrolman, Cara inched through the crowd and cornered the man. "Do you know if Harry Oberlin is here?"

"Lieutenant Oberlin is on crowd control—first floor." Cara nodded and slipped out of the room through a side door. She'd just started down the stairs when a friendly voice called up to her.

"Hey! I've looked all over for you!" Melissa announced, coming up the stairs at a dead run. "This place is a madhouse."

"Don't I know it. If I hear one more person say, 'Hey, have I got an idea for the governor!' I'm going to scream."

Melissa laughed and brushed snow off of her navy wool coat. "It's starting to snow outside," she offered. "Maybe that will drive the crowds back to whatever hole they climbed out of."

Cara ran a hand through her hair. "Don't get me wrong. I don't for a minute think they're all snakes. It just seems like a great many of them are definite opportunists."

"Where are you headed now?"

"I thought about trying to find Harry. Any ideas?"

"I saw him downstairs," Melissa admitted, "but I wouldn't go there if I were you. It would make his job ten times more difficult."

"I guess I hadn't thought of that. Oh, well, I have you here now."

"But not for long. I'm not on your staff yet, and the paper expects me to bring in good coverage of this event."

"You will be at the inaugural ball, won't you?"

"I have a flashy green sequined number just for the occasion," Melissa announced. "How about you?"

"I broke down and bought a black chiffon gown with a sequined jacket. I guess I like it more than I thought I would." Cara grinned. "Harry agreed to escort me."

"Good for you. It's about time you pressed that issue forward."

Cara frowned. "I don't feel like I can push any issue forward until I get out from under Kerns' control. What's to keep him from threatening everyone I care about if I don't do exactly as he wants?"

"Nothing. But threatening and carrying out threats are two different things."

Cara grimaced. "Tell that to Teri Davis."

Twenty-Nine

Smoothing back an imaginary strand of hair, Cara waited anxiously for Harry to arrive. The inaugural ball was the most prestigious of all the after-hours affairs, and Cara was more than a little nervous. She hurried to the full-length cheval mirror in her room and took inventory once more, while Brianna guarded the door downstairs and watched with her grandparents for Harry's arrival.

Studying her image with a critical eye, Cara made certain the hairpins were secure and that her two hours in the beauty salon weren't wasted. The stylish arrangement left her hair piled high on top of her head, with large curls making a bold statement. Wispy tendrils framed her face, and beside these were dangling diamond earrings. The earrings matched the necklace that seemed to drip diamonds across her neck and fall just above the bodice of her gown. The set was costume jewelry borrowed from Melissa, and the effect was just as her friend had suggested. Stunning!

The black chiffon gown elegantly swept the floor. It fell from spaghetti straps and a sweetheart neckline, and the princess seams made Cara appear even more slender. The short sequined bolero jacket was just the right touch to accompany the simple lines of the dress. Twirling like a young girl, Cara caught a final glimpse of her black sequined pumps. She was ready.

"He's here!" Brianna yelled up the steps.

Cara drew a deep breath and picked up her satin purse

from the bed. She prayed that the night would be magical and that Harry would be the perfect date. It was really their first private date, and yet, it wasn't going to be private at all. Cara now belonged, as Robert Kerns was so fond of reminding her, to the state of Kansas.

Pausing at the top of the stairs and out of sight, Cara heard Brianna introduce Harry to her grandparents. The exchange of pleasantries gave her a moment more to collect herself before making her grand entrance. When she heard Brianna tell Harry that her mother would be right down, Cara stepped forward.

Harry was standing in the doorway at the bottom of the stairs, as if knowing this would be the best place to view Cara's descent. Her breath caught in her throat at the first glimpse of him. Harry looked like something from the pages of a bridal magazine, she decided. This was what it would be like to come down the aisle to marry Harry Oberlin. He would be there in a black tuxedo just like this one, with his salt-and-pepper hair combed back and his dark blue eyes all afire for his bride. He would give her a look that spoke a million words of love—she saw it there now. The thought almost made Cara stumble. A year ago she wouldn't have even considered the possibility of marriage, but with Harry in her life, it was an all-consuming idea.

"You look incredible," Harry exclaimed. "I'm going to be the envy of the ball."

"Only because everyone thinks I can get them in good with the governor."

Harry laughed. "Not true. They'll all be wanting to get in good with you."

Her father attempted a whistle. "You sure did yourself up nice, Cara. It's been a long time since I've seen you look this good." Cara felt herself blush from her head to her toes.

"Oh, leave her alone, Gus," Hazel said, putting an arm through her husband's. "She's going to be too embarrassed to talk to Harry if you keep it up."

Cara was grateful for her mother's intervention. "I suppose we'd better go," she suggested.

"I'll get your coat," Brianna offered, going to the closet. "Don't forget you're going to bring me back a souvenir from tonight."

"I won't forget," Cara said, taking her wrap. "I don't think I'll wear this, but it'll be smart to take along."

Harry took the coat from her and offered her his arm. "Well, Cinderella, your chariot awaits."

Brianna thought this particularly funny. "Be home by midnight, Mom, or it'll turn into a pumpkin."

"And you'll have to leave a slipper on the steps so Prince Charming can find you again," her father chimed in.

Harry turned and looked at her with such intensity that Cara almost forgot where they were going. "I'd always be able to find you. With or without the slipper."

From the opening grand march to the final dance, Cara found herself mesmerized by Harry Oberlin. He was witty and entertaining and could maintain an intelligent conversation with any of the political elite. Cara knew she was treading on dangerous ground when she moved closer to him and allowed herself to dance cheek to cheek. *This is a magical moment,* she thought. A moment that she never wanted to forget, because even if nothing ever came of it, for the time being it was perfect.

"Are you tired?" Harry whispered against her ear.

"I should be," Cara replied, "but I'm not. I'm enjoying myself too much."

"Me too. How about we sneak out of here?"

Cara lifted her face to meet Harry's mischievous expression. "Why, Lieutenant Oberlin, whatever do you have planned?"

"Just a little peace and quiet. Maybe a long serious talk."

"Long and serious, eh?" Cara's grin matched his.

Harry led her from the dance floor and maneuvered her through the crowds. Before she knew it, Cara was waiting for Harry to open the car door. A light snow was falling, but there was no wind and the brisk air was refreshing. Cara thought a long walk would have been enjoyable, and had she been more appropriately dressed, she might have suggested it.

"What's on your mind, Mrs. Kessler?" asked Harry as he waited for her to get into the car.

"I like the way the snow is coming down," she answered softly. "I enjoyed myself this evening, despite the circumstances."

"Me too."

Cara smiled and took her place in the car. Gracefully, she arranged the gown so that Harry could close the door. With alarming revelation, she realized that with very little difficulty, she could fall in love with Harry Oberlin.

They drove in silence for several minutes before Harry spoke. "This may sound strange, but I was wondering if you would tell me about your husband."

"Jack?" Cara said in a startled voice. "You want to talk about Jack?"

Harry nodded. "I think it's important that I know all about you."

"You do?"

"Yes."

He didn't elaborate, and Cara felt her heart racing in reaction to words that went unspoken. "Well, Jack was a good man. We were longtime high school sweethearts and we both went to the same church." She thought the words sounded awkward. Not so long ago she could have talked about Jack for hours to anyone who would have taken time to listen.

"I know about that stuff," Harry replied, surprising her. He pulled the car into the lot of an all-night store and parked. "Melissa told me. I've read about your career with HEART-BEAT, and I even read about the accident. I want to know why Cara Brown married Jack Kessler."

Cara smiled, staring up at the streetlights overhead. How could she explain? When was the first moment she knew she loved Jack? Truth be told, she couldn't remember a time when he hadn't been a part of her world.

"I fell in love with his spirit," she finally said. "He was kind, generous, and very patient. While other guys were into sports or just goofing off, Jack was consumed with righting the wrongs of the world. He loved God more than anyone or anything else." She paused. "When you're seventeen and the guys your own age act thirteen, someone like Jack seems almost superhuman. It was hard not to love him, and most everyone did."

"Sounds like a tough act to follow."

Warning bells went off in Cara's head. She liked Harry, but the harsh sneering face of Robert Kerns wouldn't allow her any peace. Unable to think of anything else to say, Cara blurted out the one thing that had obsessed her mind before the dance. "Bob is sending me to Wichita."

"Just like that?" Harry seemed to take the news matter-of-factly.

"If I'm to appear cooperative, I guess I have to go. I'm terrified of where this is all going to lead, and I'm taking my parents up on the suggestion that I send Brianna home with them to finish out the school year."

"Why are you telling me all of this now?"

Cara drew a deep breath. There was no other way to deal with this issue but straightforward. "Because I care about you."

"I had planned to express similar feelings about you."

"I kind of had that figured," she whispered.

"You make it sound like something bad. What's the problem?"

Cara shook her head. "Don't ask me to detail this for you. I don't have the ability at this point." She drew a deep breath and twisted her hands together. "I'm worried about what Kerns will do if he feels threatened by our relationship."

Harry reached out to still her hands. "Kerns can't interfere here unless you let him. I can handle myself—and Kerns —if necessary."

She shook her head and was embarrassed to find tears on her cheeks. "I keep thinking about Teri Davis and her baby. I'm afraid for Brianna and my parents. I'm afraid for Melissa and Peter. I'm even afraid for you. I've selfishly put you in the middle of this melodrama, and I don't know what to do." She paused a moment and tried to steady her voice. "But I know this much. I don't have the strength to go through losing someone else. I hardly knew Teri, but her death has shaken me in such a way that I still have nightmares about it. Kerns is heartless and vicious, and he won't allow his agenda to be interrupted just because two people happen to lo—" She stopped abruptly. Looking up guiltily, she knew that Harry understood exactly what she'd left unspoken.

He touched her cheek and brushed away the tears. "Don't cry. We'll make this work."

"No," she said firmly. "I won't risk it. I can't. I lost Jack, and now Brianna is leaving to live with my parents. I can't lose anyone else!"

Harry stared at her for a moment before starting the car.

"Then I guess there's nothing else to be said." He turned the car for home and drove there in silence.

Cara kept expecting him to say something more, but he didn't. Perhaps he knew talking would only complicate the issue. This wasn't really about them. It was about the evil regime that surrounded them. Maybe Harry realized this, and because of it he knew that to react any other way would only damage their tenuous relationship.

At her apartment, Cara didn't even wait for Harry to open the door. She hurried from the car and into the apartment. Knowing that Harry hadn't even made the effort to stop her somehow made the matter worse. Closing the door behind her, Cara leaned against it and allowed the tears to fall in earnest. This was all Kerns' fault! Robert Kerns had ruined her life, and in that moment she fully understood why Teri Davis had wanted revenge.

Thirty

The move to Wichita was a lonely one for Cara. Brianna had accompanied her grandparents back to Hays only days before her eleventh birthday, and Cara had never known such an emptiness. Harry hadn't bothered to call since their fiasco the night of the ball, and even Melissa had to renege on coming on as her assistant. There was no way she could relocate to Wichita, but Melissa promised Cara she'd continue to dig into the Teri Davis story.

"Dear God," Cara whispered, looking out from her new office window, "there's no one here who knows me, and no one I can trust. I don't like the place I've been put into, and I cannot abide the lies and deceit of Robert Kerns. Please show me what I'm supposed to do. I feel so lost, so alone."

Around her were boxes of computer equipment and office supplies. Unpacking seemed an overwhelming task, and it was only made worse by the knowledge that Russell Owens was on his way to help her get started. She couldn't tolerate Owens any better than she could Kerns. In fact, there was a side of Owens she couldn't stomach at all. Owens was still not shy about his intention to date Cara. He promised her everything from a good time to an evening that would be long remembered. Cara in turn made it clear that she had no interest in advancing a relationship with him. But the suggestive remarks didn't stop. And now he was coming to Wichita to spend a week working closely with her. The entire matter made Cara shudder.

Spreading the panels of the venetian blinds, Cara choked and sputtered at the dust they raised. It appeared the office had been neglected and long deserted. No doubt Kerns planned the same fate for her. Outside, the Wichita workday went on in the streets below, but it seemed unimportant and meaningless to Cara. She had a staff to hire and an agenda to maintain, but it was all so senseless. Without Brianna, her life seemed to contain an unfillable void, and without Harry, her heart seemed hopelessly empty.

In Topeka, Robert Kerns was enjoying his ride at the helm. People were quickly learning not to cross him and that his word was the final authority on all matters. He liked having the goods on people, and he loved knowing where the bodies were buried. Whenever someone would dare to step out of line, Kerns had little difficulty in pulling one skeleton after another out of the proverbial closet. It generally took little more than this to put people back in their places.

Taking the podium for his first major press conference since the election, Kerns felt much like a king surveying his subjects.

"I am putting forth a plan today," he began, "that will change the structure of how we do business in Kansas. There is a great deal of waste in state government, and one of my campaign promises was to eliminate that waste. I propose to streamline our government and to promote efficiency in the running and management of day-to-day operations."

He held everyone's attention, and not so much as a cough was offered up in interference with his speech. "I am, therefore, proposing to begin my plan where it will be most effective—tax relief. I pledged to cut the state work force by at least ten thousand workers before the end of my term. This will in turn benefit the state in many ways. Offices will be leaner and more productive. The chances of idle workers or jobs being duplicated will be eliminated. Tax monies that now go to fund these workers and their benefits will be freed up to more vital areas such as helping to promote private industry, farming and ranching, and the individual Kansan. And, ultimately, taxes will come down for the average Kansan as privatization of government work becomes reality.

"Privatization will also allow local industries around the state to do jobs currently being done by state workers. These jobs are paid for by state taxes and are a continuous drain on the budget. If these same jobs are performed by the private sector, we benefit not only the taxpayer, but also local people who are currently jobless.

"I am also going to seek additional changes in the way purchasing is performed here in the state. I intend to see that favored status is given to in-state businesses in order to keep Kansas dollars in Kansas." He paused for effect and leaned toward the audience. "I am dedicated to seeing this state become even greater, and I believe if we work on this together, we can get the job done."

His conclusion opened the floor for questions, and Melissa Jordon managed to be the first one to speak. "How do you propose cutting ten thousand workers to be a benefit to the state? As unemployed workers, they will naturally seek compensation that will be a drain on unemployment funds."

"For the most part, we will rely on attrition for the cuts in personnel. At our last estimation, there were over three thousand people who could qualify for retirement at the present. There is also another five thousand who could qualify for early retirement if a strong incentive could be offered. As you know, we use a points system for retirement. Age plus years of service have to equal a certain number. I am proposing that number be drastically reduced in order to allow a greater number of people the opportunity to take advantage of this."

"But what happens if you can't entice people to retire?" another reporter questioned.

"If the package is good enough, they'll want to take advantage of it."

"What kind of package will you support?" the same reporter asked. "Buy-outs? Health insurance coverage? And if so, wouldn't these things defeat the purpose of trimming the budget?"

Kerns was not happy with the way the press conference was going. He'd hoped the reporters would hear tax cuts and run with the ball. He'd figured on at least partial support toward promoting privatization.

"There are currently several studies being done to calculate what would be the most beneficial to both the employees of this state and the taxpayer."

"But a state filled with unemployed people is a state in trouble. Taxpayers are working people," Melissa said boldly. "You can't pay income taxes unless you have an income."

Kerns narrowed his eyes. "That's where private industry comes in, Mrs. Jordon." He saw her as a definite adversary. He'd hoped to be rid of her by moving Cara to Wichita—after all, Cara had told him that Melissa was to be her assistant. "Private industry," he offered, "will snap up those unemployed workers as they assume the jobs once performed by the state."

"What type of jobs might this include?" a Wichita reporter asked.

"There's really no limit to the possibilities," Kerns replied. "Highway construction can be privitized, hospital and mental health workers, even clerical staff can be hired through private agencies. In some cases, this has already been tried and found to work quite well. The employee can remain the responsibility of the private company, while working for the state. This way the private sector is paying for benefits such as health insurance, retirement, and so forth."

"And you are confident that layoffs aren't in the picture?" Melissa dared again.

Kerns drew a deep breath and leaned both hands on the podium. "No, Mrs. Jordon, I'm not. As governor of this fair state, I will have to be strong enough to make some unpopular choices. Choices that may seem detrimental to the individual, while benefiting the greater masses. We have to look at the big picture here. Layoffs are a possibility. So too is the dissolving of obsolete agencies. Over all, it is my intention that the elimination of state employee positions be a voluntary thing. However, I have broad enough shoulders to square the load if that's not the case. I was elected governor because I promised to eliminate waste, and that is exactly what I intend to do."

Kerns answered only two additional questions before bringing the conference to a halt. "I will keep you informed as we have new developments. This will be a program that requires cooperation from all sides. The better we work together on it, the better for Kansas."

Thirty-One

Russell Owens listened with marginal interest as the Association wrapped up their weekly meeting. He was anxious for the various matters to be resolved so that he could get on a plane and fly down to Wichita. Cara Kessler was awaiting his arrival, probably not with the same kind of enthusiasm he had for the job at hand, but nevertheless, she was waiting.

"We took possession of an entire bag of shredded documents," Patrick Conrad was saying. "I believe it will be possible to reassemble some of these. After all, no one thought to really stir up the bag, and the shredder appears to have rather dull blades. Some of the pages are still partially intact at the bottom."

"Good. If it was worth shredding, it's worth our knowing more about it," Kerns announced. Russell watched as he picked up a neat stack of photocopied information. "This is all very helpful, Pat." For once Pat Conrad didn't seem to need a cigarette to steady his nerves.

Russell noted that George Sheldon wasn't faring as well. The EPA was formally charging him with various forms of environmental negligence, and Kerns was cutting him loose from the Association. Sheldon hadn't taken the news well. In fact, Russell had seen the man actually press a hand to his chest and grimace. Perhaps he'd have a heart attack and rid them all of the liability he was bound to become.

When Serena Perez appeared at the door, Russell was surprised to find her motioning him outside. Usually her messages were for Kerns, but this time it was evident that Owens was the object of her interest. With reluctance, Owens took up his suit jacket and followed her outside.

"What is it?" he asked, shrugging into the coat.

"You'd better get out to Clarion Estates. Debra's ranting and raving and making quite a scene. Security just called and suggested someone come talk to her. She says she's going to leave Bob because of his infidelity."

"I'm on my way," Russell said, realizing how desperate the situation could become if any of the press caught wind of this. "When the meeting breaks up, let Bob know where I've gone."

When Russell pulled into the cul-de-sac off of Clarion Drive, he was again struck by the grandeur of the palatial three-story estate. Brass lighting fixtures capped the tops of two massive brick entry posts, while black wrought iron encircled the grounds like a line of shadowy sentries. Driving through the open gates, Russell tried to imagine what it would be like to call such a place home.

Owens could understand the desire to use this as the governor's mansion instead of the ancient Cedar Crest. This impressive creation bespoke of the money and power that Kerns held. It also said loud and clear that Kerns would not conform to tradition merely for tradition's sake.

Because it was almost February, the landscaping was rather impoverished beside the $850,000 home. Stark bare ground had been covered with sod, but the lifelessness was evident, as was the case with a variety of newly planted trees. Behind the house a stand of forest seemed to help break the barren look, but even these were devoid of leaves and life. It made the house take on a haunted appearance.

Parking the car, Owens hurried up the brick walkway and

rang the doorbell. When security opened the massive oak door, Russell was immediately assaulted by Debra's tirades.

"If that's my husband, tell him he can just turn around and go back to the arms of his press secretary!"

Russell looked at the guard, who shrugged and closed the door.

"Debra, it's me, Russell Owens."

The petite blonde appeared in the arched entryway to the main living room. Her short hair was neatly sprayed into place, and her makeup was impeccably applied. She wore a gray flannel jumpsuit whose finely tailored lines promised to bear a designer label. All of these were secondary dressings, however. The rage in Debra Kerns' eyes was clearly the only thing she was interested in wearing at the moment.

"What do you want, Russell?"

"I, well . . ." He thought for a moment. It wouldn't do to tell her that security had called to report her. "I came for some papers."

She clenched her teeth and nodded. "Take whatever you want. I'll even give you the combination to the safe."

"That won't be necessary, Debra," Russell replied soothingly. "Sounds like you're having a bad day. If you want, I can come back later."

"No." A bit of the anger seemed to leave her face. "Get what you need."

Russell thought for a moment, then said, "What I really need is a drink. I think your husband's administration is taking its toll on me."

Debra smiled, sensing a comrade. "I have some very old Scotch," she offered. "A drink sounds like just the thing."

It was just as Russell had hoped. He nodded and followed her across hardwood floors into the living room. Here was more evidence of the grandeur to which Kerns was accustomed. An antique Persian rug sprayed out across the floor in reds, blues, and golds. Red and gold throne chairs sat at either end of the room, while two gold brocade antique sofas sat at right angles to the massive native stone fireplace.

"Here you are," Debra said, smiling in what might have once been an attractive manner.

Owens noted she'd poured a drink for herself, and he raised his in salute. "Cheers."

"Whatever," she answered and tossed back the Scotch as though it were nothing stronger than tea.

"Want another?" she asked. Without waiting for a reply, she returned to the bar and poured herself another drink.

"I'm still good on this one." Russell knew if he could just keep her drinking she would eventually pass out.

"Why don't you tell me what's bothering you," Russell finally said.

"Have you got a couple of years?" she questioned snidely and finished off the second drink. She poured another, and this time took the bottle with her, motioning for Russell to take a seat. "I'm divorcing Bob," she announced without fanfare. "I've absolutely reached my limit of tolerance."

"Tolerance for what?"

Debra glared at him. "What do you suppose? His affairs are driving me insane. I've had it up to here." She drew her drinking hand across her neck, sloshing Scotch on her jumpsuit. She contemplated the spill for only a moment before shrugging and continuing her list of grievances. "I have a feeling—no, I'm almost certain that Bob is sleeping with Serena Perez. That woman is always with him, always flashing her white teeth and swinging her hips. Of course, she hasn't got a thing in her wardrobe that comes below the knee. She even wore a mini to the inaugural activities."

Russell nodded. He remembered only too well. Serena

had made quite a hit in her clinging red sequined dress.

"Well, if Bob thinks I'm going to sit back and take this public humiliation, he's got another thing coming."

She poured more Scotch and sipped it awkwardly. Russell noted she was slowing down. Her rigid posture had relaxed to a kind of sprawling disinterest.

"He's an animal," she whined.

"I've never known him to dally with Serena," Russell stated honestly. In fact, for all of Serena's teasing and provocative dress, Russell had actually seen her put Kerns at arm's length.

"Bob takes what he wants," she said and downed her fourth glass of Scotch.

Now less agitated, she became almost more focused on her vocal assault. Though stammering somewhat, she managed to express every injustice, real or imagined, that Bob had ever put upon her. After an hour of listening, Russell couldn't help but wonder why Kerns hadn't at least called to find out the status of the situation.

She began to cry when the Scotch ran out, and Russell was in no way experienced in comforting drunken females.

"Come on, Debra. Let me help you to bed. Maybe you'll feel better after you sleep it off," he suggested.

"But I loved him," she said, turning mascara-smudged eyes on Russell. "I gave up my entire life for him."

Russell grew uncomfortable. He could competently handle himself in court or crisis-manage a political campaign, but weepy women were something he'd never been able to figure out. They never seemed to respond the same way, and it was almost always a real feat of mind reading to figure out just how he should react.

He offered her a helping hand, and Debra clung to it as if he were some kind of lifeline. Getting her to her feet, Russell could tell she'd never be able to negotiate the stairs. Not knowing any of the security staff by name, Russell called out in the only way he could.

"Security!"

The same man who'd let him into the house appeared from the entryway arch. "Problem?"

"Yeah, she's dead drunk. Can you carry her up to her room?"

The broad-shouldered guard nodded. Russell handed Debra over to him and glanced at his watch. He'd wasted a great deal of time here. "Go ahead. I'll follow."

The guard grunted and took off up the stairs as though Debra weighed no more than a child. Just then the front door opened.

"Mother, I'm home," Danielle Kerns called out.

"I'm afraid," Russell said, coming into the foyer, "your mother is indisposed."

Danielle paled. "What's happened?" She put her books on a small oak receiving table and pulled off her coat.

Russell imitated tossing back a drink and Danielle immediately understood. "Where is she and why are you here?"

As Danielle hung up her coat, Russell explained, "Security called me. She was drinking heavily and they were afraid she'd hurt herself. Your father was in an important meeting, so I came to see what I could do."

Danielle marched into the living room and spied the empty bottle. "It isn't like her to drink so early in the afternoon."

Russell wondered if she'd question the two drinking glasses, but with a frown Danielle turned to the stairs just as the security guard was descending.

"Hello, Pete. How's Mother?"

"I just put her in her bed. She's still pretty upset, though."

Danielle nodded. "I'll go right up." She turned back to Russell and offered a grim smile. "Thanks for helping her out."

"No problem. That's what I'm here for."

Thirty-Two

Cara was less than delighted at the prospect of spending her evening discussing affairs of state with Russell Owens. He had made it clear that he'd arrive in Wichita around five-thirty, and he'd come directly to her office after checking in at the Marriott, unless of course she wanted to meet at the hotel. She had declined and agreed to wait around for him instead. She was scarcely more settled now than she had been three weeks ago. She'd hired an older woman as her secretary and immediately appreciated her skillful organization. Liz Moore had worked in a previous gubernatorial administration and knew the job of running the Wichita office better than Cara could have hoped.

"I'm heading home," the plump dark-headed Liz announced.

"Thanks for all you've done. I'm grateful for your patience."

Liz smiled. "Hope your meeting with Mr. Owens goes well. Are you sure you won't need me to take shorthand?"

"No. Supposedly he's bringing me copies of everything important. The rest I'll just depend on remembering and take my own notes if necessary."

"Well, if you're sure. Don't forget we're interviewing office staff tomorrow."

"Right." Cara watched Liz gather up her things and cross the outer office. Just as her secretary opened the door, Russell Owens appeared in the opening.

"Well, hello," he said with a suave kind of smile. He noticed Cara and motioned to Liz. "Care to introduce us?"

"Liz Moore," Cara replied, "this is Russell Owens. Liz is my new executive secretary."

"Nice to meet you, Mr. Owens. I've heard a great deal about you."

"All good I hope." Russell took hold of Liz's hand and turned on the charm. "I'm looking forward to spending this week with you both."

Cara felt like rolling her eyes, but instead she waited for Russell to wrap up his performance. "Liz has an important date this evening with her granddaughter, otherwise she'd be staying for our meeting tonight."

"Well, perhaps tomorrow we'll have a chance to discuss matters more thoroughly."

Liz murmured something Cara couldn't quite make out before closing the door, leaving Cara to face Russell alone.

"Well," she began reluctantly, "we might as well get right to it. My office is in here." She stepped back and pointed the way.

"You're looking great, Cara. Wichita must agree with you."

"Not particularly," she replied dryly. "I miss my friends and my daughter, as well as the life I'd grown accustomed to. But I'm certain that is of no concern to you." Her hostility was clear.

"Moving you to Wichita wasn't my idea. I wanted you in Topeka. I was kind of hoping we might get to know each other better. I know we got off on the wrong foot, but I want to set things right and start over."

"Start what over?" Cara asked. She stepped around to her desk chair, happy for the chance to put something between her and Russell.

"Us."

He said the word so nonchalantly that Cara couldn't help but pick up on his lead. "What do you mean, 'us'?"

Russell put down his briefcase. "Come on now, Cara. You know I find you attractive. I just want a chance to get to know you better."

"I see. Well, as far as I'm concerned, Russell," she said, taking her seat, "you are as much to blame as Kerns for my being forced into an uncomfortable situation. What makes you think I would ever be interested in you?"

Russell appeared unconcerned. "You can't blame me for Kerns' actions. I'm in the same boat as you are. Just his hired man."

"Well, that definitely separates us," Cara replied, barely able to control her anger. "I wasn't hired."

"Look, Cara"—Russell's voice dropped an octave—"I don't want you to associate the way Kerns does business with the way I feel about you." His expression was turning into a leer.

"I don't think this conversation bears any further consideration," Cara interjected. "I want to know what messages you've brought from Topeka and to see the agenda Bob has lined out for me. Other than that, I have no use for you here."

Russell surprised Cara by coming around the desk. Without thought as to what she was doing, Cara jumped to her feet and put the chair between them.

"Don't be like this, Cara."

"I told you I'm not interested."

"But you aren't giving me a chance."

Cara moved around the desk. "That's right. I'm not."

Russell smiled. "I don't think that's fair." He moved toward her with slow deliberate steps. "After all, you really aren't in a position to deny me." His eyes narrowed behind the wire-framed glasses.

"What's that supposed to mean?" Cara felt her heart beat faster and goosebumps formed on her arms. She was genuinely afraid. There was no one else in the office to help her, and much of the building would be deserted because of the hour. She was sorry now that she'd rejected the idea of a bodyguard.

"What about your daughter? What about HEARTBEAT and your friends there?" Russell pushed the chair aside and Cara went to the door.

"You are threatening my child?"

"I'm merely pointing out that you have a lot to lose, and if you give me a chance, I could help you hang on to what's important. Otherwise," he shrugged, "who knows what will happen."

"Get out!" Cara exclaimed and moved into the outer office. She hurried to the door and managed to unlock it, but Russell pulled her back, trying hard to embrace her. "Stop it! Let me go!"

"Cara, I'm not such a bad guy. I know how to treat a lady."

"Then demonstrate it now and let me go!"

"You just don't understand," he whispered against her ear. "I get what I want . . . and I want you."

Cara brought the heel of her shoe down on his foot. The action caused Russell to release her only momentarily. It was enough time for Cara to move away from him, but Russell maintained his wits enough to put himself between her and the door.

"Fighting will get you nowhere."

"Get out of here, Russell, or I'll resign my position as lieutenant governor and I'll tell the papers and anyone else who will listen just why I'm doing it. Furthermore, I'll sue you for sexual harassment."

Russell laughed and moved toward her. "And how are you

going to prove such a charge?"

She gritted out, "I will find a way." Cara glanced around and knew real panic. She barely had time to form a desperate prayer before Russell lunged at her and forced her back across an empty desk.

The smell of his musk was overpowering and the feel of his hands on her body was more than Cara could stand. Without giving thought to anything else, Cara screamed as loud as she could.

Russell forced his hand across her mouth and pounded her head back against the desk top. "Stop it!" he demanded. "If you'd just get off your prudish pedestal, you'd enjoy what I'm offering you."

Cara shook her head furiously from side to side. She tried to bite him and slapped at him with one hand while the other remained firmly pinned by his body.

"I mean it, Cara. There's no sense fighting this." With his free hand, Russell was unbuttoning the top button of her blouse. "There's no one to help you."

"Oh, I wouldn't say that," a voice sounded from the outer office door. It was Harry in full uniform.

Cara felt almost faint with relief as Russell released her and stood to face his intruder. Without caring what Russell thought, Cara rolled off the desk and ran to Harry. He put an arm around her, leaving his gun hand free. She hid her face against him and forced her knees not to buckle.

"Get out of here, Owens. Get out of here or I'll tear you apart."

"You?" Russell questioned without seeming the least bit disturbed by the interruption. "If you interfere, I'll see you terminated. You won't work in law enforcement again."

"You talk big, but what kind of power are you going to have after Cara brings you up on charges of attempted rape?"

Cara forced herself to look at Owens at this point. "Get out!" she demanded again, and this time Russell shrugged, retrieved his briefcase, and walked toward the door.

"She enticed me, Oberlin," he said at the door. "She told me to meet her here after hours and offered to come back to the hotel with me. I don't think it's rape when they're willing."

Harry started after Owens, but Cara held him back. "Don't. He's only trying to provoke you. Just let him go." She stared past Harry to where Russell stood smirking. "I'm smarter than you give me credit for, Mr. Owens. I'll receive your report tomorrow, and then I'll expect you on the next flight to Topeka."

"We're supposed to tackle a week's worth of work, or did you forget?"

"I didn't forget, I'm just pulling rank."

"Have it your way, Cara," Russell answered with a hint of malice in his tone. "For now."

He left the office, and only after his presence had been completely removed did Cara give in to her emotions and begin to cry.

Harry wrapped her in his arms and pulled her close against him. "I missed you," he said, as though nothing bad had happened.

Realizing it was the first time she'd allowed Harry to embrace her, Cara suddenly felt rather shy. She pushed away gently and looked up at him with tear-filled eyes. "Thank you, Harry. If you hadn't come . . ." Her voice broke.

He put a finger to her lips. "I know."

She shuddered and crossed her arms defensively. "I just don't know what I'm going to do. Owens won't stop at this."

"Probably not," Harry agreed somberly.

She'd hoped for a contradiction from Harry, but Cara

knew she wouldn't have believed him anyway. She was already too familiar with Russell Owens' ruthless nature. After all, he'd had the perfect teacher.

Trying to collect her thoughts, Cara was only mildly aware that Harry had moved closer. "Come here," he whispered.

Looking deep into his midnight blue eyes, Cara realized she trusted him implicitly. Without hesitation she allowed him to encircle her with his arms.

"I drove down here today because I waited three weeks for you to call me and you didn't," he said gently.

"I thought maybe—"

"Just hear me out," Harry interrupted. "I know you're afraid and I can well see why, but I don't like it coming between us."

"Me neither," she managed to whisper.

"So we're friends again?" he asked, pulling back enough to see her face.

"We were always that." Her heart raced so hard that she was sure Harry could hear its pounding beat.

"For now," he said with the same grin that had first won him a place in Cara's heart, "I'll settle for that much."

"For now?" she questioned, almost hoping he'd take the bait.

"For now."

Thirty-Three

Melissa Jordon once again climbed the steps of the Capitol and made her way to the second-floor conference room. Robert Kerns was to make additional announcements today regarding the future of various agencies, and Melissa was relishing another confrontation with the governor she'd come to despise.

Taking her place with a number of other reporters and television camera crews, Melissa caught sight of Serena Perez. The woman had been placed in charge of public relations. As Kerns' press secretary, Serena was the one Melissa had to deal with for information. She was cordial enough, but there was something about her that just didn't seem to fit.

As Kerns came into the room with Russell Owens two paces behind, a hush came over the chattering reporters and cameras began to hum. Melissa was taking her own photographs today, since Gary had called in sick and the other photographers were assigned elsewhere. Clicking off several pictures, Melissa focused first on Kerns, then Owens, and finally on Serena.

The conference moved at a rapid pace. Kerns lost little time in announcing that he had put into motion the demise of several small defunct agencies. Every attempt would be made to reassign the workers into other agencies, while the responsibilities that needed to be maintained would be passed on to larger ones. He further revealed, through a graph held up by

Owens, that these actions would save the state millions in tax dollars.

When questions were allowed, Melissa waited her turn and finally asked, "What if there are no available positions for the displaced workers?"

"As I stated," Kerns began without looking directly at Melissa, "every attempt will be made to find new positions for them. These will have to come from available positions, because obviously creating new ones will defeat the purpose of downsizing."

"And if there are no available positions?" Melissa pressed.

"Then they will remain displaced." Kerns' voice registered irritation.

"So, you may indeed have as many as fifteen hundred unemployed former state employees?" This question came from a *Kansas City Star* reporter.

"That would be an unlikely scenario," Kerns replied. "There are already positions available within the state—positions from which other employees have quit or retired. I am not opposed to filling these positions, if the position is deemed necessary. The displaced workers would be first in line to assume these jobs."

"What if the positions are in no way equal to the positions they've left?" Melissa shot out.

"Under Civil Service regulations," Kerns said in a tight manner, "workers may transfer in this manner to positions of equal or lower status and maintain their current salaries."

"Can you give us a list of the agencies you are closing?" a television interviewer asked.

"Certainly. Ms. Perez will hand out a complete list to each of you. I'm afraid that's all the time we have. I will keep you apprised of the situation either in person or through my office. Thank you for coming today."

Kerns got to his feet with a parting glance in Melissa's direction. His gaze bore through Melissa's self-sufficient exterior into the depths of her soul. *He'd like to eliminate me like he did Teri and Cara,* she thought. *I'm in his way, and I ask too many difficult questions.*

Packing her notebook and camera into a canvas tote bag, Melissa edged her way through the crowd, snapping up a copy of the list from Serena. The affected agencies were spread out over the state, and in many situations were located in such remote areas that workers would have to travel for hours or relocate in order to be placed with other agencies. Naturally, it wouldn't be Kerns' fault if these rural community folk refused to make such a move.

She rounded the corner at the south end of the second floor and heard muffled talking coming from a partially opened door. Easing close enough to hear, Melissa could make out the voices of Kerns and Owens.

". . . he's a problem and I want to eliminate him from the Highway Patrol."

Kerns' low chuckle was unmistakable. "Your jealousy is showing. I take it Lieutenant Oberlin is a hard act to follow."

"He's insubordinate and out of line when he comes between me and my job."

"Is it really your job that's at issue here? Or might I suggest it's a certain brunette in Wichita."

Owens' irritation was evident. "I want to fire him. Is that acceptable?"

"Do what you want with the man. I certainly don't care, but—and I stress this point—make it a clear-cut case of employee conflict and failure to comply with job standards. I don't want this thing back in my lap in six weeks."

"No problem there," Owens answered. "I just want to do a little housecleaning."

Melissa moved quickly away from the door and hurried to her car. Climbing in, she punched in Harry's number on her cellular phone and waited.

"Lieutenant Oberlin," a voice sounded on the other end.

"This is Mrs. Wipple. I'm calling about my impounded car again." The code had been established by Melissa and Harry to avoid assisting anyone who might be listening in on their conversation via Harry's state office line.

"I understand you're anxious," Harry replied.

"Yes, it's urgent. I need that car immediately."

"The matter is under consideration and we will be in touch." The click on Harry's line told Melissa he understood exactly what needed to be done.

Ten minutes later, Melissa arrived in the parking lot of Stormont Vail Hospital. The multiple levels of above-ground parking seemed to swallow up the light and left Melissa in the shadows until she spotted Harry's car. Stepping forward, she motioned to him and Harry pulled alongside.

"What's up?" he asked, jumping from the car. "Is it Cara?"

"No. As far as I know Cara is fine. I overheard Russell Owens and the governor talking. Russell wants your blood and Kerns just handed him the axe. I think the time has come for you to lay low."

"I think exactly the opposite is in line," Harry said with a grin. "Cara and I have already discussed this. We decided if Russell tried to have me fired or otherwise discredited, Cara would transfer me to Wichita as her personal bodyguard."

Melissa laughed. "Well, that will certainly make Owens' plans for romantic dinners with Cara a little less romantic."

"That's the idea. Kerns doesn't have too much to say about who Cara takes on staff."

"So you aren't concerned?"

"Not for me," Harry replied. "But I'm very worried about Cara."

"You love her, don't you?" Melissa was surprised that she'd thrust the question into the light. She'd guessed Harry's feelings for a long time but knew he'd gone far to keep them hidden. The blank expression on his face clearly answered her question.

"You are a good reporter," he said with a bit of a smirk. "But please keep this news flash under wraps, okay?"

"I'm glad about it, Harry. I think Cara probably feels the same way, although she's never said it in so many words."

"Well," Harry said, with a quick glance at his watch, "she'll come around to our thinking in time."

"So, where do we meet next time?" Melissa questioned.

"If there's a next time, Mrs. Wipple, let's meet at the zoo."

"Good enough. I'm certainly glad you're not worried about this."

"God looks out for us, Melissa. You'd do well to consider the way He works in your own life."

Melissa frowned. "You and Cara both seem so sure of where you stand with God, and yet I feel most of the time like God is just this entity out there somewhere."

"He's only as close as you let Him be." Harry's words struck a chord.

"You make it sound so simple." Melissa tried to sound lighthearted about the matter, but truth be told, she didn't feel so lighthearted about it anymore. "Besides, how do you explain Cara's situation if God is so close?"

Harry leaned against the car and crossed his arms. "The way I've seen it so far, God has walked every step of the way with Cara. How else could she deal with such ruthlessness and lack of conscience? God is watching over her, protecting her, and guiding her to make the right choices. I don't know that I would have given in to Kerns' demands, but Cara did what she thought she had to. If it isn't right for her to be lieutenant governor, God will show her."

"I wish I had your faith," Melissa replied.

"It isn't all that hard to get," Harry answered, a broad smile lining his tired face. "Accept that Jesus came to offer you salvation, confess and repent of your sins, and turn your worries over to God. Faith comes along the way, kind of out of practice, so to speak. You have to step forward, trusting that God will be there. If you give it a shot, you'll find that He never lets you down."

"Explain Teri Davis, then." Melissa really wanted answers. She hoped, almost prayed, that Harry could make sense of the conflict inside her.

"I can't. I can't explain Teri, or the hundreds of other things I've seen while on the force—things that seem heinous and unjust, without reason or explanation. But," Harry said, reaching out a hand to Melissa, "God gave me a peace about trusting Him with the details. I may get frustrated because I don't have all the answers, but God always reveals that He has it under control."

"And that's enough for you?" Melissa felt the firm grasp of Harry's large hand.

"It's all you'll ever need. If God's in control, then we don't have to be. And if the alternative is that we take control and God gets a seat out there somewhere, as you put it, the picture becomes pretty grim."

"I guess that makes sense. Thanks, Harry."

He gave her hand a squeeze and droped his hold. "Anytime."

Cara was working to satisfy one of her more demanding deadlines when Liz announced that Harry Oberlin was there to see her. Perking up, Cara felt her pulse quicken. It had been less than a week since Harry had rescued her from Russell, and in that short time they'd talked nearly every night.

"Hello there."

Cara looked up to find him dressed very casually in jeans and a white button-down shirt with the sleeves rolled up. He was smiling at her like he did most of the time, looking for all the world like a man with a secret.

"Hi." She cleared her desk. "What brings you to Wichita?"

"I'm job hunting."

"What?"

"Russell Owens has asked King Kerns for permission to be 'off with my head,' and I thought I'd check out greener pastures."

Cara sighed. They'd both anticipated this action after Russell's thwarted attack. "Harry, if you don't want to move down here, I'll put my foot down with Kerns and—"

"You'll do nothing of the kind. And why wouldn't I want to move to Wichita? Long-distance dating is kind of hard on the wallet and the heart."

"Is that what we're doing?" Cara laughed and tried to hide her nervousness. She'd found herself thinking a great deal about Harry these last few days. Sometimes she even wondered what Jack would have thought of him.

"I think so," Harry finally answered, shutting her office door. "Although at times I question exactly what it is myself. Look, I want to say something, and I'd appreciate it if you would agree to hear me out."

His sudden seriousness worried her. They'd never resolved her rejection of him on the night of the inaugural ball. Even after the incident with Russell, Harry had never said a word to her about it. Perhaps now she was being called to account for it. When Cara found it impossible to reply, Harry continued.

"I'm able to take care of myself. With God, I'm a pretty heavy-duty force. So I don't want you thinking you have to baby-sit me or offer me a hand-out. Kerns and Owens don't worry me for myself. It's you that concerns me."

"I know," she said in a whisper.

"I'm glad. I guess since you stormed off the night of the ball, I've been trying to figure out what I did wrong and how I could have handled that situation better."

"But you didn't do anything wrong," Cara argued. "I just can't deal with everything at once. Kerns scares me, and his agenda is weighing heavily on me. Then Russell comes down here and tries to threaten me with Brianna. . . ."

"He did what?"

Cara swallowed hard, remembering that Harry knew nothing of Russell's threats. "It's not important now." She got up and started to pace. "I think I'm going to have to get out of this job. I don't know exactly when or how, but perhaps if I'm out of the picture, Kerns can assign whomever he chooses to be lieutenant governor." It was as if the idea had come to her for the first time.

"That's a decision only you can make," Harry replied. "I'm only here because I want to protect you, if you want me. Otherwise, I'm perfectly capable of looking for work elsewhere."

"No! I want you here," she said, stopping suddenly. She couldn't bear the idea of Harry getting too far away. It was still a mystery to her exactly what she was going to do with him, but keeping him close sounded very reasonable.

Harry smiled. "I'm glad. I can start immediately. Oh, and I expect some pretty good job benefits."

Cara tried to ignore the nagging reminder of Kerns and returned the smile. "I'll just bet you do."

Thirty-Four

By August, Bob Kerns was finally able to see some results to his no-nonsense approach to government. Not only had he reduced the state employee numbers, but he had managed to arrange some very comfortable deals on the side with private businessmen. Deals that would continue to support his affluent lifestyle and buy him the power he craved.

He was, in fact, leading what many people called a "charmed life." His political hard lines were taking the state by storm, and while employees who stood to lose their jobs were less than satisfied with Kerns' style, taxpayers loved the idea of cuts that would trickle down their way via tax reductions slated for the next year.

He smiled at his reflection and finished running an electric razor over his face. Even Cara Kessler was less of a problem than he'd anticipated. She'd vexed Russell Owens by assigning Harry Oberlin to her personal security staff, but Kerns couldn't have cared less. If it kept her feeling some portion of control—control that was unimportant to Kerns—then it made for good politics and a quiet lieutenant governor.

Coming out of the bathroom, Kerns pulled on a fresh shirt and prepared to face a new workday. He glanced with something akin to indifference at a Kansas City newspaper article that spoke of the suicide of George Sheldon. The article indicated Sheldon's trouble with the EPA along with his waning health as reasons for the depression that led to suicide. *Good riddance*. One less problem for him to address.

"Who are you sl . . . sleeping with this week?" Debra slurred, coming into the room. The drink in her hand at seven in the morning was either an indication of an all-night pity party or an early morning jump on the day.

Kerns glanced at his watch. "Isn't it a little early to be drunk, even for you?"

"I hate your guts!" Debra cried and stumbled forward as if she might throw the drink at Kerns. He easily knocked it out of her hands and onto the thick mauve carpet below.

"Stay away from me, Debra, or I'll have you committed."

She rushed at him with her nails bared upward to his face. "You're a lying conniving cheater!"

"What's going on?" Danielle had come to the doorway just as Bob had taken hold of Debra's flailing hands.

"Your mother is out of control. I'm afraid we're going to have to put her in a hospital."

Danielle looked mortified. "You don't mean you're going to force her into a psychiatric ward, do you?"

"I mean exactly that!" he yelled. "Look at her! She's drunk before eight in the morning. She goes through the stuff like water, and there's no telling when she'll get behind the wheel in this condition and kill someone. Don't you think we owe it to her and the rest of the world to put her into rehab?"

Danielle hurried forward to encircle her mother's shoulders. "Please calm down, Mama. You've got Dad all upset. If you don't calm down, he's going to send you away."

Debra seemed to ease back a little, but Bob still held her arms at the wrist. "It's too late for that, Danielle. She will be sent to get the help she needs. If nothing else, it will get her out of my hair and leave me free to do what I have to do."

"Don't you mean *who* you have to do?" Debra screeched. "You lousy two-timing . . ." Kerns freed a hand and slapped her hard.

Danielle began to cry. "Please stop. Please don't do this to each other."

Kerns looked at his daughter in complete disgust. "Get her out of my sight," he told her and thrust Debra into Danielle's embrace.

By this time Grace Gleason, their housekeeper, had appeared to offer her assistance. She frowned at her employer, but Kerns had never cared about winning domestic popularity contests. He grabbed his tie and coat and turned at the door. "This matter will be settled tonight!"

Unable to control his temper, Kerns pounded his fist against the wall outside his door. It left an indentation from the blow and sent shooting pain up his arm. In his mind, he blamed Debra for the discomfort.

"I guess you heard about Sheldon," Russell said when Kerns got into the car.

Scowling, Kerns motioned to the road. "Just drive and we'll talk about something important."

"I figured it was important by the look on your face." Russell pulled out of the drive with only a single side-glance at Kerns.

"The time has come to put Debra into a hospital," he announced. "I want you to call Menninger's Pyschiatric Clinic and make the arrangements."

"Are you sure? I mean, this is going to be hard on your public appearance." Russell merged into the main thoroughfare.

"Not if we do it right." Kerns was working hard to regain control of his anger. He'd had it with Debra's morning brawls and nightly drunken tirades. More than once security had called at the Capitol and relayed their serious confrontations with a very drunken first lady. It was all more than he should have to handle. Perhaps when he went public with the seriousness of Debra's problem, Serena Perez would offer him a bit of comfort. She had been such a perplexing woman. Kerns found it a personal challenge to discover a way to get her into his bed. So far, however, she'd flatly refused him. Maybe sympathy was the right approach. Maybe his broken heart over Debra's condition would win him some intimate comfort.

The day passed in humid muggy heat, and even though August was usually a drier month in Kansas, the skies promised rain and perhaps a thunderstorm or two. By nine o'clock that night, Kerns was more than ready to sign the papers that would take Debra out of his life. She had called no less than forty times to harass and harangue. The calls were always intercepted for him by Serena, but it was clearly a situation out of control.

"Have you been in my office today?" Russell questioned Kerns. He came into the governor's inner office with a jumble of papers and files. "I found this mess on the floor, and it would appear that someone had knocked it from my desk."

Kerns shook his head. "I've been too busy to make pit stops in your office. What are the papers, anyway?"

"Nothing of great importance, but I'm missing a couple of tapes."

"Tapes?" Kerns asked warily. "What tapes?"

"The tapes we make from each of our meetings with the Association. At least I think that's what they were."

"Imbecile!" Kerns jumped up, completely enraged. He could feel his patience give out. "Those tapes in the wrong hands could bury us forever. Find them!"

"I will," Russell replied. "There aren't too many possibilities, you know. I leave the office locked and only my secretary and yours have the key."

"Along with security."

"Look, I only mentioned it because I thought maybe you took them. They might just have fallen behind some papers. I'll do a more thorough search tomorrow. After all, if someone has taken them, there's not a lot we can do about it but wait."

"I'm out of here. Take me home." Kerns picked up a briefcase and crammed it full of files.

"How about a drink first? I thought we might stop off on the way and discuss a few other things."

"Such as?" Kerns asked.

"Such as the trip I plan to take to Wichita."

Kerns suddenly thought a drink and maybe even dinner sounded like a great diversion. "You never stop, do you?"

"Not until I get what I want," Russell replied.

Outside, the distant rumble of thunder attracted both men's attentions. Flashes of lightning could be seen in the western skies, but neither one gave it much consideration.

"Maybe if it rains it'll bring down the temperature," Russell suggested as they moved from the lighted tunnel to where the governor's car was parked.

"Not likely," Kerns said, suddenly hesitating as he heard a rustling in the bushes that lined the walk in front of the cars. He held out a hand to stop Owens. "What was that?" His skin began to crawl.

Just then two shots rang out and Owens and Kerns hit the ground. Bob could hear the running of feet hurrying off into the distance. Next came shouts from the Capitol Area Security as they emerged from the building.

Dusting himself off, Kerns got to his feet. "He's getting away!" he yelled to the security guards. "He headed straight west." The guards took off in the direction Kerns had motioned.

"Well, I guess that was a close call," he said to Owens, who had yet to pick himself up.

When Russell didn't respond, Bob reached down to touch his shoulder. "Russell?"

Rolling him over, Kerns was stunned to see a bullet hole in his chief of staff's forehead. A trickle of blood ran down his face and across his left eye. He was very much dead.

"Are you all right, Governor?" a man asked from behind him.

Kerns nodded, still stunned by the knowledge that Russell had taken a bullet intended for him. "Mr. Owens is dead," he told the guard.

Immediately the guard called for help and knelt at Russell's side to feel for a pulse.

"They've caught the man!" another guard announced, coming at a dead run upon the scene. "We're taking him into custody right now. Are you hurt, Governor Kerns?"

"No, but he is." All eyes traveled to Russell.

"We'll take care of him. Come on, we can drive you home and the police can contact you for a statement there. We don't want you standing out here as a target. The man might not have acted alone. After all, you've got a good bunch of people pretty mad at you right now."

The man's words seemed to shock Bob Kerns back into reality. "Mad at me? Because I'm trying to cut expenses and deal out tax breaks? They hired me because I promised change!" His voice raised in anger. "They wanted me to make a difference, and then they come after me with guns when I accomplish their desires!"

Sirens sounded in the distance.

"Come on, Governor, at least come back inside the

Capitol." By now there were four guards surrounding him and staring out into the dimly lit night. The storm was approaching ever closer, and a brilliant flash of lightning betrayed the dark red stain growing under Russell Owens' head.

"Yeah, let's get inside," Kerns finally agreed. With one last glance over his shoulder, he let out his breath. *It could have been me,* he thought over and over. *Just a few inches closer and it would have been me.*

Thirty-Five

The ringing of a distant telephone brought Harry out of his dreams.

Shaking himself awake, he picked up the receiver. "Hello?" His voice was gravelly and low.

"Harry, this is Klark Anderson in Topeka."

"Klark, it's the middle of the night. What's up?" Harry tried to wake himself up by rubbing the sleep out of his eyes.

"There's been a shooting. Someone tried to kill the governor earlier this evening."

"Was he successful?"

"No, but Russell Owens is dead. He took a bullet in the head."

After the initial shock, Harry tried to feel bad or at least sorry that Owens had been killed, but he kept thinking about the attack on Cara. There was no sense holding a grudge against a dead man, he reminded himself. "The governor wasn't hurt?"

"No," Klark answered. "They are stepping up security, however. Kerns and his family are to have round-the-clock protection. So is the lieutenant governor. I figured since you're in charge of Mrs. Kessler's security, I'd call you rather than her."

"No doubt someone from Kerns' staff will call her," Harry replied, dreading the thought of her facing the news alone. "I'll step up security down here. Don't give it a second thought."

"We knew you would handle it."

"Who did the shooting?" Harry asked.

"Disgruntled former employee of the state. Seems he was among those people laid off, and he wasn't able to find work to support his family. The man is a raving loony, if you ask me. He hasn't shut up in over four hours."

"He may only be the first of many. I'll call you if I need anything, but I think for now I'd better get over to let Mrs. Kessler know what's happened." Harry hung up the phone, now fully awake and fully distracted by the circumstance.

Harry pounded a third time on Cara's door. "Come on, Cara, wake up," he muttered and reached his fist up to the door once again.

"Who is it?" Cara's frightened voice called from inside.

"Cara, it's Harry, let me in."

"What are you doing here?"

"Just open the door."

He heard her unfasten the chain and turn the dead bolt. *Hurry, Cara,* he thought. *Hurry and let me see that you're safe. Hurry and let me hold you.*

She opened the door and brushed back disheveled brown hair. With a yawn, she tightened the sash of her satin robe and repeated the question. "What are you doing here, Harry?"

He wanted to grab her and pull her hard against him. He wanted to surround her with his protection and love and keep her safe from the horrors outside her door. "Has Kerns' office called you tonight?"

"No, why?"

Harry closed the door. "Cara, there's been a shooting in Topeka."

Her wide-eyed expression told him the sleep had just

cleared from her head. "A shooting?"

Harry led her to the sofa and forced her to sit down. "A former state employee took shots at Kerns and Owens."

"And?"

He could see she was trembling. "Owens is dead, Cara." He heard the sharp intake of breath and put his arm around her shoulder, hoping she wouldn't feel the shoulder holster he was wearing. "We're stepping up security and I've already called to put extra men on the job down here. You'll have twenty-four-hour protection."

"Why did this happen?" She looked at Harry with an expression that pleaded for explanation.

"I'm not sure. I guess the guy was unhappy about being laid off. From what I was told, the man was pretty depressed over not being able to support his family. He wanted to make Kerns feel just as bad, I guess."

"But that means someone might want to make me feel bad, too," Cara said, her voice rising in fear. "I mean, I'm the lieutenant governor. People who don't know me are going to associate me as a member of Kerns' team. Oh, Harry, they're going to believe I condone Robert Kerns' actions."

"It's going to be okay. I promise. I'm going to keep you safe from harm," he said, pulling her into his arms. He would, too. If it cost him everything, even his life, he would protect Cara.

"But Kerns is powerful and so are his enemies," Cara said, pushing away. "He's evil and people have a right to be angry."

"Then God will protect us both," Harry countered.

Reluctantly she nodded. "No doubt God's the only one who can."

Melissa had taken the mass confusion surrounding the

governor's office as an opportunity to accomplish some extra snooping. Working at a blinding pace, she made her way to the coroner's office and just happened to catch the doctor as he was concluding his workday.

"Doctor Bains?" Melissa asked, blocking the door to his office.

"Yes?" The middle-aged doctor looked startled.

"I've tried for almost a year to talk to you. I'm Melissa Jordon with *The Capital-Journal*. It seems someone would rather I didn't talk to you."

The man shrugged indifference. "What can I do for you, Mrs. Jordon?"

"I'm digging into a number of cases that involved drug-related deaths. Of particular interest to me is the Teri Davis case."

"I'm not sure I know who that is. Did she pass through this office?"

"Yes. Like I said, it was about a year ago, and the death was listed as heroin overdose. Teri Davis's body was found floating in the river."

"I remember now," the man said, his facing lighting up with understanding. "I thought you folks already did a thorough report. What else did you want to know?"

"Well, you see," Melissa began to falter. "The fact is, Teri was the friend of a friend. And she had a baby that disappeared after her mother's death."

"I don't remember anyone saying anything about a baby," the coroner admitted.

"They didn't. In fact, as far as I could tell from my investigation, there was no baby. But my friend saw the child and had discussions with the mother regarding the infant. What I'm looking for is clinical confirmation, one way or the other, that Teri Davis had given birth."

"Surely there would be a hospital record of the birth," Bains offered.

"Normally that would be true. But I have looked and believe that because of various circumstances, the mother gave birth without the assistance of a doctor or hospital."

"So why come to me?"

Melissa stepped closer. "Perhaps your autopsy report would confirm whether or not Teri Davis had given birth?"

Dr. Bains shook his head. "I doubt it. I didn't do a complete autopsy. Once lab work revealed the heroin overdose, there was little reason to go on digging. After all, the county was footing the bill."

"Could you at least pull the records and check? Anything at all would be more than I have now."

He turned to five silver filing cabinets. "The autopsy report should be in here." He pulled out a drawer, thumbed through it for a moment, then closed it and went to another drawer. "Here it is. I suppose it can't hurt to glance at whatever is here." He pulled out a surprisingly thin folder and opened it.

The silence of the room was broken only by the few file pages being turned. "Like I thought, the report is very brief."

Melissa's shoulders slumped dejectedly. "I was so hoping—"

"Wait a minute," Bains said, sounding rather excited. "I think I just found what you're looking for."

"What?" Melissa hurried forward and put her hands on the desk. "What did you find?"

"Teri Davis was lactating." The doctor looked to Melissa and held up his report. "I noted it here on the last page. If she was lactating, then it would stand to reason that she'd given birth in say, the last year or so, and that she was nursing a baby."

"Can I talk you out of a copy of that report? I mean, if she didn't have any family and the death was pretty cut and dried, could you make an exception and at least let me have that much of your report?"

"I normally wouldn't, but I'll make an exception on one condition."

"Anything!" Melissa held perfectly still in anticipation. "Name it."

"You didn't get it from me."

"Agreed."

Thirty-Six

After the attack on Kerns and Owens, Cara found herself jumping at every noise. Once on the way up to her apartment, the elevator had stopped between floors and Cara had nearly panicked. Even after Harry's constant assurance that he was on the job, as well as an army of comrades he could trust, Cara refused to relax.

Then, too, her concern for Brianna was tenfold stronger than it had been last January when she'd agreed to let Brianna move in with her parents. She'd hoped to bring her daughter to Wichita for the new school year, but now she wanted to keep her as far away from the political arena as possible. And even though it seemed the right decision, it was killing her.

Using a lace-edged handkerchief, she dabbed at her eyes. Given to afternoon fits of tears, Cara tried hard to keep her grief from Harry. She knew he cared very deeply for her, and if she stopped hiding from her feelings long enough, she knew she cared for Harry as well. But life as she knew it had no room for romance.

Staring out her office window, Cara nearly screamed aloud when Harry came in from behind and called her name.

"Are you okay?" he asked sympathetically. "I'm sorry I startled you." Then he noticed that she'd been crying. "Cara, you don't have to bear this alone."

That was enough to break her. With sorrowful anguish, she dropped into her chair and put her face in her hands. Painful sobs filled the silence.

Harry knelt beside her and gently stroked her hair. "It's okay, honey."

"No, it's not," Cara replied from behind her hands. "It's never going to be okay again."

"Nonsense. You listen to me, Cara Kessler." He pulled her hands away and forced her to face him. "We're going to get through this together. You aren't going to shut me out and bear this alone. I won't let you."

"I miss Brianna, but I'm so afraid to go see her. What if some madman follows me to Hays? Worse yet, what if someone is already there stalking her?"

"Your imagination is running rampant. I've already seen to it that Brianna has security. I'll take care of you both," Harry promised.

"You can't be with me all the time," Cara protested.

"I could be if we were married."

The words were so startling to Cara that she pushed Harry away, almost toppling him over backward. "What?"

"You heard me. I love you, Cara. I can't deny that any longer. I've loved you for a long, long time now. Probably from the first moment we ran into each other at the Capitol. I know you care for me, and I'd be willing to risk a marriage on it that you love me as much as I do you."

Cara wanted to cry all over again. He loved her, and in a roundabout way, he'd just asked her to marry him. For some odd reason she thought of Jack and knew that he'd be pleased. He always worried about Cara being able to take care of herself. It was why she'd worked so hard to prove to everyone around her that she was as independent and self-sufficient as they came.

"Oh, Harry," she managed to say before breaking into tears anew.

Much to her surprise, he chuckled and stood up, pulling

her into his arms. For several minutes all he did was hold her and stroke her hair, and when he spoke, it wasn't of his love, but of Brianna.

"We'll arrange for you to take a week off, and then I'll drive you to Hays. I'll take care of everything and then we can both see Brianna. I love her, too, you know."

"Yes," she managed between sobs, "I know you do."

He lifted her face to his and pressed his lips against her tear-stained cheek before gently kissing her on the lips. "And I love you," he whispered against her mouth.

Cara had always expected their first kiss to come in a more romantic setting. She'd dreamed of it and wanted it, just as Harry had suspected. She knew he was waiting for her to admit her feelings. He wanted to hear her tell him that she loved him, too, but could she say the words? Her heart was in turmoil, and it seemed an unlikely setting for sorting through the mess. She had to be sure of this. Because of Brianna and her own convictions about love and marriage, Cara knew that there could be no doubts in a commitment to Harry.

He was looking down at her with those wonderfully intense blue eyes when Cara opened her mouth to speak. Just then the telephone began ringing and Cara straightened her shoulders.

"Saved by the bell, eh?" Harry grinned. "Don't think I won't expect an answer after you take that call."

Cara dried her eyes and smiled for the first time that day. "I don't remember there being a question." She reached for the telephone, but Harry's large hand covered hers and kept her from lifting the receiver.

"I'll refresh your memory after you answer the phone."

Cara trembled slightly and picked up the call. "Hello?"

"Cara, it's Bob."

She felt the color drain from her face. "What is it, Bob?"

Harry pulled out her chair and motioned her to sit.

"In light of the recent events," Bob began, sounding much like a press release, "I'm bringing you back to Topeka. I believe in the long run it will provide for a more secure administration."

"I see. How soon?" Cara saw Harry's puzzled expression but didn't want to give away his presence to Kerns.

"Immediately. Leave the staff to close out the office and head back today."

"I can't," Cara told him. "I'm taking a week off. I need the space and the time. I'm going to see my daughter, and I won't take no for an answer."

"I see." Bob sounded surprised but did nothing to refuse her. "When will you be back in the office?"

"Well, this is Thursday, so I guess a week from Monday should allow me enough time to clear my head." Harry was nodding approvingly.

"You'll still need to have security with you. There have been some additional threats up here, and . . ."

"What kind of additional threats?" Cara questioned, eyeing Harry to see if he knew about them. When he shrugged and shook his head, she felt better. At least he wasn't trying to keep anything from her.

"I'll fill you in on it when you get back to Topeka. In the meantime, tell your Lieutenant Oberlin to give my office a call. I'll have him completely apprised of the circumstances so that he can better deal with your security."

"I'll tell him," Cara replied.

"I guess, then, I'll see you a week from Monday. Do I have a number where I can reach you?"

"Probably," Cara said, feeling rather snide, "but don't use it." She hung up the phone a little harder than she'd intended and turned to Harry. "You're supposed to call the governor's office for details on developing problems."

"Will do," answered Harry with a mock salute. "Now, about our unfinished business . . ."

Bob Kerns listened for a moment to silence on the other end of the receiver before hanging up the telephone. His call to Cara had been less than satisfying. He felt as though the world had suddenly turned upside down, and now the inmates were running the asylum.

More disturbed by Russell's death than he liked to admit, Kerns hadn't known a decent night's sleep since the shooting. Every time he stepped out of his office he was surrounded by no fewer than six armed men. This was supposed to discourage any further attempts on his life, but it didn't stop the threat of those attempts. Daily hate mail revealed a variety of methods in which people hoped to rid the state of his presence. Most came anonymously, but surprisingly, a few came signed. Of course, those didn't usually bear any real or intended threat, but spoke with the same hatred and malice that was evident in the other letters.

Kerns was scared, and for the first time in his life he knew what it was to feel hunted.

"I've arranged for Russell's office to be inventoried and packed," Serena Perez announced, bringing a cup of black coffee to Bob. "I've also sent press releases regarding the funeral and closing of state offices on Friday."

"Thanks," Kerns replied, taking the cup. He was grateful for the shapely brunette's ingenuity and organization.

"Is there anything I can take over in Russ's absence?" Serena questioned softly.

Kerns looked up, taking in her stylish silk dress. She looked stunning as usual, but her trademark flirtatiousness was gone. There was nothing but true concern in her voice this time, and for some reason Kerns found it comforting.

"I'm going to have to replace Russell, but I just don't trust that many people."

"What if I were to take over his duties until a replacement can be found?"

Kerns took a drink and shot a grateful look at Serena as he tasted the liberal amount of brandy she'd added to the coffee. "Do you think you want that kind of headache?"

"I've had worse jobs. Handling people is my specialty."

Kerns nodded. "Okay, the job is yours."

"Just like that?" Serena sounded surprised.

"Why not? You've been faithful and beautiful and everything . . ." Kerns paused, putting down the cup and getting to his feet. "Well, almost everything a man could want."

Serena smiled and fairly purred a reply, "I try to please."

Kerns stood directly in front of her. "Not hard enough," he said suggestively.

Serena pouted. "Poor Bob, as if you didn't have your hands full enough." She smiled and put her arms around his neck. "I suppose, just this once, we could seal the deal with a kiss."

Kerns couldn't believe his good fortune. Wasting no time, he pulled her roughly against him and kissed her hard.

"Daddy!" Danielle Kerns exclaimed from the door.

Bob looked up at the sound of his daughter's voice. Beside her, his wife stared daggers at him. Danielle put an arm around her mother in a defensive response to the scene, while Serena discretely moved away from Bob.

"How could you do this, Dad?"

"Yes, Bob, tell our daughter how it is that you could do such a thing. And while you're at it, explain all the other times to her, as well."

"I don't owe any explanations. Now, please tell me why

you're interrupting my day." He refused to be intimidated by the women in his life, even though he'd faced it from all corners on this particular day.

Debra stared at Serena until the brunette offered a smile and walked from the room. "At least your taste in bimbos has improved. This one wears designer clothes."

"Isn't it a little late in the day for you to be sober?" Bob questioned sarcastically. "Tell me why you've come here and then get out."

"I want to know what gives you the right to go behind my back and make arrangements to put me in Menninger's."

"If you'd stay dry long enough, you'd have learned that this is old business, Debra. I'm not sure how you found out about it, but I'm serious about the conclusion. You will go into rehab for your drinking problem."

"Never!" Debra railed and lunged at her husband.

After a quick trip home to Lawrence, where Melissa deposited the coroner's papers, she was back in Topeka for some answers. Outside the open door of the governor's office, Melissa Jordon heard and saw the showdown between Kerns and his wife. She'd come to the Capitol in hopes of securing a brief visit with Bob Kerns regarding Teri, but this was proving to be even better. Whipping out a notebook, she began to shorthand the entire affair.

"I don't think it would be wise to make the governor and first lady front-page news because of this," Serena said from behind Melissa.

"Everything they do holds potential for being front-page news."

"But this is a private family matter. Surely you don't want to tear them any further apart by speculation and false rumors."

Melissa shook her head. "These are hardly false rumors. This is a firsthand account of the situation. No grapevine or 'He said-she said' from the staff." Her hands fairly flew to keep up with the scene.

"Mom, please," Danielle was begging her mother, "let's just go." Debra turned and without warning slapped Danielle hard across the face.

Everything stopped.

Kerns froze in place, as did Serena and Melissa. Even Danielle did nothing more than put a hand to her cheek. The shocked expression on her face mirrored everyone's feelings.

It was at this point that Melissa made eye contact with Kerns. He was very angry, and seeing her only seemed to expand his rage. He went quickly to his desk and pressed a button. Immediately the side door opened and three armed security guards entered the room.

"Take Mrs. Kerns into protective custody. We'll be escorting her to Menninger's very shortly."

Debra threw her purse at Kerns, hitting him in the middle of his chest. Danielle did nothing, still stunned by her mother's reaction.

Melissa noted it all and knew it was clearly the story of the year. As Debra began to scuffle and fight with the guards, Kerns called to Serena to bring in more help.

Never once did Melissa fear for her own safety. She was a newspaper reporter, after all. She'd been in worse situations than this. *What I wouldn't give for a camera*, she thought.

As the security guards pulled Debra out the side door, Danielle followed in silence while Kerns spoke in low tones to an awaiting bodyguard. The man looked up, saw Melissa, and nodded. Suddenly Melissa felt the hairs at the back of her neck stand straight up. It was the kind of feeling she got whenever she was in real trouble.

Sensing she'd worn out her welcome, Melissa eased away from the inner office and backed toward the outer-office door.

"You aren't going anywhere, Mrs. Jordon," Kerns announced, walking very slowly into the outer office.

By this time Melissa had backed into the solid wall of security guards and knew a feeling of desperation as one of the guards took hold of her.

Kerns walked toward her with deliberate slowness. "You and I are going to have a little talk," he said, lifting an auburn curl from her collar. "A very important talk."

Thirty-Seven

Going to Hays had been the very best thing Cara could have done. Seeing Brianna and taking her into her open arms, Cara felt whole again. Harry stood several feet away, but Brianna instantly saw him and ran to offer him the same greeting.

"Harry!" She dove into his arms and squealed as he lifted her in the air.

Cara watched the display, thinking of the three different times Harry had tried to bring up the idea of marriage on the drive up from Wichita. Brianna would be pleased if she agreed to marry Harry. Her mom and dad were beaming smiles from the porch, and Cara could well imagine that with Harry accompanying her, they'd instantly assume an announcement might be forthcoming.

"Mom! Dad!" Cara exclaimed with a wave. She hoped they wouldn't be too brazen about Harry's appearance. She would, of course, explain the need for security and ease out of speculation that way. At least that was the plan.

"I see you've brought Brianna's favorite highway patrolman," her father said, coming down the walk to embrace Cara. "My guess is," he said when he was close enough to whisper, "he's more than just Brianna's favorite."

"Harry is my full-time bodyguard," Cara explained.

"I'll bet he hates that job." Her father's laughing face was enough to cause her to blush.

"Harry's going to stay with us, Grandpa. Isn't that great!"

Brianna exclaimed, bringing Harry along with her as if he were on a leash.

"I'll say. How do we rate such a treat?" Gus questioned, rubbing Brianna's head lovingly.

"He's got to guard Mama. There's been a lot of trouble, you know."

She spoke very authoritatively, and Cara thought her daughter had aged at least five years in the last three weeks. Talking every night on the phone was definitely not enough exposure to her rapidly changing child.

Considering how she might rectify the situation, Cara missed much of the exchange between her parents and Harry. She heard her mother offer Harry the guest bedroom and suggest that Cara and Brianna sleep together in Cara's old room.

"You'll just be down at the end of the hall," Brianna told Harry very seriously. "Will that be close enough to guard us? I don't think anybody could sneak into the house so fast that you couldn't just run down the hall. But they could throw a bomb," Brianna said, seeming to consider all of the possibilities. "If the room down the hall isn't close enough, you could—"

"I'm not having him sleep on the floor at the foot of the bed, if that's what you were going to suggest," Cara interjected. She hated that the situation seemed so matter-of-fact to Brianna. When did her young daughter take terroristic acts as commonplace occurrences in their lives?

Harry smiled at her over Brianna's head. No doubt he thought the issue could be quite easily resolved with a trip to the nearest parson. "The guest room sounds like it will work out just fine," Harry assured Brianna.

"You two must be just about famished."

Cara was grateful for her mother's interruption. "We are," she answered and made her way to give her mother a hug. "What's for supper?"

Later that night, Cara slipped into bed with Brianna and pulled the sleeping child close. The smell of freshly washed hair and bubble bath reassured Cara that Brianna was really there. Suddenly the world seemed less crazy.

Her mind wandered down the hall to where Harry would sleep. He fit in well with her family, and having lost his own parents at an early age, Cara thought he more than welcomed the mothering of Hazel Brown.

"Marry me," he had insisted, taking the Hays exit from Interstate 70. She'd only smiled and kept her mouth shut. It was exactly what she'd told Harry she'd do until some of the more complicated matters in her life were worked out. It didn't seem to discourage him from asking.

Brianna sighed and rolled away from her, leaving Cara with an empty feeling. It wouldn't be long before Brianna was grown and gone. For years she'd pleaded for a baby brother or sister, and for just as long, Cara had insisted they were enough family for each other.

"I've cheated you out of some of the very best things in life," Cara whispered, stroking back long brown strands of hair from Brianna's face. "You didn't ask for much. A father. A family. I thought I could be everything to you, but I was wrong. I'm sorry."

Cara thought of how their lives had changed because of her involvement with Kerns. She was working at a job she hated, caught up in a lifestyle where she felt like a foreigner, and everyone she loved was in danger because of the slash-and-burn tactics of the governor. Anger overwhelmed her. This had all happened because Kerns had threatened HEARTBEAT and Suzanne Milken.

Thoughts of Suzanne made her believe her choice had

been the right one. Their baby boy had arrived safe and sound just months after Cara had turned the ministry over to Joe. But instead of a comforting thought, this only made her angrier. Kerns didn't care who he destroyed. It didn't even matter if he knew the people involved. If he wanted something, he took it. Whether it was a person's livelihood or their life.

Teri and Jamie Davis came to mind. They were both so young and innocent, but again Kerns had seen a way to take something precious and corrupt it. No longer able to lie beside her daughter and feel so angry, Cara got up and paced the room. Throwing on a robe, she decided to go outside for some air.

It was nearly midnight, and because their farm was well away from Hays proper, the night held nothing but the chirping of crickets and the occasional lowing of milk cows from her father's barn. Walking out past the barn and livestock pens, Cara's thoughts were consumed with her anger. *Kerns. Kerns. Kerns.* Her feet seemed to march in rhythm as she moved farther away from the soft glow of the porch light. This was Bob Kerns' fault and Bob Kerns should pay.

Overhead, moonlight brightened the pathway to the pond. Cara had swum here as a child, enjoying long lazy summer days. Now she just wandered aimlessly, no purpose, no direction. Pausing by a collection of farm debris, she picked up a rock from the path and threw it at the water's silky reflection of trees.

"I hate you!" she yelled and threw another rock and then another.

Soon she was reaching for whatever she could find. Rocks, branches, old rusty buckets, and pieces of pipe. Wherever something appeared to have collected, Cara pulled it from its peaceful rest and threw it as hard as she could.

Splash! Crash! The sounds alternated, depending on whether she hit the water or the rocky ledge beside the pond.

"This is all your fault!" At one point she knew that she'd cut her hand, but she didn't care. Somehow, someway she had to get Bob Kerns out of her mind. She had to let go of the anger within or go mad.

"Cara?"

Turning around, Cara could see the outline of Harry's silhouette. Kerns had even ruined this for her.

"No, I won't marry you. I can't marry you or anyone!" she declared to the imagined question. "Bob Kerns would just kill you or force you into some sort of hardship." She picked up a wooden crate they'd used for sitting to fish and heaved it into the water.

"Stop it, Cara," Harry said, coming forward.

"Make him stop first!" she said, sounding like a preschooler fighting over toys. "You make him stop."

She reached down for something else but found nothing. By this time Harry had crossed the distance between them and encircled her with his arms.

"Make who stop?" he asked softly.

Cara struggled against him but knew it was no use. Finally tiring of her fight, she grew still in his arms. "Kerns," she said in a whimper.

"Is that what all this is about?"

She nodded. "He's cost me so much. I know it may sound stupid, but I couldn't sleep beside Brianna knowing that I put her in the path of danger."

She was calmer now, so Harry dropped his hold. Reaching down, he rubbed her cheek with his thumb. "So quit your job. Resign the position."

Cara looked at him blankly. "It isn't that easy."

"Why not? Kerns can't want anything else from you. You

got him into office, and now that he's beginning to have more trouble than he'd planned, what's to stop you? Kerns certainly isn't going to want you to go public with accusations of inappropriate behavior."

"What if he threatens me? What if he threatens Brianna?"

"Take witnesses. Make a public declaration first, without telling him. Call Melissa and get the press together and announce that because you're marrying Harry Oberlin and moving far, far away to raise a large family, you can no longer continue with the duties of lieutenant governor."

Cara smiled. "You just never stop, do you?"

Harry grinned and pulled her gently against him. "I've been called determined. I mark a course, set my sights, and follow it."

"And you've set your sights on me, I suppose."

Harry kissed her slowly and very gently. It was almost as if he knew that to present too harsh a force would cause Cara to run, even from him. She allowed herself to be lost in his touch for just a moment. Perhaps Harry was right. Perhaps the only thing to do was walk away while she still had something to salvage.

Pulling away first, Cara said, "I'll do it. We'll go back to Topeka tomorrow. If I wait, I might not go through with it."

"Good girl," Harry said approvingly. "You'll announce your resignation at a press conference?"

"Yes." Cara was beginning to feel some control return to her life.

"And what about the rest?" Harry questioned.

"The rest?"

His lopsided grin was enough to warn her. "About marrying me and moving away to raise a large family," he said rather innocently.

Cara pushed at him with her hands and would have

quipped something sarcastic, but the moonlight revealed that she'd just smeared something across his white shirt. Looking closely at her hands, Cara gasped to realize it was blood.

"What's the matter?" Harry asked, taking her hand in his. Holding it up to the light, he could see the problem for himself. "Nasty cut there, Lieutenant Governor. I guess I didn't guard you well enough."

"I got blood all over your shirt," she said, pulling back her hand.

Harry would have no part of that and held her fast. "The shirt will wash, but we need to see about this first. Are you up-to-date on your tetanus shots?" he asked, taking her down the path toward the house.

"Yes, and I can take care of this myself, Harry."

"Sorry, ma'am, it's my job to see to your well-being." He tried to take on the airs of a serious state trooper, but he couldn't hold the pose without chuckling. "Come on, I promise I won't use the stuff that stings. Just let me practice on you, and you'll see how good I can be with real children."

Cara sobered. "I already have," she murmured, remembering him with Brianna.

Harry caught her serious tone. "And did I pass inspection?"

Nodding, Cara replied, "Most definitely, Lieutenant. Most definitely."

With a promise of a quick return to Hays, Cara and Harry left the Brown farm and made their way back to Topeka. It was a straight shot on the interstate, and Harry calculated they could arrive in little more than four hours.

"If I use my siren we can be there in even less time," he teased.

When they were less than an hour away from the capital,

Cara turned the radio on and was surprised to hear Kerns' voice.

"It has been a difficult decision to make. . . ."

Cara glanced at Harry in surprise. "It's Kerns," she said, then turned the volume up.

"Debra and I appreciate the show of support from those around us, and we know our friends will continue to offer us encouragement in the days to come."

The news commentator came on at that point and said, "That was Governor Kerns announcing the family's decision to seek medical treatment for First Lady Debra Kerns. Debra has suffered from years of alcohol abuse, and in his speech the governor bravely related that the family will stand by her as she undergoes treatments at Menninger's."

Cara turned the radio off and stared at the highway as it stretched out in front of them. "He's getting rid of everyone," she finally spoke. "One by one, anyone who's crossed him is being eliminated."

"Debra's had a problem for a long time, as I hear it."

"You would, too, if you were married to Kerns," snapped Cara. "Sorry, Harry, I didn't mean to . . ."

"I know," he said, reaching to hold her hand.

"It's just that he manages to come out smelling like a rose. It isn't just the campaign or Teri Davis, or even this. Bob has systematically arranged for the demise of all complications in his life."

"Well, you'll be out of it soon enough."

Cara knew that Harry was trying to ease her concern, but it only served to further her worry. "But who else will he go after?"

"It's not your problem, Cara. Think of Brianna and even of HEARTBEAT. You're needed elsewhere. Don't give Kerns and his games another thought."

"I can't do it, Harry." She made the statement without considering the consequences.

"What are you saying?"

"I'm saying that I can't resign my position. Not now. Don't you see? Bob would want me to resign. He knows I'll stand up to him eventually. He knows I'm only here because he pulled the right strings. But now with Russell gone, and Bob slowly taking out any competition to his will, there won't be anyone to stand up to him."

"It isn't your battle, Cara. Resign your position and let God deal with Kerns."

"But what if I'm the way God intends to deal with him? Don't you wonder why I got caught up in this in the first place?" Cara shifted as much as the seat belt would allow her. She looked hard at Harry's tight-lipped expression. He wasn't happy with her decision, and she felt that somehow she had to convince him to see things her way. "Before, I could never see a reason for me being forced into this campaign in the first place. But now . . . just maybe . . . I do." She waited a moment for the words to sink in before continuing.

"Bob Kerns is used to dealing with people as if they were commodities to be bought and sold. He uses them one by one, until he uses them up, and then he casts them aside for something or someone new. Debra drinks to forget what he is and to ignore what she's become with him. Even his daughter, Danielle, slinks around in silence, trying to be whatever it is she can be in order to please him. He hardly even notices that she's alive."

"But, Cara, think about last night. Think about your own losses because of Kerns. He's keeping you from Brianna."

"No," Cara said firmly. "My *fear* is keeping me from Brianna. I haven't trusted God on this, Harry, and He's straightening me out about it even as we speak. I've let Bob

Kerns run my life, not God. I've let Bob Kerns dictate my attitude and environment, but no more. If I don't stand up to him, who will?"

"There are bound to be others who feel just as you do," Harry offered, glancing at her for only a second before turning his attention back to the road.

"Yes, but others won't be in the position I am."

"Which is?"

Cara drew a deep breath. "I'm the lieutenant governor of Kansas. I can cite Kerns for inappropriate activities and behavior if I'm there to witness them. I'll have to get proof, but once I do, I won't have anything to lose in using it against him."

Harry said nothing for several minutes, and Cara knew he was trying to deal with her decision. Reaching out, she put her hand on his arm.

"Harry, we have to let God work through us, but He can't do that if we run away from our responsibilities."

"Yeah, I guess Jonah in the Bible proved that," Harry said unwillingly. "I just don't like worrying about you and knowing that you'll be putting yourself into the thick of things."

"But you'll be there to protect me, won't you?" She smiled at him, hoping that he'd understand her need to see this through.

"You'd better believe it," he assured. "And when this is all over with, you're going to marry me, right?" He grinned at her to let her know all was well between them.

"I'll think about it," she replied, crossing her arms and looking ahead.

Thirty-Eight

With a minor exception to the seasonal change, Topeka looked no different than it had when she'd left eight months earlier. Outside the Capitol, carefully tended flower beds displayed a variety of roses and the air hummed with the sound of lawn equipment. Harry dropped Cara off at the tunnel entrance on the south side.

"I'll be right up," he told her.

"Meet me in my office," she replied. "I'm going to see Kerns first and let him know that I'm back."

"Be careful."

Cara's heels clicked against the highly polished floor as she made her way to the governor's office. Kerns wouldn't expect her until next week, and she hoped that by catching him off guard, his defenses would be down. What Cara found instead was an empty office and a noncommittal Serena Perez.

"I really have no idea when Bob will be back. He wasn't expecting you until next week, you know."

"Yes, I'm quite aware of that," Cara answered and glanced at her watch. "Look, I've got something else to take care of, but I'll be back. If Bob calls, tell him I need to talk to him right away."

Serena flashed a smug smile, suggesting that if it wasn't too inconvenient she'd pass the message along.

Cara turned to head out the door just as the telephone rang. Pausing outside, she heard Serena answer brightly,

"Governor Kerns' office."

She started to leave, but at the way Serena dropped her voice in the charade of seductress, Cara couldn't help but eavesdrop.

"No, I have no idea," Serena was saying. "Her name is Melissa Jordon. She was here the day Debra Kerns went berserk."

At the mention of Melissa's name, Cara felt a blanket of dread wrap itself around her. Was Melissa in danger?

"Kerns had her removed, that's all I know." There was a long pause and Serena finally said, "Okay, I'll let you know if I learn anything." Another pause. "Yes, I know he has to pay. There are a great many things he's going to answer for if I have my way."

Cara hurried from the office, remembering to stay on her toes until she was well away from the door. What was going on? And who was Serena talking about? She burst into her own office and found Harry reading a copy of *The Capital-Journal.*

"Something's wrong!" she declared, reaching for the telephone.

Harry threw the paper down and got to his feet. "What?"

"I just overheard Serena talking to someone on the telephone. She mentioned Melissa being taken away on Kerns' orders and something about someone having to pay for what they'd done."

Harry frowned and sat back down. "Who are you calling?"

"Peter."

"Where's Kerns?"

Cara shrugged. "Serena was unable to pinpoint a location for him." She held up her hand to stop Harry's next question. "Peter, it's Cara. Is Melissa there?"

Cara grimaced. "When did you last talk to her?" Pause.

"Two days?" Harry came to the edge of his chair as Cara continued. "No, I haven't seen her either. Look, we need to talk. Harry and I will come to Lawrence. Stay home. We should be there in about half an hour."

She hung up the telephone and turned to Harry. "Melissa's been missing for two days, and Peter's half out of his mind."

"I want you out of this."

"I can't, Harry. Now he has Melissa. I got her into this and I have to get her out."

"It may already be too late."

"Don't say that!" Cara exclaimed, then lowered her voice. "Come on, I told Peter we'd come to the house. We need to work together."

They rushed out and had just reached the elevator when the gate-styled door opened and Danielle Kerns hurried off. She seemed to be crying and, from the look of her puffy eyes, had been doing quite a bit of it.

"Danielle?" Cara called out, but the girl would have nothing to do with her and hurried around the corner and into her father's office.

"I wonder what that was all about," Cara said, getting on the elevator.

"It may all be related," Harry said, then nodded his head to the elevator attendant. "First floor," he instructed.

Cara remained silent until they were safely in Harry's car. "Forty-eight hours is a long time," she whispered.

"Yeah, I know."

Melissa pushed at the steel door one more time, as though the other fifty or more times had never occurred. Kerns had locked her in a basement area of the Capitol building, nicknamed "The Dungeon." This area, now used for storage, had once housed state prisoners in bygone days. The walls were thick stone, and with the steel doors, they became silent tombs from which no cry could be heard. This particular cell was far removed from any traffic flow, and after two days of confinement, Melissa knew this cell might be her final resting place.

The heavy musty smell was overwhelming, and the only thing that brought her any comfort at all was that the light switch was on the inside of the cell and couldn't be turned off by Kerns. She paced the small room and knew by heart that it was ten steps to the end and five steps across. There had once been a stack of boxes at one end because the dusty outline was still imprinted on the floor. Apparently, Kerns had emptied the room to house her.

The rattle of a key in the lock and the sliding bolt being pulled back caused Melissa to come to attention as Kerns appeared with two security guards. Unsure of what he planned, Melissa blurted out the first thing that came to mind.

"Kerns, I want to make a deal."

"You have nothing I want," the governor replied with a humorless smile.

"I think I might," Melissa hurried on. "Maybe we could discuss this without your sidekicks. After all, it has to do with a certain baby."

Kerns' lips tightened as he clenched and unclenched his jaw. With a flick of his wrist, he motioned the two guards outside. When the door was closed, he turned back to Melissa.

"If you and Cara would have stayed out of things, you wouldn't be here now."

"If I'd stayed out of things, I wouldn't have proof of Jamie Davis's existence."

"There is no proof."

"Ah, but that's where you're wrong." Melissa summoned all of her courage. "I finally had my audience with the coroner."

"So?" Kerns seemed unconcerned.

"I talked the man out of papers. Papers that confirm that Teri Davis had given birth recently, enough to be nursing a baby."

"Mrs. Jordon, if you thought to win your freedom by this, you're gravely mistaken. If anything, you are only making it clear that I can never let you go."

Melissa swallowed hard. "My husband knows about the papers. If I'm gone much longer, he'll turn them over to the police."

Kerns' face contorted and he took a menacing step toward Melissa. Cowering back a pace, Melissa pressed her case. "I could turn the papers over to you. But only if I'm released. You could then eliminate the originals, and no one would be the wiser."

"I could just kill you and your husband and put an end to this nonsense once and for all."

Melissa could stand it no longer. Surprising both Kerns and herself, she charged at him, connecting her fist to his chin. It was the only strike she made, as Kerns easily maneuvered her arms behind her back, pivoting Melissa until her face was just inches from his.

"You've just signed your death warrant," he said, his breath landing hot against her cheek. "Maybe your husband's as well."

"No! He hasn't done anything to deserve this!" She struggled against him, but he pushed her away, knocking her onto the damp floor.

Kerns pulled open the steel door and looked down at her,

the thrill of power evident on his face. "You should have played the game my way."

The door closed, shutting her off from the world and life. The only thing left to Melissa was her tears. Breaking into sobs, she laid her head against her knees and gave in to despair. Her bluff had failed. Now she would die.

"But, Peter, there has to be some clue as to what she was doing—what she was working on." Cara looked at Melissa's husband with hopeful eyes.

"I was gone for two weeks," he said, getting up to pace for the fifth time. "We talked on the telephone, but only briefly and never about much of anything related to her job. Two days ago, she stopped returning my calls, and when I got back I found all my messages still on the machine." He paused and shook his head. "I called the newspaper thinking that maybe they'd sent her out on an assignment somewhere."

"And?" Cara questioned.

"And her last assignment was to get an interview with the budget director regarding state finance."

"That would have put her at the Capitol," Cara said, looking at Harry.

Harry asked, "Have you checked with the budget office?"

"She never made it there," Peter said dejectedly.

Cara looked around the room. "Does she have an office here?"

Peter nodded. "Sure, we share the second bedroom as an office. I have a desk and so does she."

"Can we look?"

"Of course," Peter said, sounding completely exhausted.

"Hey, buddy, why don't you rest," Harry suggested. "Cara and I might be able to spot something quicker."

Peter laughed dryly. "I haven't been able to rest since I got back, and I doubt you could either if it was your wife involved instead of mine."

Harry said nothing, but Cara felt his eyes on her as Peter led the way through the house. He showed them to the office and stood aside while Cara and Harry rummaged through papers and folders.

"We've got to find out what she was doing apart from her assignment at the paper. My guess is that somehow Kerns got wind of it and didn't like what he heard. Melissa probably knew too much and he felt threatened."

"So you think Kerns has her?" Peter asked in a voice that broke. "But why?"

It was obvious to Cara that Melissa had told Peter very little of their concerns regarding Kerns. Finding nothing that seemed to make any sense, Cara straightened up and tried to smile sympathetically. "I can't tell you everything, Peter. But I will find her, and I will see that Kerns pays for this."

Her hand was on the corner of the desk where a manila envelope sat precariously perched on the edge. Moving her hand, the envelope fell to the floor. All three stared at it for a moment before Cara reached down and picked it up. Somehow knowing this was the key, Cara opened the envelope and read through the contents.

"She found proof of the baby," Cara said, meeting Harry's questioning gaze. "These are papers from the coroner's office."

"What baby?" Peter asked, but both Harry and Cara ignored the question.

"She must have told him," Harry said, looking at Peter with a pained expression.

"Told him what?" Peter demanded to know.

Cara replaced the papers and folded the envelope in half. "Melissa has probably told Governor Kerns that she has proof of his illegitimate child. A child he may already have murdered as he did her mother."

Thirty-Nine

"Cara, you have to let the professionals handle this," Harry said, unlocking the door to his apartment. "I want you to stay completely out of this. Call in sick for the next week. Tell Serena you've changed your mind and you're heading back to Hays for your full vacation. Just leave it to someone else to find Melissa."

"I can't," she said with quiet resignation. "I'm the reason she's in danger. If she hadn't joined up with me—"

"She would have found herself involved in some other way," Harry interrupted.

He flipped on the light and pulled Cara through the door into the very masculine apartment. Stacks of trade magazines related to piloting and law enforcement were strewn on the counter of the breakfast bar, while unopened mail was tossed on top of the television.

"I'm not the world's best housekeeper, but that should just prove to you how much I need a wife."

Cara shook her head. "Not a wife, a maid."

"Okay," he said, trying hard to get a smile from her, "I need both."

"Look, Harry, I appreciate what you're trying to do, but I can't stay here." They'd argued all the way from Lawrence as to where Cara was going to live until the matter was settled.

"You don't have a place to stay and there's no security for you in a hotel."

"It's not proper for me to be here with you." She stared

266

him down with hands on hips. "You may think you own the rights to me, but we're not married."

"Not yet. We could easily fix that, though," Harry stated with a devilish grin. "I have a friend who's a judge—"

"Harry, stop it! Melissa's in danger and you aren't taking this seriously."

Harry sobered and came to where Cara was making her determined stand. Taking her face in his hands, he thought of how very frightening the situation was for her. He loved this woman as he'd loved no other, and if Kerns was systematically eliminating people who dared cross him, Cara was no doubt on the list. *I can't lose her,* he thought and gently stroked her cheeks with his thumbs.

"I'm taking it very seriously." His breath seemed ragged in his own ears. "More seriously than you'll ever know. I can't bear the thought of you having to face what Teri Davis faced —what Melissa must be facing now. I won't let him have you, Cara." He paused and pulled her close. "I need you," he whispered against her hair. "I love you."

Cara wrapped her arms around him. "I know. But loving someone doesn't keep them from harm. I loved Jack and he was killed by a drunk driver. I love my daughter, and yet she's hundreds of miles away because of people like Kerns. Now Melissa's in danger, maybe even dead. I loved her as a dear friend, but that didn't protect her from harm."

Harry knew her despair. He pulled her closer, wanting nothing more than to wrap her in a cocoon of protection. His protection. *But what of God's protection,* a voice seemed to say in his head. Harry felt a great deal of turmoil from that one thought. He wasn't trying to do God's job, he reasoned. He was trying to do the job God had given him. Wasn't that right? Wasn't that why he'd been placed in a position to legitimately work as Cara's security?

"I think we're sidetracked again," he said, feeling the full impact of his awakening.

"What do you mean?" Cara asked and looked up to search for the answer in his face.

"I mean, I'm trying too hard to do God's job. I need to turn you over to His care and do the job intended for me. I have friends at the Kansas Bureau of Investigation and the Highway Patrol. I can contact them and get their help in finding Melissa. I guess my mind is so consumed with guarding you and keeping you safe that I forgot the tools available to me. Serena must know something, given what you overheard. If we find Melissa alive, she and Serena can both testify against Kerns and end his corruption once and for all. I just want to be assured that you will be safe."

He looked at her for several seconds before releasing her. If she chose to walk out of the apartment and go to a hotel, he wouldn't stop her. *Okay, God,* he prayed silently, *she's all Yours and I trust You to know what's best.*

Cara smiled, seeming to sense his need. "I'll stay here, Harry. If that gives you peace of mind to do your job, I'll stay here as long as it takes."

"You're sure of your facts, Harry?" a KBI officer asked. The KBI agents and the Highway Patrol troopers all looked to Harry for assurance.

He nodded. "I am positive Governor Kerns has taken Melissa Jordon hostage or arranged for it. It's the only answer. She has information that he would kill to keep quiet. In fact, he's already killed in order to keep it quiet."

"What are you saying, Harry?" Klark Anderson asked.

Harry looked around the room at the men in his office. They were trusted friends and people he knew would work with him to resolve this problem. "About a year ago, Teri

Davis turned up dead in the Kansas River. The coroner listed her death as an accidental overdose of heroin. That girl was a former friend of the Kerns family, and she was raped on numerous occasions by Kerns and gave birth to his child."

The eyes of his friends widened in surprise. No one said a word as Harry continued. "Melissa and Cara Kessler knew about the baby. They were trying to help the young woman, but Kerns had Cara's telephone wired and he found out about it before Cara could intercede."

"Do you have proof?" one of the KBI officers questioned.

"We have a dead body, a missing baby and reporter, and a coroner's report that shows that Teri Davis was nursing a baby—one that everyone swears doesn't exist. I believe Melissa confronted Kerns with this information."

"Where do we start?" Klark asked.

"Serena Perez," Harry replied. "It's my guess that Serena has her own agenda when it comes to Kerns. The lieutenant governor overheard her having a telephone conversation with someone in which she spoke of him removing Melissa. She also spoke of making someone pay for their actions. Cara wonders now if Serena isn't plotting something against Kerns."

"One of us can make a visit to her," a KBI officer suggested.

"But not at the Capitol," Harry replied. "We'll need to get her alone, away from Kerns. If she is planning something, it might be wise not to expose her to question. And, too, she might even cooperate with us and make our job a little easier."

A knock at Harry's closed door brought all eyes to the turning knob. A young secretary peeked through the opening.

"Harry, I'm sorry to bother you, but there's someone here who says they must talk with you."

"Can't it wait?" he snapped irritably.

"I don't think so. She says it has to do with the lieutenant governor's safety."

Harry caught on to two things. The refence to Cara was one, and the "she says" was the other. Perhaps it was Melissa. With a surge of hope, Harry nodded and motioned to the woman. "Send her in."

Silence fell across the room as the shapely form of Serena Perez entered. With the trained expression of a professional, she reached into her purse and produced her FBI identification. Flashing it to every member of the room, she nodded to Harry. "We need to talk."

Cara paced Harry's living room and wondered if she'd done the right thing by agreeing to wait things out here. She tried to watch television, but most of the networks were showing movies dealing with murder, and the other channels seemed to have one form of violence or another on their programs. She clicked the remote to turn the set off. Silence descended upon the room, leaving Cara very aware that she was alone.

Harry had been gone for over six hours, and Cara could barely stand not knowing what was happening. She'd locked the door behind him, using both the dead bolt and the sliding chain lock, but somehow just knowing that he was out there and she was in here left Cara feeling an unexplained emptiness. *I should have told him how I feel,* she thought, stretching out on the couch. She stared up at the white spackled ceiling.

"I love you, Harry," she whispered to the air. "I should have told you that before you left, but I'm scared and I don't want to love you because you might die." She thought of Jack, and for the first time in a long time, his face flooded back in a clearly defined image. She could almost hear his voice. The scene was from a youth rally at their church, and Jack was telling a group of children how risky it was to care about people and things.

"Things get wrecked, worn out, or broken," he had said. *"If you put your affection into things, then you will have to constantly redirect your loyalties, because things don't last. If you put your affection on people, you might also have to redirect. Sometimes feelings aren't returned, and sometimes relationships get broken, especially when they aren't centered around God's purpose and will. And,"* Jack had added with a special tenderness, *"sometimes people die, and then what do you do?"*

The conversation had been meant to make the kids think long and hard about relationships and setting their affections on God before focusing on people.

"God is a constant," Jack had told the kids. *"His love never changes, never redirects, never ends. No matter how many things you own or how many own you. No matter who you love or who loves you. God's love will never change. His love is perfect, and in it there is no fear. No fear of death or life or the changes that come along with either one."*

Cara felt warm tears on her cheeks. "No fear in God," she whispered. "No fear in His love." Why was this such a hard lesson to learn? How many times had she walked down the same path? Like a frightened child, Cara could remember hours of pleading with God for answers and direction, when all along the answer was already within reach. God's love was perfect, and in it she had all she would ever need. . . .

She hadn't realized that she'd fallen asleep, but the ringing telephone brought her instantly up off the couch. No doubt Harry was calling to let her know how things were going.

"Hello?" Nothing but silence greeted her.

"Hello?" Cara repeated.

"Mrs. Jordon will be moved at midnight. She'll be transported in a dumpster from the Capitol to a janitorial truck. Stay where you are. You'll be contacted later." *Click.*

The dial tone sounded in Cara's ear, leaving her stunned at its finality. The caller had sounded surprisingly enough like Serena Perez, but how would she know to call here?

Cara felt her heart race and her breath quicken. She glanced at her watch and saw that it was a little after eleven-thirty. Where was Harry? She dialed his beeper number and waited several precious minutes for him to return her call. When he didn't answer, she searched the apartment for a pen and paper. There was no way she was going to obey the voice on the phone. Melissa needed help and Cara reasoned that she might be her only hope.

Pulling out a drawer in the kitchen, Cara startled at the sight of a revolver. She knew a little about guns from her days on the farm. Rattlesnakes were often a problem during the summer, and Cara had learned how to handle her father's rifle and pistol in order to combat any threat. Carefully picking up the revolver, she checked to see if it was loaded. It was.

A feeling of power coursed through Cara, and in her mind's eye she thought of what it would be like to confront Kerns with gun in hand. He delighted in controlling and bullying people weaker than himself. How would he feel if he had to come face-to-face with something more powerful than his ego?

A part of her wanted to replace the gun and close the drawer, but a stronger part made up her mind to take the weapon and rescue Melissa on her own. Harry was nowhere to be found and he wasn't answering his beeper call. With new self-determination, Cara put the gun in her purse, her search for a pen and paper forgotten.

Her next concern, transportation, was answered when she

realized that Harry had left a set of keys on top of the breakfast bar. What was it he had said about the patrol car? Had he left his own car in the parking lot? Chiding herself for not having paid better attention, Cara knew that all she could do was go downstairs and search things out on her own.

Sliding the chain from the lock, she turned the dead bolt and drew a deep breath. She opened the door, feeling every nerve in her body come alive. Looking first left and then right, Cara entered the balcony hall and peered over the edge of the railing into the parking lot below. Easily spotting Harry's car, she let out her breath and hurried for the stairs.

The short drive to the Capitol left Cara nerve-wracked and questioning the validity of her actions. Perhaps she should have called the police.

Trembling from anxiety, Cara checked the darkened parking area surrounding the Capitol. There was no sign of a janitorial truck or a truck of any type for that matter. The grounds seemed completely silent, void of life. Pulling into a space marked "Reserved for Legislators," Cara shut off the engine and wondered what to do next.

The voice on the telephone had said Melissa would be moved at midnight. But moved from where? It was ten minutes until the hour and still no sign of anyone. Guardedly, Cara opened the car door and got out. The bushes where Russell's killer had hidden were directly in front of her, and thinking about the murder made Cara's skin crawl.

"I shouldn't have come here," she whispered. A warm summer breeze seemed to confirm her words as it picked up and rattled the brush ominously. Instantly, Cara's hand went inside her purse and took hold of the gun. Just as her fingers closed around the revolver's grip, Cara caught sight of something she'd missed earlier. There was a light shining from the governor's office on the second floor.

She hurried across the parking lot and entered the building. Security should have been posted at the entryway, but no one was in sight. She glanced down the long hall to where the rotunda's information desk usually housed one or more security people. This, too, was deserted.

Closed doors lined the dimly lit hallway on either side of her. The ornate ceiling hovered overhead like an apparition, with shadows that swallowed up the light, leaving veils of black and gray. It seemed to Cara that the once warm classic appearance of this seat of government had now taken on the face of evil.

Slipping to the right, Cara eyed the brass capping of the staircase rail and wondered again if she was doing the right thing. Directly overhead were the governor's offices, and if her hunch was right, Kerns would be firmly ensconced on his throne.

Melissa. The name brought with it new courage to go forward. Pausing only long enough to pull the gun from her purse, Cara crept up the stairs in silence.

Forty

Bob Kerns looked again at the clock on the wall. Midnight, straight up. Within minutes his troubles would be over.

Going to the window, he glanced across the grounds and then below to the street. With any luck, Patrick Conrad would already be in position, ready to receive the dumpster holding Melissa Jordon's unconscious body. The plan was too simple to fail.

He sat down and smiled. *Simple,* he thought again. All he had to do was drug Melissa's food and send security to load her in an empty trash dumpster. From there, who would question the governor's men emptying a trash container? If someone did stop them, all they'd have to do was announce the bin held secured materials and pass without question to the awaiting truck. Conrad would have crews cleaning in other parts of the Capitol, so his trucks on the premises would be quite understandable. It was really quite ingenius.

He looked at the clock again. 12:03.

The silence surrounding him was nothing to cause fear or trepidation. It was the brief scuffing sound from the outer office that caught Kerns' attention. Feeling an awkward sensation of confusion, Kerns called out, "Who's there?"

The only light he'd turned on in the suite of offices was his own desk lamp. The outer office remained shrouded in blackness, which made it impossible to perceive motion. It wasn't until the scuffing sounded again that Kerns was sure someone was there.

"Look, I don't know who you are, but you'd better make yourself known."

In the doorway a movement caught his eye, then Bob gasped to hide his surprise as he made out the barrel of a leveled gun.

"Who are you? What do you want?"

Silence.

"I'm not armed, so why not come inside and discuss this like reasonable people?" His mind was racing through a list of potential assailants. Of course, so many people were angry with him. People he didn't even know in many cases.

The gun remained fixed, almost as though the owner had yet to make a final decision about his fate.

"Look, if you're a state employee—or used to be," Bob offered, "and you're upset about the layoffs, we can talk about it. There's no need to resort to violence."

Kerns felt an unwelcomed desperation. His stomach churned and he actually thought he might be sick. With a wavering voice, he tried again. "There's always an alternative to violence."

Cara tripped up the final step and caught herself just before falling. Her hands felt clammy and the gun slipped, nearly dropping onto the floor. Steadying herself against the wall, Cara took slow deep breaths, wondering if it was too late for God to show her what to do next.

Peering into the darkness, Cara was tempted to return to the lighted hall below. The soft glow of the first-floor lighting penetrated the blackness through the open rotunda, but for some reason the normal second-floor illumination had been removed. Perhaps Kerns had thought it would work to his advantage in moving Melissa. Cara couldn't help but worry that the whole security team had sold out to Kerns.

Looking down at the gun in her hand and realizing her own feeble attempt at sleuthing, Cara wanted to laugh out loud. How could she hope to overcome Kerns and rescue Melissa? Suddenly she felt very foolish. This was the stuff television shows and movies of the week were made of. She started to put the gun away, when much to her surprise a hand reached out to pull her through an open door.

Breaking away, Cara whirled around, gun in hand.

"I'll shoot!" she said in what she'd planned to be quite a yell, but what was in fact hardly more than a whisper.

"Cara?"

"Harry?" She felt sick inside. She'd almost put a bullet into the man she loved. Lowering the gun, she began to tremble from head to foot. "Oh, Harry," she moaned as a haze seemed to settle over her mind.

"Where in the world did you get a gun?" he asked angrily, taking the revolver from her hands. He pulled her farther into a dimly lit room. "Are you all right? What are you doing here?" Then, without giving her a chance to answer, he exclaimed, "This is my revolver!"

"I know. I know. Listen, Harry." Gasping for breath, she seemed to snap out of her daze. "I tried to call you, but you didn't answer your page. Somebody telephoned at the apartment and said Melissa was here at the Capitol. They're going to move her tonight."

"I know."

His matter-of-fact statement held no emotion, no thought of comfort. "You know?" She looked up into his face, seeing the harshness soften at her questioning expression.

"Yes. I can't explain now, but Melissa is safe. She was pulled out of a trash dumpster about ten minutes ago and Kerns' men were taken into custody."

"There's a light on in Kerns' office. When I didn't see anything going on outside, I thought I'd go to his office and . . ." Her voice trailed away.

"And what were you going to do? Shoot him?" Harry asked, the anger subsiding from his voice.

What had she planned to do? Would she have burst into the office waving the weapon around, demanding answers? And what if Kerns had refused to comply with her wishes? Would she have shot him?

"I don't know. I just thought—"

"No, you didn't think, that's the problem."

Cara grew angry. "I did what I thought was the only answer. I had to try to help Melissa and I couldn't find you!" she declared accusingly.

"I was already on the job. I couldn't answer any pages."

His explanation made perfect sense, but Cara felt her pride gravely wounded. "I just wanted to help. I didn't know you'd be here."

A gunshot rang out from several offices away, seeming almost like the popping of a firecracker.

"What is it?"

"Gunshots."

"No," Cara said, refusing to believe him.

"Stay here," he said, going to the door.

"No." She came up behind him. "I'm going with you."

"Then stay low and keep behind me."

Harry's refusal to argue with her made Cara fully aware of the severity of the moment. She tiptoed behind him, wondering what they'd find and praying that no one was hurt.

It was the sobbing sound that first reached her ears. Cries that sounded like those of a hurting child. She'd heard the same cry from Brianna.

Harry motioned her to stop at the doorway to the governor's outer office. They could both see the silhouette of a person at the entrance to Kerns' private office. It was that person who appeared to be crying. It was also that person who held a gun.

"How could you do it, Daddy? How could you kill Teri?"

Cara thought her heart would break at the emotionally torn voice of Danielle Kerns. She couldn't see Kerns' face, but she could tell he was sitting at his desk.

"You don't . . . don't know . . ."

Kerns was gasping to say the words, and Cara knew that Danielle's bullets must have found their mark.

"Daddy, you killed her. You got her pregnant and you killed her. I know!" Her voice raised hysterically. "I found the tapes. I found the recordings in Russell's office. I found papers, too. Things Russell had written down."

"That's his doing, then," Kerns said, forcing his voice to be steady.

Cara could see him lift his arm and pull it to his chest. Harry motioned her to remain still while he crept forward. Neither one had any idea if Danielle meant to shoot again, but it was evident to Cara that Harry meant to disarm her if possible.

Danielle was crying again. Crying and straining to say what had to be said to the father who'd never bothered to give her the time of day.

"You made Mom drink. You slept with other women and broke her heart. You were never there for Gary or me, and I hate you!" she shouted. "I hate you! Do you hear me?"

Harry was almost to the door and within reach of Danielle's arm.

"Danielle, I'm not that bad. I didn't do the things—"

"Stop it! Stop lying to me!"

Just as Harry reached out a hand, Danielle crossed the room to her father's desk. Cara held her breath as Harry struggled to regain his balance.

"All of my life I watched other kids with their dads, and I kept wishing I could have a father like they had. Their fathers played games with them, but not the kind you played." Danielle's voice was full of emotion. "I needed you. I needed you to take away the monsters in my world, but instead you became one of them."

"Dani, listen—"

"No! You listen. I needed a father and you were never there. I needed to be able to count on you, but I couldn't. You never cared about anything or anyone but yourself."

"I cared." Kerns gasped for air. "I worked hard so that you and your brother could have the best."

"No, you lived your life to be in control. You forced everyone around you into the cruel devious world that you designed. You don't deserve to live. You arranged for Russell to kill Teri so that you didn't have to live with your mistakes. You put Mama in Menninger's and drove Gary away from our home. What did you plan to do to me? When would I have become a liability like them?"

"I wouldn't . . . have hurt you, Dani." Kerns' voice was growing weaker.

"Well, I'm hurting you. I'm making you pay for all that you've done." She paused and the hurtful childish voice added, "And for all you didn't do."

Cara could see Kerns clearly now. He was slumped back in his chair, a crimson stain spreading out across the right side of his chest.

Danielle's hands were shaking and the gun bobbed up and down with the motion. "You need to die!"

Without regard to her well-being and ignoring Harry and his orders, Cara came out from her hiding place.

"If you kill him, Danielle, we won't find Teri's baby."

Danielle turned to face the darkness. "Mrs. Kessler?"

"Yes, Danielle. It's me."

"He hurt you, too. He made you join the campaign. I read Russell's notes. You didn't want to do it."

"No, I didn't," Cara admitted, coming into the office.

Harry walked in behind her, as though nothing at all was amiss, while Danielle moved to the far side of her father's desk.

"You want him dead, too, don't you?" Her voice begged for assurance that she was doing the right thing.

"It won't change anything," Cara said softly, studying the girl for any change in expression. "It won't bring Teri back to life, and it won't help Jamie."

"Jamie?"

"Teri's little girl. Your sister, actually."

Danielle glanced from Cara's face to Kerns and back again. The young woman seemed to be trying to assimilate this new information.

"Before you do anything else," Harry said, maneuvering between Cara and Danielle, "we should find out where Jamie is."

Danielle nodded and turned to her father. "Where is my sister?"

"Don't call her that!" Kerns exclaimed with more strength than anyone had expected. The words came at a price and he broke into a fit of coughing and gasping.

"Where is she?" Danielle brought the gun up and leveled it at Kerns' head.

"A family in Great Bend has her. All the information is on a computer disk in the safe at home."

Danielle looked at Cara and Harry as if to question what she should do next. Harry stepped forward and held out his hand.

"Give me the gun, Danielle. Your father is wounded and

needs medical attention. Killing him won't make him pay for what he's done, but providing evidence will."

"It's true, Danielle," a recognizable feminine voice sounded. "You and I can bring him to justice."

Lights came on in the outer office and Serena Perez stepped into the now crowded room. Behind Serena, Cara could see several men in dark blue with gold KBI letters marking their identity.

"I've been playing your father's game in order to get enough evidence to send him to prison for a long, long time," Serena said while Harry reached for the gun.

"I'm sorry that you and your mother had to suffer because of my part in this mess," Serena said, holding up an identification badge for Danielle to see. "If you'll look this over, you'll see that I'm telling the truth. Your father has caused a lot of problems over the last few years and he's broken a lot of laws. You don't need to worry about him anymore. Where he's going"—Serena paused to look at the bleeding Kerns —"he won't be hurting anyone else."

Danielle looked at Serena's badge, while Cara nervously twisted her hands together. If Danielle went berserk, Harry would be the first one to get it. *Please God,* she prayed, *let Danielle give up the gun.*

"How can I believe you?" Danielle asked, eyeing each of the players in the macabre scene.

"Who do you think called Harry and Cara?" Serena asked gently.

Cara nodded, knowing now for sure that Serena had placed the mysterious call to Harry's apartment. "She's right, Danielle. You may think that no one else cares about you, but it isn't true. I care and I want to help you." Danielle looked at her, as though weighing the truth of her words. Cara stepped forward. "Please give them the gun."

And then without further complication, Danielle did just that.

Handing the revolver to Harry, Danielle buried her hands in her face. "I hate him for what he's made me."

Cara put her arm around Danielle. "It's all right, Danielle. He can't hurt you anymore, not if you don't let him."

Danielle looked up, fresh tears streaming down her face. "Are they going to put me in prison?"

Cara looked to Harry and Serena for answers. It was Serena who came to take Danielle by the arm. "I don't think you'll have to go to jail, Danielle, but it would be best if we check you into the hospital. Would that be okay?"

Serena talked to Danielle as though she were a child, and in many ways, Cara thought, she really was.

Danielle went willingly with Serena, leaving Harry to take Cara in hand. The office was a mass of confusion, so he led her into the semi-quiet of the hall.

"Are you okay?" Cara asked, suddenly concerned about Harry's well-being.

Harry drew a deep breath and pulled her into his arms. Cara went stiffly, but at the wonderful way Harry tucked her against him, she relaxed and sighed.

"You should have stayed put, like I told you," Harry said softly. "I love you, or have you already forgotten?"

Cara smiled against the cold metal of his badge. It was suddenly all so clear. Her heart seemed to take flight. "I love you, too, Harry," she whispered.

Harry dropped his hold on her and stepped back to look at her very sternly. Cara thought for a moment that she'd said the wrong thing.

"You what?" he said, registering disbelief.

Cara crossed her arms and raised a single brow. "You heard me, Oberlin."

"No, I don't think I did. The words I heard couldn't have come out of that mouth, because I remember a time when that same mouth told me that you wouldn't say those words until you were ready to accept the responsibilities of a commitment to me."

"Yeah, what of it?" She tried to assume a tough facade, but her happiness and relief at having come through the night unscathed got the better of her and she grinned from ear to ear.

"Say it again," he demanded, still not smiling. "Say it again, and this time sound like you mean it."

Cara made him wait for several silent moments in which she did nothing but meet his stare, hardly daring to blink. Then, stepping forward very slowly, Cara reached up her hand to his face. She felt his stubbly cheek before slipping her hand behind his neck.

"I love you, Harry."

She pulled him down to meet her lips and kissed him warmly on the mouth. Pulling away only far enough to speak, she whispered the words again, "I love you."

Harry pulled her hard against him and kissed her as though his life depended on it. Cara felt a surge of elation. For that moment, there was only Harry.

But it was only a matter of minutes before the traffic in the hallway doubled and the fragile silence was broken.

With a firm arm around her waist, Harry suggested, "Let's get out of here and go check on Melissa at the hospital. You can elaborate on your statement on the way over."

Cara nodded, then gazed down at the floor like a nervous schoolgirl as she answered, "I'd like that, Lieutenant Oberlin."

"And we'll discuss your future as the governor of Kansas," Harry replied casually.

Cara's head snapped up to meet his amused expression. "What?" Her gaze traveled to the governor's office and back to Harry. "What are you talking about?"

"Kerns is going away for a long, long time. Maybe even for the rest of his life. Within hours he'll be formally removed from office and his lieutenant governor will assume the position of governor."

Cara felt the color drain from her face. "I think I'm going to need to sit down."

Harry laughed and pulled her along with him. "I'll carry you if the shock is too much, soon-to-be Governor Oberlin."

"Governor Oberlin," she repeated, looking at Harry in complete wonderment.

Forty-One

Cara sat behind the governor's desk, feeling the edges of the wood surface, wondering what the future would hold. In a matter of months her entire world had turned upside down, and now she was responsible for the state of Kansas. In front of her was a newspaper that blared the headline, "Robert Kerns Indicted on Eighteen Counts." The by-line read, "Melissa Jordon."

"How does this look?" Liz Moore questioned. Coming into the room, she held up a large bronze and wood nameplate.

"Governor Kessler." Cara read the words and shook her head. She smiled at Liz, who'd eagerly made the transfer to Topeka in order to be executive secretary to the new governor. "It just doesn't seem real."

"Well, it is," Harry announced, surprising her.

She looked up at him with a shy smile. "Hello, Lieutenant Oberlin." He looked glorious in his uniform, and Cara couldn't help but stare at him. Harry just grinned at her appraisal and winked.

Liz noted the looks between them and graciously put the nameplate down and exited the room, making a special point to close the door securely behind her.

Harry tossed his hat to an empty chair. "I got a message that you wanted to see me."

"I understand you've asked for the next two weeks off. I wondered if you were going away." She was trying hard not to sound worried or overly interested.

Harry came around the desk and held out his hand to her. "I have some plans."

Cara let him pull her into his arms. "I suppose we're scandalizing the office," she murmured.

"After the last governor, you've got to be kidding." Harry kissed her ever so gently on the lips, then abruptly let her go. He reached into his dark blue slacks and pulled out a jeweler's box.

Cara was unable to hide her sharp intake of breath. Harry opened the box to reveal a solitary diamond engagement ring. Tears came to her eyes, blurring her vision. Taking the ring from the box, Harry lifted her left hand and slipped it on.

Then holding her fingers to his lips, he asked, "Will you marry me, Cara Kessler?"

"Oh, Harry, it's beautiful."

"You're avoiding the question."

"I guess I've been avoiding this particular question for some time, huh?" Cara looked up into his face and saw the reflection of all the love she felt in her heart.

"Too long, as far as I'm concerned. Now how about an answer?"

"Are you sure you aren't just asking me to be your wife so that you can be married to the governor of Kansas?" Cara teased.

Harry laughed and pulled her into his arms again. "You need me to keep you out of trouble."

"Who, me?" she said, looking wide-eyed and innocent.

"Stop putting me off," he said, tightening his hold on her. "I'm not letting you go until I get an answer."

"Hmmm." Cara snuggled against him. "I may have to think on it for a minute or maybe . . . an hour or two."

Just then the door opened and Brianna burst in with

Melissa and Peter not far behind.

The lively eleven-year-old danced around them chanting, "Harry's going to be my new daddy."

Cara eyed Harry with a questioning look. He shrugged and smiled sheepishly. "I had to get her permission first, didn't I?"

Melissa and Peter laughed, but Harry maintained a hold on Cara with one hand and motioned everyone else to quiet down. "She's just about to answer an important question," he said rather dramatically. All eyes turned to Cara in anticipation of her reply.

"What question did you ask her, Harry?" Brianna looked up intently.

"I asked if she'd marry me," Harry said, putting his free arm around Brianna. "I've been asking her for ages and she always manages to avoid giving me an answer."

"Oh, that," Brianna said, as though Harry had said nothing of importance. "Of course she'll marry you."

Melissa and Peter broke out in laughter again, while Harry turned to Cara. "Smart kid. I'm going to like being her new dad."

Cara shook her head. "I guess I don't have a choice," she said, feigning a pout.

"The only choice you have," declared Harry with a firm grasp on her waist, "is the right to remain silent, only if you don't love me enough to say yes."

Cara nodded. "In that case, I love you, Harry Oberlin, and I will marry you."

"Yea!" Brianna cheered and began to dance around again while Harry kissed Cara solidly on the mouth.

"Well, now that we have that settled," Melissa said, sweeping back waves of auburn hair, "when is the big day?"

"Next week," Harry said without batting an eye.

Cara looked up at him in stunned surprise. "Next week?"

"Sure. I'm not giving you room to get into trouble without having the ability to offer you twenty-four-hour protection."

"No more sleeping down the hall, eh?" Cara teased.

"Nope."

"It's just as well. I feel the same way," Cara replied. Growing serious, she looked at her friends and daughter. "You know, I'm really sorry I got you all into this mess. So many lives were affected by the deception of one man, and when I relive that night and see Danielle holding a gun to her father . . ." Her voice trailed off as she shuddered. "She just wanted to be loved," Cara murmured and pulled Brianna close. She smiled down at her daughter. "She just wanted a father's love."

"She's got us now, right, Mom?" Brianna asked enthusiastically.

"What's that?" Melissa questioned.

Cara stroked her daughter's hair. "Danielle has been given her freedom, on the condition that she perform community service and remain in counseling for a year. I suggested her community service be performed with HEARTBEAT Ministries."

Melissa nodded. "Was she open to the idea?"

"Very much so, especially now that she's interested in learning more about God," Cara replied. "She has a great deal to work through, but she's a strong sweet-spirited girl. It took the evil of Kerns to push her to the edge of destruction, but I know the love of God will bring her back. When I think of how tragically it could have ended, I can only thank God for the protection He offered each of us."

"Me too," Melissa said as Peter put his arm around her shoulder. "It made us both think more about what life had to offer and what we want out of it. I can't say that I understand everything about this faith stuff, but I do know that I plan to investigate it in more detail."

"And she's going to have plenty of time on her hands for personal investigation," Peter joined in. "At least when she isn't busy running after a very lively one-year-old."

"What?" Cara's eyes widened in surprise. "What are you talking about?"

"We're adopting Jamie Davis," Melissa announced with a glowing expression that left no one in doubt of her happiness.

"Congratulations!" Harry and Cara exclaimed in unison.

"I guess everything really does happen for a purpose," Melissa said, glancing at Peter.

"This calls for a celebration," Harry stated. "We'll celebrate our engagement and your adoption."

"Don't forget me," Brianna said, taking Harry's big hand in hers.

"Never in a million years!" Harry declared and reached down to lift Brianna into the air.

Cara watched the scene with a great deal of satisfaction. So many lives had been demaged by the actions of one man. She thought sadly of Teri and of the baby who would never know her birth mother. Then seeing the joy on Melissa's face, Cara knew that Jamie would never want for love. Feeling her heart swell with happiness, she studied Harry and Brianna as if seeing the hand of God in motion. The past was clearly settled, and the future held a great deal of promise. They were caught up together in love, and to Cara it seemed the very best way to be.